Short Stories

The Dark Corners of the Human Soul

A Modern Translation

Adapted for the Contemporary Reader

Fyodor Dostoevsky

Translated by Tim Zengerink

Table of Contents

Preface - Message to the Reader

What If You Could Help Rebuild the Greatest Library in Human History?

Thousands of years ago, the Library of Alexandria stood as the crown jewel of human achievement — a sanctuary where the collected wisdom of every known civilization was gathered, preserved, and shared freely.

And then, it was lost.

Through fire, conquest, and the slow erosion of time, humanity lost not just books — but ideas, dreams, discoveries, and stories that could have changed the world forever.

Today, the Library of Alexandria lives again — and you are invited to be a part of its restoration.

Our mission is simple yet profound:

To rebuild the greatest library the world has ever known, and to translate all timeless works into every language and dialect, so that no seeker of knowledge is ever left behind again.

By joining our movement to rebuild the modern Library of Alexandria, you become part of an unprecedented mission:

Unlimited Access to the Greatest Audiobooks & eBooks Ever Written:

Instantly explore thousands of legendary works—Plato, Shakespeare, Jane Austen, Leo Tolstoy, and countless more. All instantly available to read or listen, placing a complete literary universe at your fingertips.

Beautiful Paperback & Deluxe Editions at Printing Cost

Own any title as an elegant paperback, deluxe hardcover, or stunning collectible boxset—offered to you at true printing cost, delivered straight to your door. Build your personal Library of Alexandria, crafted for beauty, built for durability, and worthy of proud display.

Fresh Translations for Modern Readers—in Every Language & Dialect

Enjoy timeless masterpieces reimagined in clear, contemporary language—no more outdated phrases or obscure references. Alongside the original versions, we're tirelessly translating these classics into every language and dialect imaginable, ensuring accessibility and understanding across cultures and generations.

Join a Global Renaissance of Literature & Knowledge

You directly support expanding our library, publishing deluxe editions at true cost, translating works into all global languages, and bringing humanity's greatest stories to people everywhere. By joining today, you're not just preserving a legacy of masterpieces; you set in motion a powerful wave of literary accessibility.

Become a Torchbearer of Knowledge.

Join us for free now at **LibraryofAlexandria.com**

Together, we will ensure that the light of human wisdom never fades again.

With gratitude and a shared love of knowledge,

The Modern Library of Alexandria Team

Visit:

www.libraryofalexandria.com

Or scan the code below:

Introduction

Windows into the Abyss:
Dostoevsky's Psychological Miniatures

Fyodor Dostoevsky is best known for his sweeping novels—epic works such as Crime and Punishment, The Idiot, The Brothers Karamazov, and Demons—that wrestle with philosophy, theology, morality, and the harrowing contradictions of human nature. But to read only his major novels is to miss a crucial part of his literary brilliance: his short stories. These compact, intense, and often experimental pieces serve as laboratories for Dostoevsky's deepest obsessions. They give us snapshots of human suffering, conscience, delusion, and redemption—rendered with brevity and precision that often make them more psychologically explosive than his larger works.

Collected under the title Short Stories, this modern edition brings together some of Dostoevsky's finest shorter fiction, including early works such as Mr. Prohartchin and A Faint Heart, as well as late parables like The Dream of a Ridiculous Man. These stories span the full arc of his career, offering both stylistic variety and thematic consistency. Whether capturing the comic absurdity of social misfits, the tortured psyche of sensitive souls, or the desperate rationalizations of petty criminals, Dostoevsky's short stories showcase his unmatched ability to render the human soul in crisis. Each tale invites readers to step into the mind of a person on the verge—of breakdown, of discovery, or of moral reckoning.

This introduction explores the evolution of Dostoevsky's short fiction, the recurring themes that animate these stories, and how these tightly focused works offer unique insight into Dostoevsky's artistic and philosophical worldview. While often overshadowed by his more famous novels, these stories demonstrate that no human soul was too small, no experience too minor, to warrant the full force of Dostoevsky's empathy and intellect.

Conscience in Fragments
The Form and Function of the Dostoevskian Short Story

Dostoevsky's short fiction is not bound by genre expectations. Some stories lean toward satire, others toward tragedy; some are psychological case studies, while others approach spiritual allegory. Yet all share a common urgency. The short story form allows Dostoevsky to strip away the elaborate scaffolding of plot and dwell instead on a single moment of human experience—a moral test, an inner crisis, a flash of insight or collapse. These are stories of revelation. Whether the revelation is hopeful or devastating depends on the character, the context, and the fragile moral calculus at the heart of each tale.

The brevity of the short story serves Dostoevsky's psychological intensity. In stories like Polzunkov, Mr. Prohartchin, or A Little Hero, the reader is quickly immersed in the protagonist's subjective reality. The line between narrator and character blurs, and we experience shame, fear, love, or existential dread through the protagonist's own distorted perceptions. In others, such as The Crocodile or Bobok, satire provides a sharp counterpoint to the darker undercurrents, allowing Dostoevsky to critique bureaucracy, nihilism, or vanity with bitter humor.

In these brief pieces, Dostoevsky often experiments with narrative voice, tone, and pacing. The stories are intimate and volatile, constructed not to comfort but to provoke. Many begin in mundanity and spiral into the surreal or philosophical. And nearly all of them confront a fundamental question that preoccupied Dostoevsky throughout his life: How can one live with a conscience in a world that mocks, crushes, or ignores it?

These stories are populated with the kinds of characters that Dostoevsky championed throughout his career: clerks, misfits, children, old maids, fallen women, self-deceivers, and spiritual seekers. Their voices may be small in society, but in Dostoevsky's world they are given full moral dimension. In this lies the democratic genius of his short fiction: everyone suffers, everyone questions, and everyone is worthy of attention.

This modern translation presents these stories in updated, emotionally accessible language, while preserving Dostoevsky's irony, nuance, and thematic urgency. Each story has been rendered to speak directly to the contemporary reader, without diminishing the philosophical and emotional density of the original.

In conclusion, Short Stories is not merely a collection of minor works—it is a concentrated vision of Dostoevsky's lifelong preoccupations. These stories plunge into the dark corners of the human soul and return with fragments of truth. They challenge readers to witness suffering without turning away, to understand the grotesque without dismissing it, and to believe that even in humiliation, madness, or despair, the human spirit endures. Through these small windows, Dostoevsky illuminates the infinite complexities of conscience, making his short fiction not a footnote to his greatness, but a vital expression of it.

An Honest Thief

One morning, as I was getting ready to leave for work, Agrafena, my cook, washerwoman, and housekeeper, came into my room and, to my surprise, started a conversation.

She had always been a quiet and simple person. For the past six years, the only words I'd heard from her were her daily question about dinner. So, this was unusual.

"I came to talk to you, sir," she said abruptly. "You should rent out the little room."

"Which little room?" I asked.

"The one by the kitchen, of course," she replied.

"And why should I rent it out?"

"Why? Because people rent out rooms, don't they?"

"But who would want to rent it?"

"Who would want it? A lodger, of course," she answered confidently.

"But the room is too small for a bed. There's no space to move. Who could live there?"

"Who said anything about living there? He just needs a place to sleep. He could sit in the window during the day."

"In the window?"

"Yes, in the window," she said as if it were obvious. "The one in the passage. He could sit there and sew or do whatever work he has. He could even sit on a chair if he wanted. He has a chair—and a table, too. He has everything he needs."

7

"And who is this person you're talking about?"

"Oh, he's a good man, experienced. I'll cook for him, and I'll charge him three roubles a month for board and lodging."

After much effort, I finally managed to get the full story from Agrafena. It turned out that an elderly man had convinced her to let him rent the kitchen as a lodger and boarder. When Agrafena got an idea in her head, it was impossible to change her mind. If I didn't agree, I knew she'd give me no peace. She would sink into one of her moods, brooding and becoming deeply unhappy for weeks. During those times, my dinners would be ruined, my clothes misplaced, and the house left uncleaned. I'd noticed long ago that she wasn't capable of coming up with ideas on her own. But once someone planted an idea in her mind, not allowing her to carry it out felt like committing a great injustice against her.

Since I valued my peace of mind more than anything, I agreed.

"Does he have a passport or some kind of paperwork?" I asked.

"Of course, he does. He's a good man, an experienced man, and he promised to pay three roubles," she said.

The very next day, the new lodger moved into my modest bachelor apartment. Surprisingly, I wasn't bothered by this; in fact, I was secretly pleased. I usually led a very lonely, hermit-like life. I had almost no friends, and I rarely went out. After ten years of living this way, I had grown used to solitude. But when I thought about spending another ten or fifteen years in the same isolation, with only Agrafena and these same bachelor quarters, it felt like a bleak prospect.

So, having a new tenant, as long as he behaved himself, felt like a blessing.

Agrafena was right—my lodger, Astafy Ivanovitch, was indeed a man of experience. His passport showed that he was a retired soldier, something I could have guessed just by looking at him. An old soldier is easy to recognize. Astafy Ivanovitch was a good example of his kind, and we got along very well. The best part was that he sometimes told stories about his life, and in the monotony of my days, his storytelling was a real treasure. One of his stories made a deep impression on me, and here's what led to it.

One day, I was alone in the apartment; both Astafy and Agrafena were out on errands. Suddenly, I heard someone enter from the inner room. I thought it might be a stranger. When I went to check, there really was a short man standing in the passage without an overcoat, even though it was a chilly autumn day.

"What do you want?" I asked.

"Does a clerk named Alexandrov live here?"

"There's no one by that name here," I replied. "Goodbye."

"But the dvornik told me it was here," he said, cautiously moving toward the door.

"Get out, brother. Move along," I told him, and he left.

The next day, after lunch, while Astafy was fitting a coat he was altering for me, someone came into the passage again. I opened the door just a little and saw the same visitor from the day before. Calm as could be, he grabbed my quilted greatcoat from the peg, stuffed it under his arm, and bolted out of the apartment. Agrafena just stood there, staring at him in shock, without lifting a finger to stop him.

Astafy immediately ran after the thief but returned ten minutes later, out of breath and empty-handed. The man had completely disappeared.

"Well, that's some bad luck, Astafy Ivanovitch," I said.

"It's a good thing he didn't take your cloak too, or you'd be in real trouble!"

The whole event left such a strong impression on Astafy Ivanovitch that I soon forgot about the theft and became more interested in watching him. He couldn't let it go. Every few minutes, he'd stop whatever he was doing and recount the entire incident again—how he'd been standing there, how the thief had taken the coat right in front of him, and how he hadn't managed to catch the man. Then he'd go back to his work, only to stop again and start retelling the story.

Eventually, he went downstairs to the dvornik to give him a piece of his mind for letting something like this happen. Then he came back and started scolding Agrafena for not acting. Finally, he returned to his work, but even hours later, he was still muttering to himself, replaying the scene over and over in his mind—how the coat had been taken, how he'd been standing there, how I had been here, and how the thief had gotten away right under our noses.

Astafy knew his business well, but he was a terrible slowpoke and a bit of a busybody.

"He really made fools of us, Astafy Ivanovitch," I said that evening as I handed him a glass of tea. I was trying to pass the time by bringing up the story again. His repeated retelling, combined with the seriousness he gave it, had started to become quite entertaining.

"Fools, indeed, sir! Even though it's not my coat that was stolen, it makes me angry. A thief is the worst kind of vermin. If someone takes something you can spare, that's one thing, but a thief steals the work of your hands, the sweat of your brow, your time. Ugh, it's disgusting! I can't even talk about it without feeling upset. How can you not be bothered by losing your property, sir?"

"You're right, Astafy Ivanovitch. It would have been better if the coat had just been burned. It's frustrating to let a thief have it—it's unpleasant."

"Unpleasant? I should think so! But still, there are different kinds of thieves. You know, sir, I once came across an honest thief."

"An honest thief? How can a thief be honest, Astafy Ivanovitch?"

"Well, you're right, sir. A thief can't really be honest. What I meant is that he was an honest man in general, but he still ended up stealing. I actually felt sorry for him."

"Why was that, Astafy Ivanovitch?"

"It happened about two years ago. I'd been out of work for almost a year, and just before I lost my job, I met this poor, lost soul. We got to know each other at a tavern. He was a drunk, a vagrant, a beggar. He used to have some kind of job, but his drinking habits cost him everything. He was such a hopeless case! God only knows what he had on—it was hard to tell if he even had a shirt under his coat. He drank away everything he could get his hands on.

"But he wasn't the type to argue or cause trouble. He was quiet, soft-spoken, and good-natured. He was so ashamed to ask for anything, but you could see it in his eyes when he wanted a drink. So, you'd buy him one. That's how we became friends—or rather, he just latched onto me. I didn't mind. He was like a little dog, following me everywhere I went, even after just one meeting. He was so thin he looked like a wisp of thread!

"At first, he just asked if he could stay the night, and I let him. I even looked at his passport; everything seemed in order. The next day, it was the same story. Then, on the third day, he came back again, sat in the window all day, and stayed the night. That's when I started thinking, 'He's attached himself to me. Now I have to feed him, give him drink, and let him sleep here. I'm barely making ends meet myself, and now I have someone else to take care of!'

"Before he came to me, he used to do the same thing at a clerk's place. They'd drink together all the time. But that poor clerk eventually drank himself to death. My man's name was Emelyan Ilyitch. I didn't know what to do with him. I felt too ashamed to kick him out. He was such a pitiful, God-forsaken creature. I'd never seen anyone like him. He didn't ask for anything, either. He'd just sit there, looking at me like a dog. It was heartbreaking to see how far drinking had brought him down.

"I kept wondering how I could tell him, 'You need to leave, Emelyanoushka. You've come to the wrong place. I can barely feed myself, let alone take care of you.'

"I could picture how he'd react. He'd sit there, staring at me, not understanding what I was saying. Then, when it finally sank in, he'd get up, take his little bundle—this red-checked handkerchief full of holes with God knows what inside—and try to adjust his shabby old coat so it would look decent and keep him warm. He was a man with delicate feelings, you know. Then he'd open the door and leave, tears in his eyes.

"No, I couldn't do it. I couldn't let him go like that. You just feel sorry for someone like that."

"And then I started thinking about my own situation. 'Wait a bit, Emelyanoushka,' I said to myself. 'You won't be staying with me much longer. I'll soon be moving, and you won't be able to find me then.'

"Well, sir, my employer, Alexandr Filimonovitch, who has since passed away—God rest his soul—told me, 'I'm very pleased with you, Astafy Ivanovitch. When we come back from the country, we'll hire you again.' I had been working as their butler, and he was a kind gentleman, but he passed away later that same year. So, after I saw him off, I took what little money I had and decided to take a break. I rented a corner in the room of an old woman I knew. She had once been a nurse and now lived off a small pension.

"'Goodbye, Emelyanoushka,' I thought to myself. 'You won't be able to track me down here.'

"But what do you think happened? One evening, after I'd gone out to visit someone and returned, the first thing I saw was Emelyanoushka sitting on my box with his ragged little bundle beside him. He was in his tattered coat, waiting for me. To pass the time, he'd borrowed a church book from the old woman and was holding it upside down. He had sniffed me out! My heart sank. 'Well,' I thought, 'there's no getting rid of him now. I should've turned him away in the beginning.'

"So I asked him right away, 'Did you bring your passport, Emelyanoushka?'

"I sat down and started thinking. 'How much trouble could this vagabond really cause me?' I figured it wouldn't be much. I'd give him some bread in the morning, maybe an onion to help it go down. At midday, more bread and another onion, and in the evening, bread, onion, and kvass. If we happened to come across some cabbage soup, we'd both be satisfied. I don't eat much myself, and everyone knows a drunkard doesn't care about food—just vodka or some herb-brandy. 'He'll ruin me with his drinking,' I thought, but then another idea struck me, and it really took hold. I started feeling like I wouldn't have anything to live for if Emelyanoushka left.

"I made up my mind to take care of him, to save him from himself. 'I'll wean him off the bottle,' I decided. 'You just wait, Emelyanoushka. You can stay, but you'll have to behave. You'll follow my rules.'

"I thought I'd start by giving him a small job to do, but not right away. First, I wanted him to relax a little. 'I'll find something you can handle, Emelyanoushka,' I told myself. After all, every job requires a certain skill. So I began to keep an eye on him. It didn't take long to see he was a hopeless case.

"I tried talking to him. I gave him advice. 'Emelyanoushka,' I said, 'it's time to clean up your act. Stop drinking! Look at the state of your clothes! That coat of yours is so full of holes it might as well be a sieve. You've got to draw the line somewhere.'

"He'd sit and listen to me with his head down. Would you believe it, sir? He was so ruined by drink he could hardly string a sentence together. Talk to him about cucumbers, and he'd answer with something about beans. He'd sigh deeply after listening to me.

"'Why are you sighing, Emelyan Ilyitch?' I asked.

"'Oh, nothing, Astafy Ivanovitch. Don't mind me. Did you know there were two women fighting in the street today? One accidentally knocked over the other's basket of cranberries.'

"'And what of it?'

"'Well, the second woman knocked over her cranberries on purpose and stomped on them.'

"'And what's so important about that, Emelyan Ilyitch?'

"'Oh, nothing. I just thought I'd mention it.'

"'Just thought you'd mention it!' I thought to myself. 'You've drunk away your wits, Emelyanoushka.'

"Another time, he said, 'Did you hear about the gentleman who dropped a money note in Gorokhovaya Street—or maybe it was Sadovaya? A peasant picked it up and claimed it was his, but another man saw it first and said it was his. They fought over it until a policeman came, took the note, and gave it back to the gentleman.'

"'And what of that, Emelyanoushka?'

"'Nothing much. Folks laughed, Astafy Ivanovitch.'

"'Ach, Emelyanoushka! What do folks matter? You've thrown your life away for nothing! Listen to me, Emelyan Ilyitch, get a job! Have some mercy on yourself!'

"'What kind of job could I do, Astafy Ivanovitch? No one will hire me.'

"'That's why you're in this mess, Emelyanoushka. Because of your drinking.'

"Yet he'd keep dodging responsibility. And if I got angry, he'd grab his old coat, slip out, and be gone all day, only to return at night drunk. Where he got the money for his drinking, I have no idea. It certainly wasn't from me."

"No, Emelyan Ilyitch," I said, "you'll end up in a bad place if you keep this up. Stop drinking, hear me? Give it up! And let me warn you—next time you come home drunk, you'll sleep on the stairs. I won't let you in!"

Hearing my threat, Emelyanoushka stayed home that day and the next. But on the third day, he disappeared again. I waited and waited, but he didn't return. I admit, I felt a mix of fear and pity. What had I done to him? Had I scared him away? Where could he have gone now? He might get lost or worse. "Lord, have mercy on him," I prayed.

When night fell and he still hadn't returned, I became even more anxious. The next morning, I went out to the porch, and there he was, lying on the steps, his head resting on the cold stone, frozen to the bone.

"What on earth are you doing, Emelyanoushka?" I exclaimed. "God have mercy on you! What's going to happen to you now?"

He looked up at me with those weary, sad eyes of his and replied softly, "You were angry with me the other day, Astafy Ivanovitch. You

15

said I'd have to sleep in the porch, so I didn't dare come inside... I thought it was better to stay out here."

His words cut me deeply. I felt both anger and sorrow.

"Surely, Emelyanoushka," I said with frustration, "you could find something better to do than lie here guarding the steps like this?"

"What else can I do, Astafy Ivanovitch?" he asked simply, his voice almost resigned.

"Look at the state of your coat," I said, unable to hold back my irritation. "It's already in tatters, and now you're sweeping the stairs with it! Couldn't you at least sew up the holes, as any decent man would? Pick up a needle and fix it!"

To my surprise, he actually tried. Of course, I had said it as a joke, but he seemed so shaken by my scolding that he immediately set to work. He took off his coat and tried to thread a needle. It was painful to watch. His hands were trembling, and his red, swollen eyes squinted as he struggled to get the thread through the eye of the needle. He wet the thread, twisted it, and tried again and again, but it was no use. Finally, he gave up and looked at me helplessly.

"Well," I said, "what am I supposed to do with you? If anyone saw this, I wouldn't know where to hide my face! Stop this nonsense, Emelyanoushka. Sit quietly and don't make a spectacle of yourself. Don't sleep on the stairs and embarrass me like this."

"But what am I to do, Astafy Ivanovitch?" he said, his voice trembling. "I know I'm a drunkard, a worthless man. All I do is trouble you... my benefactor..."

And with that, his lips began to quiver, and a single tear rolled down his pale, stubbly cheek. Suddenly, he broke into sobs. The sight of him crying like that struck me like a knife to the heart. I had never imagined such sensitivity in him. I had thought he was beyond feeling, that he was too far gone.

At that moment, I felt a wave of despair. "No, Emelyanoushka," I thought, "I can't keep you here. You're hopeless. Go your way, and let it be."

But life went on, and soon after, an incident occurred that I'll never forget. I had a pair of fine riding breeches—blue with a check pattern. They had been custom-made for a gentleman from the country, but he decided they weren't full enough and refused to take them. I figured I could sell them to a secondhand dealer for five roubles or repurpose them into two pairs of trousers and a waistcoat. Every little bit counts when you're living hand-to-mouth.

Around this time, Emelyanoushka seemed to be changing. He wasn't drinking, not a drop, and spent his days sitting quietly, lost in thought. It was as though he was turning over a new leaf. I dared to hope that perhaps he had finally come to his senses.

Then, one holiday, I went to vespers. When I returned, I found Emelyanoushka sitting by the window, rocking back and forth. He was drunk.

"So that's what you've been up to," I thought. Feeling uneasy, I went to my chest to check on my belongings. The riding breeches were gone. I searched high and low, but they were nowhere to be found. A cold fear gripped me. I questioned the old woman we were living with, but she swore she hadn't touched them.

"Who else could it be?" I asked. "Who's been in here?"

"No one," she insisted. "Emelyan Ilyitch went out and came back. Ask him."

I turned to Emelyanoushka, still rocking in his seat. "Did you take the riding breeches, Emelyanoushka? You know, the ones I made for the gentleman from the country?"

He looked at me with wide, glassy eyes. "No, Astafy Ivanovitch," he said. "I didn't—sort of—touch them."

But something about the way he said it, the way he avoided my gaze, made my heart sink. Still, I couldn't bring myself to accuse him outright. What had become of those breeches? Where could they have gone?

"No, Astafy Ivanovitch," he said quietly, "I've never seen them."

"Never seen them?" I replied. "So, what are you saying, Emelyan Ilyitch—that they've simply gotten up and walked off on their own?"

"Maybe they have," he muttered, avoiding my eyes.

When I heard that, a wave of anger washed over me. I got up immediately, went to light the lamp, and sat down to work on a waistcoat I was altering for a clerk who lived below us. But the rage and ache in my chest wouldn't subside. It was as if I had thrown all my belongings into a fire. Yet somehow, I could feel Emelyanoushka sensing my anger. A guilty man, they say, can sense trouble before it strikes, like a bird feels a coming storm.

"Do you know, Astafy Ivanovitch," he started hesitantly, his voice trembling, "Antip Prohoritch, the apothecary, married the coachman's widow this morning. She's the one who—"

I cut him off with a sharp look. He got the message. Silently, he rose from his spot, shuffled over to the bed, and began rummaging around under it. He muttered to himself, "No, not here. Where on earth have they gone?"

I watched him for a while, waiting to see what he would do next. He stayed busy, crawling under the bed on all fours. Finally, I couldn't bear it any longer.

"What are you doing under there, Emelyan Ilyitch?" I asked coldly.

"Looking for the breeches, Astafy Ivanovitch," he replied earnestly. "Maybe they fell under the bed somewhere."

"You've no need to go crawling about for me, a poor, simple man like myself," I said, my frustration boiling over. "What are you trying to prove by this nonsense?"

"Oh, it's nothing," he said softly. "I'll just keep looking. Maybe they'll turn up somewhere."

I stood there, staring at him as he continued his fruitless search. Finally, I couldn't hold back any longer. "Emelyan Ilyitch," I said firmly, "have you simply stolen them from me? Is this how you repay the bread and salt you've eaten in my home?"

At that, he froze, still lying on his stomach under the bed. He didn't answer for a long time. When he finally crept out, his face was as pale as a sheet. He sat down near the window and stared into the distance, silent for what felt like hours.

"No, Astafy Ivanovitch," he finally said, his voice shaking. He stood and came toward me, his entire body trembling. "No, I swear, I never touched your breeches."

His hands shook as he pointed to his own chest, as if trying to affirm his honesty, but his words wavered so much that I felt a pang of fear. He looked so pitiful, I was rooted to the spot.

"Well, Emelyan Ilyitch," I said at last, trying to calm myself, "if that's how it is, then forgive me. Maybe I was wrong to accuse you. Forget the breeches; let them go. We'll get by without them. Thank

God we still have our hands to work and earn our bread. There's no need to resort to thieving."

He listened to me, standing there with an expression of deep sorrow. Then, slowly, he sat back down in the same spot near the window. He stayed there, unmoving, for the rest of the evening. When I finally lay down to sleep, he still hadn't moved. In the morning, I found him curled up on the bare floor, wrapped in his old coat. He hadn't even bothered to come to bed.

From that day on, something changed between us. I couldn't feel the same toward him anymore. At first, I even hated him. It was as though my own son had betrayed me. I couldn't shake the feeling of loss and disappointment.

Meanwhile, Emelyanoushka sank deeper into his misery. For two whole weeks, he drank himself into oblivion, coming home late at night, stumbling and drunk. He didn't say a single word during that time. It was as if he was punishing himself, letting his grief and shame eat away at him.

When his drinking finally stopped, he sat by the window in silence for three days straight. On the third day, I noticed tears streaming down his face. He wasn't making a sound, just sitting there, crying like a child. Seeing him like that broke my heart.

"What's wrong, Emelyanoushka?" I asked softly, breaking the silence for the first time since that awful day.

He began trembling all over. "Nothing, Astafy Ivanovitch," he said, his voice barely audible.

"Come now," I said gently. "Don't carry on like this. What's done is done. Let it go."

"Oh, it's nothing," he replied. "I just... I need to find some work, Astafy Ivanovitch."

"What kind of work?" I asked.

"Anything," he said. "Maybe I can find a job like I had before. I don't want to be a burden on you anymore, Astafy Ivanovitch. I'll pay you back, every bit of what I owe you, and make up for all the kindness you've shown me."

"Let bygones be bygones, Emelyanoushka," I said, trying to comfort him. "Stay here. We'll manage, just like we did before."

But he shook his head. "No, Astafy Ivanovitch. I can't stay. You've been locking up your chest ever since... it makes me feel terrible. I can't bear it anymore."

"Where will you go?" I asked, alarmed. "You'll be lost out there, like a child without a home."

"I have to go," he insisted. Tears welled up in his eyes again. "Forgive me for all the trouble I've caused. I can't stay here any longer."

And just like that, he left. For days, I waited for him to return. Each night, I hoped he would come back, but he didn't. By the fourth day, I couldn't bear it any longer. I went out looking for him, checking every tavern and corner of the city. But there was no sign of him.

On the fifth day, just as I was losing all hope, the door creaked open. There he was, my Emelyanoushka. He looked thinner than ever, his face blue with cold and his hair matted with dirt. He sat down silently on the chest, too weary to speak.

Seeing him like that filled me with both relief and sadness. I began to care for him again, speaking gently and trying to lift his spirits. I couldn't abandon him, no matter what.

"Well, Emelyanoushka," I said gently, "I'm glad you've come back. Had you stayed away much longer, I'd have had to go looking for you in the taverns again today. Are you hungry?"

"No, Astafy Ivanovitch," he murmured.

"Come now, aren't you really? There's no point hiding it. Look, there's some cabbage soup left from yesterday—it even has meat in it. It's good stuff. And here's some bread and an onion to go with it. Come on, eat up—it'll do you good."

I made him eat, and as I watched him, I realized just how hungry he was. The poor man devoured the food like a starving wolf. It struck me that he hadn't eaten in days, and the thought broke my heart. He hadn't returned out of pride or a sense of guilt—he had come back because hunger had driven him to it.

Seeing his desperation, I couldn't stay angry. My heart softened, and I decided to make peace with him. "Let me run to the tavern," I thought, "I'll get him something to lift his spirits, and we'll put this behind us. I can't stay mad at you, Emelyanoushka."

When I returned, I had a bottle of vodka in hand. "Here, Emelyan Ilyitch," I said, pouring him a glass. "Let's have a drink to mark the holiday. It'll do you good."

He reached for the glass eagerly but hesitated just as his fingers brushed it. His hand wavered, and I could see him wrestling with himself. A moment later, he lifted the glass to his lips but paused again, then set it back down on the table.

"What's the matter, Emelyanoushka?" I asked, puzzled.

"Nothing, Astafy Ivanovitch," he said, his voice low and trembling. "I just… I'm not going to drink anymore, Astafy Ivanovitch."

"Do you mean you've given it up for good, or is it just for today?" I asked, surprised.

He didn't answer. Instead, he rested his head on his hand, looking worn and distant.

"Are you feeling ill, Emelyanoushka?" I pressed, concerned.

"Yes, Astafy Ivanovitch," he replied softly. "I don't feel well."

I helped him to the bed and laid him down. His forehead was burning hot, and he shivered uncontrollably. I sat by his side all day, watching over him as his fever worsened. Toward evening, he seemed weaker still. Desperate to help, I mixed him a simple meal—oil, onion, kvass, and bread—but he shook his head.

"No, Astafy Ivanovitch," he whispered. "I don't want anything to eat today."

I even made him tea, fumbling around the kitchen in a panic, but it didn't help. On the third morning, I decided to fetch a doctor I knew, a man named Kostopravov who had treated me before. When he came, he examined Emelyanoushka briefly and shook his head.

"He's in a bad way," the doctor said. "There's little I can do now. But I'll leave you a powder if you want to try."

I didn't bother with the powder—it felt futile. By the fifth day, Emelyanoushka was clearly dying. He lay there, frail and pale, as I sat by the window pretending to work. The old woman who lived nearby was heating the stove, and the room was silent, heavy with sorrow. My heart ached as I watched him. He looked at me several times, his eyes filled with a deep, unspoken misery, but each time I met his gaze, he quickly looked away.

"Astafy Ivanovitch," he said finally, his voice barely audible.

"What is it, Emelyanoushka?" I asked, leaning closer.

"If you took my coat to a second-hand dealer," he began hesitantly, "how much do you think they'd give you for it?"

"Perhaps a rouble," I said, though I knew no one would pay that much for the tattered old thing.

He was silent for a moment, then added, "I was thinking, Astafy Ivanovitch, that they might give you three roubles for it. It's made of cloth, after all."

"Maybe," I replied gently, "if you ask for three roubles, they might give it to you."

He nodded, falling silent again. An hour passed before he spoke once more. "Astafy Ivanovitch," he said.

"Yes, Emelyanoushka?"

"When I die," he said slowly, "sell my coat. Don't bury me in it. It might still be useful to someone."

His words hit me like a blow, and I had to look away to hide my tears. I couldn't bear to see him like this, so resigned to his fate.

An hour later, he asked for water. I brought him a cup, and he drank slowly. "Thank you, Astafy Ivanovitch," he said, his voice weaker than before.

"Is there anything else you need?" I asked.

He hesitated. "No, Astafy Ivanovitch. But... those riding breeches... it was me... I took them..."

"God forgive you, Emelyanoushka," I said, my voice breaking. "Depart in peace, you sorrowful soul."

He tried to say more, his lips trembling as he struggled to sit up. His face turned red, then suddenly white as snow. His head fell back, and with one final breath, he was gone.

A Novel in Nine Letters

Chapter 1

From Pyotr Ivanitch

To Ivan Petrovitch

Dear Sir and Most Esteemed Friend, Ivan Petrovitch,

For the past two days, I have been diligently pursuing you, my dear friend, as I urgently need to discuss a matter of great importance with you. Yet, despite all my efforts, I have not been able to find you anywhere. Yesterday, while we were visiting at Semyon Alexeyitch's home, my wife, with her characteristic wit, made a humorous remark about you. She joked that you and Tatyana Petrovna are like two birds, always on the wing. Imagine, you've been married less than three months, and already your domestic hearth seems neglected! We all laughed heartily, of course, out of genuine fondness for you, but in all seriousness, my dear friend, you've put me through quite the ordeal.

Semyon Alexeyitch suggested that you might be attending the ball at the Social Union's club. Leaving my wife with Semyon Alexeyitch's good lady, I hurried off to the club in search of you. Picture my predicament—me at the ball, alone, without my wife! The ever-cheeky Ivan Andreyitch spotted me in the porter's lodge and immediately jumped to conclusions. He assumed, quite mistakenly, that I have some hidden passion for dances. Grabbing my arm, he tried to drag me to a dancing class, claiming the Social Union was too crowded for anyone with a fiery spirit, and he was suffering from the overwhelming scent of patchouli and mignonette.

Alas, I found neither you nor Tatyana Petrovna at the club. Ivan Andreyitch, with his usual certainty, declared that you must have gone to the Alexandrinsky Theatre to see Woe from Wit. Off I dashed to the theatre, but once again, you were nowhere to be seen.

This morning, I hoped to find you at Tchistoganov's residence. But there was no sign of you there either. Tchistoganov suggested the Perepalkins' place, but that search, too, proved fruitless. In short, my dear friend, I am completely worn out from chasing you across the city. You can see for yourself the trouble I've gone through. Left with no other option, I am now writing to you directly.

My business is of such a nature that it requires a face-to-face discussion; it's vital and cannot be delayed. I beg you, therefore, to visit us this evening with Tatyana Petrovna. Join us for tea and a chat. My Anna Mihalovna would be delighted to see you both. I assure you, your visit would mean the world to me, and I would remain forever grateful.

Since I have already taken up my pen, allow me to air a small grievance. My dear friend, you have played a seemingly innocent trick on me, though I must say it has caused me considerable inconvenience. You are quite the rascal, a man utterly without conscience! Do you recall introducing your acquaintance, Yevgeny Nikolaitch, into my home about a month ago? You vouched for him with your sacred recommendation, and I, trusting in your word, welcomed him warmly.

At first, I was pleased to host such a pleasant and amiable young man. But what a situation it has turned into! I don't have the time—or the nerve—to explain it all in writing, but suffice it to say, my dear friend, that his frequent visits have become too much for me to bear. Could you, in your tactful way, subtly suggest to Yevgeny Nikolaitch that there are many other homes in this great city where he might find equal hospitality? It's not that he's been rude or unpleasant—far from it. But, as Semyonovitch might say, it's simply too much.

You introduced him, so I believe it falls to you to handle this matter delicately. I would do it myself, but you know me—I just can't bring myself to address such things directly. We can discuss this further when we meet tonight.

Finally, on a more somber note, my little boy has been unwell for a week now. His teething pains grow worse by the day, and my poor wife is utterly consumed with caring for him. She is exhausted and deeply worried. Your visit would be a great comfort to us both, my dear friend.

Until then, I remain, as ever,

Your devoted friend,

Pyotr Ivanitch

Chapter 2

From Ivan Petrovitch

To Pyotr Ivanitch

Dear Sir, Pyotr Ivanitch,

I received your letter yesterday and must admit, it left me thoroughly puzzled. You claim to have searched high and low for me, yet the truth is, I was simply at home the entire time. Until ten o'clock, I was waiting for Ivan Ivanitch Tolokonov, expecting him to arrive at any moment. Upon reading your letter, I wasted no time. I immediately set out with my wife, hiring a cab at my own expense, and reached your house by about half-past six in the evening. To my disappointment, you were not at home, but your wife kindly received us.

Hoping to catch you later, I waited until half-past ten, but as there was no sign of you, I had no choice but to leave. Once again, I went to the expense of hiring a cab to see my wife safely home. Afterwards, I decided to head to the Perepalkins' residence, thinking perhaps I might find you there. But, alas, my calculations were once again wrong, and you were not there either.

That night, I hardly slept. I was uneasy, constantly wondering about your whereabouts. Determined to find you, I visited your house three times the next morning—at nine, ten, and eleven o'clock—each time hiring a cab, each time returning empty-handed. And yet, after all this, you write to me as though nothing had happened!

Your letter has left me amazed and even more perplexed. You mention Yevgeny Nikolaitch and request me to "whisper a hint" to him, yet you don't explain what it is I should hint at or why. I commend your discretion, but let me remind you that not all letters fall into careless hands, and I do not give documents of importance to my wife for curl papers. What exactly was your intention in writing to me about this matter without providing any clarity?

To be honest, I am baffled about what role you expect me to play in this. Why should I involve myself in such an ambiguous affair? If Yevgeny Nikolaitch's visits are bothersome, simply make yourself unavailable to him. As for me, I see no reason to meddle. That said, it seems this situation calls for a brief but decisive conversation between us, as time is slipping away, and there are matters that cannot wait.

Let me remind you that a journey for nothing is not without cost—financial or otherwise. And now my wife is pressing me for a velvet mantle, insisting it must be of the latest fashion. These domestic concerns only add to my exasperation.

Regarding Yevgeny Nikolaitch, I made inquiries during my visit to Pavel Semyonovitch Perepalkin's yesterday. From what I learned, Nikolaitch owns five hundred serfs in the province of Yaroslav and stands to inherit an additional estate of three hundred serfs near

Moscow from his grandmother. However, I cannot provide any details about his financial liquidity; you would likely know more on that front.

Once and for all, I urge you to appoint a time and place where we can meet and resolve these issues. Furthermore, you mentioned in your letter that Ivan Andreyitch told you I was at the Alexandrinsky Theatre with my wife. I must state plainly that he is lying. This is yet another example of how unreliable his word can be, as only two days ago he swindled his own grandmother out of eight hundred roubles.

I remain, as ever,

Yours sincerely,

Ivan Petrovitch

P.S. My wife is expecting a child soon and has been feeling rather nervous and low-spirited lately. For this reason, I avoid taking her to the theatre, where the sound effects—like firearms and artificial thunderstorms—might unsettle her nerves. Truth be told, I am not much of a theatre enthusiast myself.

Chapter 3

My Dearest Friend, Ivan Petrovitch,

I am entirely to blame, undeniably at fault, a thousand times over. Yet, I beg you to allow me to explain myself, for my actions have not been without reason. Between five and six yesterday, as we were speaking of you with the deepest affection, a sudden and urgent message arrived from Uncle Stepan Alexeyitch. A messenger, nearly breathless from his haste, brought the news that my dear aunt was in a dire state.

Out of fear of distressing my wife, I kept the true gravity of the situation from her and used the excuse of pressing business to leave the house. Upon arriving at my aunt's, I was greeted with the heartbreaking sight of her nearly on her deathbed. She had suffered yet another stroke—the third in just two years. Karl Fyodoritch, their family physician, offered little hope, stating gravely that she might not survive the night.

Imagine, dear friend, the state I found myself in. The household was gripped by grief and anxiety, and none of us could rest. We remained on our feet throughout the night, consumed by worry. As dawn broke, I was so utterly drained—both in body and spirit—that I finally collapsed onto a sofa in exhaustion. Foolishly, I forgot to ask anyone to wake me, and I only stirred at half-past eleven in the morning.

Thankfully, my aunt's condition showed some slight improvement by then. Relieved but still anxious, I hurried home to my wife. Poor thing, she had been frantic with worry over my prolonged absence. I reassured her as best as I could, embraced our little boy, and managed to grab a quick bite to eat before setting off to see you, eager to explain myself and set things right.

To my dismay, you were not at home when I arrived. Instead, I found Yevgeny Nikolaitch at your flat. After returning home, I immediately took up my pen to write to you, for I could not bear the thought of leaving this misunderstanding unresolved. My truest friend, please do not let this incident cloud the bond we share. Scold me if you must; I will accept your rebukes without hesitation. Punish me however you see fit—beat me, castigate me, or even take my guilty head from my shoulders—but do not, I beg you, withdraw your affection from me.

From your wife, I learned that you plan to be at the Slavyanovs' this evening. I will be there without fail, for I cannot wait to see you and put this matter to rest. Let us meet and reconcile, my friend, as I look forward with the greatest anticipation to being in your company once again.

I remain ever yours,

Pyotr Ivanitch

P.S. We are in utter despair over our little boy's condition. Karl Fyodoritch has prescribed rhubarb, but the poor child moans constantly. Yesterday, he didn't seem to recognize anyone, not even his own parents. This morning, however, there was a glimmer of hope—he recognized us and began to softly lisp "papa, mamma, boo." My wife, overcome with emotion, has been in tears all morning.

Chapter 4

My Esteemed Sir, Pyotr Ivanitch,

I find myself writing to you from your own room, seated at your bureau, where I have now been waiting for over two and a half hours. Allow me, without any pretense, to express my candid thoughts about this troubling and frankly unacceptable situation. From the contents of your last letter, I understood quite clearly that you were expected to be at the Slavyanovs', and that you had extended an invitation for me to meet you there. Dutifully, I went, and I remained there for no less than five hours, yet you never appeared. Now, I ask you plainly, do you truly believe it is fitting to subject a friend to such treatment? Am I to become a mere object of ridicule to those who were present?

Forgive my forthrightness, but this incident has deeply offended me. This morning, I resolved to come to you directly, confident that a visit to your residence would yield the explanation that your previous absences have failed to provide. Yet, once again, you were not at home. It seems you have chosen to avoid me entirely. Restraint alone prevents me from delivering the full measure of my grievances in this letter, though I must state that your behavior suggests an abandonment of our mutual understanding and agreement.

The more I reflect upon recent events, the more convinced I am that your actions are not merely accidental but calculated. It is becoming increasingly clear that you have long harbored some unspoken design against me. My suspicion finds validation in the way you have handled our dealings. Only last week, in a manner that bordered on impropriety, you removed a letter addressed to me, a letter in which you yourself outlined, albeit vaguely and with little coherence, the terms of our agreement regarding certain matters I need not detail here. Your aversion to written records is apparent; you seem intent on erasing any evidence that might hold you accountable, thereby attempting to confuse or even outmaneuver me.

I assure you, Pyotr Ivanitch, such tactics will not succeed. I have never been considered a fool, and I refuse to allow you or anyone else to treat me as one. The incident with Yevgeny Nikolaitch is yet another instance of your disingenuous behavior. Rather than providing clarity, your correspondence of the seventh of this month has only served to obfuscate matters further. When I sought a direct and honest explanation from you, you responded by setting ambiguous appointments and then failing to appear. Surely, you do not think I am oblivious to these maneuvers?

Furthermore, you cannot possibly believe I have overlooked the financial aspect of this matter. While you promised to reward my efforts—efforts that you are fully aware have been of great service to you—you have instead managed to borrow considerable sums of money from me without issuing any form of receipt or acknowledgment. This occurred as recently as last week. Having secured the funds, you now evade both my company and my inquiries, all while dismissing the assistance I provided concerning Yevgeny Nikolaitch.

If your plan is to rely on my impending departure for Simbirsk to avoid settling this matter, let me disabuse you of that notion. I am fully prepared to delay my journey by two months, if necessary, to remain in Petersburg and see this through to its proper resolution. Rest assured, I am more than capable of countering such tactics.

I must now demand that you provide a detailed and satisfactory explanation by the end of today. This explanation must come first in writing and then in a face-to-face meeting. You must clearly restate the key points of our agreement and offer a full account of your position regarding Yevgeny Nikolaitch. If you fail to meet these conditions, I will be left with no choice but to pursue actions that, while deeply unpleasant for both of us, will be necessary to resolve this matter.

Awaiting your prompt response, I remain, etc.

Chapter 5

November 11

My Dear and Honoured Friend, Ivan Petrovitch,

Your letter has truly cut me to the heart. I must confess, I am deeply pained that you, my dear and cherished friend, could have acted so hastily and without giving me the benefit of the doubt. How could you, without seeking clarification, wound me with such grievous and unfounded suspicions? I cannot imagine what prompted this. Nevertheless, I feel compelled to respond immediately, if only to correct the misunderstandings that have evidently taken root between us.

Allow me to explain why you were unable to find me yesterday. Quite unexpectedly, I was called away to a deathbed—a deeply sorrowful occasion that left no room for delay. My dear aunt, Yefimya Nikolaevna, passed away late last night, at eleven o'clock. Her departure has brought great sorrow to our family. By unanimous agreement among the relatives, I was tasked with organizing the necessary arrangements for her funeral. It was a duty I could not refuse, though it left me overwhelmed with responsibilities and entirely without time to write even a brief note to you, let alone to meet you in person.

I am grieved beyond words at the misunderstanding that seems to have arisen between us. Your interpretation of my casual and lighthearted remark about Yevgeny Nikolaitch has astonished me. What was said in jest, with no intention of offense, you appear to have taken in a manner that is entirely foreign to my meaning, ascribing to it implications that are deeply hurtful to me. This is not like you, my friend.

As for your mention of money, I cannot allow this point to go unanswered. I see now that my reliance on your understanding may have been misplaced, though I continue to trust in your innate sense of fairness. Let me state unequivocally: the three hundred and fifty roubles I received from you last week were not a loan. The transaction was made under the terms of an agreement we had both reached—a mutually understood arrangement. Were it otherwise, I would, of course, have provided a receipt, as is proper. But as I value our friendship, I am willing to address any concerns you may have. Should you still harbor doubts, I am fully prepared to settle any claims you wish to make, not because they are warranted, but because I value your peace of mind above all else.

I must admit, however, that some of the additional accusations in your letter have left me profoundly disappointed. They seem to stem from a misunderstanding and, perhaps, from the quickness of temper and stubbornness that you, my friend, are not wholly free from. Yet I know your open and generous nature, and I trust that once your indignation cools, you will see the matter clearly. When that moment comes, I am certain you will be the first to offer your hand in reconciliation, for such is the kind of man I have always known you to be.

Although your letter has caused me great distress, I would come to you even today, humbling myself to apologize if it would restore harmony between us. Alas, I am utterly worn out, both in body and spirit. Since yesterday, I have been consumed by an endless rush of obligations, and to add to my troubles, my wife has taken ill. Her condition appears serious, though I remain hopeful. Our little boy, thank God, is showing signs of recovery, but I dare not take that for granted.

Even now, I can hardly hold my pen. Urgent matters press on me from every side, and I find myself utterly drained. Yet, I could not let another day pass without reaching out to you, my dear friend. Let us not allow this misunderstanding to fester. I ask you to set aside your doubts and remember the bond of trust and affection we have long shared.

I remain, with all sincerity, your devoted friend,

Pyotr Ivanitch

Chapter 6

November 14

Dear Sir, Pyotr Ivanitch,

I have waited patiently for three days, using the time as constructively as possible, all the while reflecting on how politeness and good manners serve as the greatest adornments for any individual. Since my last letter on the tenth of this month, I have refrained from making any verbal or written reminders of my existence. This restraint was not out of indifference but rather out of respect. I wished to give you uninterrupted time to attend to your Christian duty regarding your late aunt, and I also required the time to consider certain matters and conduct investigations concerning the business that you are fully aware of.

Now, however, I feel compelled to address you directly and with full clarity. It is high time that we dispel any ambiguity. When I first read your initial letters, I found myself genuinely perplexed. I believed you might have misunderstood my intentions or perhaps failed to grasp the nature of my concerns. For that reason, I sought to meet you face to face, hoping that direct communication might resolve the matter. I hesitated to write in detail because I doubted my ability to articulate myself clearly on paper. After all, I am not a man of formal education or polished manners, and I avoid the empty affectation of gentility, having learned through bitter experience how deceitful appearances can be. As the saying goes, a snake may lie hidden beneath a bed of flowers.

However, it has since become apparent that you understood my meaning perfectly well. Your failure to respond appropriately was not due to any confusion but rather a calculated decision stemming from treachery. You had already resolved to break your word of honor and betray the friendly relationship that once existed between us. Recent events and your behavior leave no doubt of this.

From the beginning of our acquaintance, I was captivated by your charm, your keen intellect, and your apparent mastery of worldly affairs. I believed I had found in you a true friend and ally, someone whose association would bring mutual benefit. Now, however, I see that I was gravely mistaken. Beneath your polished exterior lies a heart filled with venom. You have wielded your intelligence not for good but to ensnare others, to deceive, and to manipulate. Worse still, you have employed fine words and flowery expressions not to uplift others but to confuse and bewitch those who placed their trust in you.

Your treachery is evident in numerous ways. First and foremost, when I wrote to you in plain and unmistakable terms to outline my position and sought clarification about your intentions regarding Yevgeny Nikolaitch, you evaded my inquiries. Instead of addressing my concerns, you deflected, sowing seeds of doubt and suspicion, all while sidestepping the matter entirely. Your subsequent letters, which claimed you were wounded by my accusations, further reveal your duplicity. What else could such behavior signify but a deliberate attempt to confuse and mislead me?

Moreover, when every moment was critical, you sent me on a wild goose chase across town, wasting my time and energy while offering no meaningful explanation. Your letters, filled with irrelevant details about your wife's illness and your child's teething troubles, served only to insult me. While I sympathize with your domestic concerns, such matters are entirely out of place when urgent business requires our attention.

Your deceit reached new heights when you invoked the sacred context of family bereavement to excuse your absence. You claimed to have been called away to your aunt's deathbed at a specific time, yet my inquiries have revealed this to be false. Your aunt's stroke occurred well before the date you cited, and her passing was likewise misrepresented. Such distortions of truth for personal gain are not only shameful but deeply offensive.

Beyond these personal affronts, your principal act of betrayal lies in your persistent silence regarding our mutual business interests. You have deliberately avoided addressing the matter of the three hundred and fifty roubles, which you borrowed under the guise of partnership but without providing any receipt. Your defamatory remarks about Yevgeny Nikolaitch further compound your wrongdoing. You attempted to portray him as ineffectual and unworthy of trust while exploiting his resources for your gain.

In light of these transgressions, I am left with no choice but to demand immediate restitution. You must, without delay, return to me the three hundred and fifty roubles, as well as any other sums owed to me under our agreement. Should you fail to comply, I will resort to every legal and lawful measure at my disposal to secure what is rightfully mine. Furthermore, I must inform you that I am in possession of certain facts that, if disclosed, could irreparably damage your reputation.

I urge you to reflect on your actions and to act honorably. This is not merely a matter of money or business but one of integrity and trust.

Allow me to remain, etc.

Chapter 7

November 15

Dear Ivan Petrovitch,

When I first read your letter—so peculiar in tone and vulgar in expression—I was seized by an immediate impulse to tear it into shreds. However, I decided to keep it, not for its merit, but as an example of what one might call an oddity or even a curiosity. Despite my initial reaction, I want to express my genuine regret for the misunderstandings and the unpleasant turn our relationship has taken. Such strained interactions bring neither satisfaction nor benefit to either party, and it is deeply unfortunate that things have come to this.

To be honest, I did not intend to respond to your letter at all, but circumstances compel me to do so. Therefore, I must inform you that it would be extremely disagreeable for me to have you visit my home again under any pretense. My wife shares this sentiment entirely. Her health is fragile, and, as you may know, she is particularly sensitive to certain odors, including, regrettably, the smell of tar, which causes her great discomfort. I trust you will understand that her well-being must take precedence over any social calls, however well-meaning they may be.

On a separate note, my wife has asked me to extend her gratitude to your wife for her gracious loan of the book, Don Quixote de la Mancha. She has read it with great enjoyment and sends her heartfelt thanks as she now returns it. It was a kind gesture, and my wife appreciates it deeply.

Regarding the galoshes you mentioned in your letter, which you believe you left behind during your last visit, I regret to inform you that they have not yet been located. Our household staff has been instructed to search thoroughly, but as of this moment, they remain missing. If they cannot be found in due course, I will ensure that a new pair is purchased for you as a replacement. I trust this will settle the matter to your satisfaction.

While I remain saddened by the recent strain in our interactions, I hope this correspondence will clarify any lingering misunderstandings. It is my sincere wish that you will respect the boundaries I have outlined and allow us both the space to navigate our respective affairs in peace.

I have the honor to remain, your sincere friend,

Pyotr Ivanitch

Chapter 8

On the sixteenth of November, Pyotr Ivanitch received two letters in the post. Both were addressed to him, and as he opened the first envelope, he noticed immediately the faint fragrance of perfume and the pale pink hue of the paper. It was carefully folded and bore the unmistakable handwriting of his wife. Inside the envelope, there was only the note—nothing more, no explanation, no additional correspondence. The note was addressed to Yevgeny Nikolaitch and dated November the second. With a sinking heart and trembling hands, Pyotr Ivanitch began to read:

"Dear Eugène,

Yesterday was utterly impossible. My husband was at home the whole evening. Be sure to come to-morrow punctually at eleven. At half-past ten my husband is going to Tsarskoe and not coming back till evening. I was in a rage all night. Thank you for sending me the information and the correspondence. What a lot of paper. Did she really write all that? She has style though; many thanks, dear; I see that you love me. Don't be angry, but, for goodness' sake, come to-morrow.

A."

Pyotr Ivanitch stared at the words in stunned silence. The betrayal implied in the note hit him like a thunderclap. His breath caught, and for a moment he could not move, as if rooted to the spot by the enormity of what he had just read. The casual tone, the mention of love, and the precise instructions—it all painted a picture he could scarcely bring himself to confront. The letter slipped from his fingers onto the table, but he could not tear his eyes away from it.

Feeling a wave of dread and rage surge within him, he reached for the second envelope. This one felt different—colder somehow, as if it carried no trace of sentiment, only purpose. He tore it open with less care than the first and unfolded the letter inside. The words, stark and direct, were like a slap to the face:

"Pyotr Ivanitch,

I should never have set foot again in your house anyway; you need not have troubled to soil paper about it.

Next week I am going to Simbirsk. Yevgeny Nikolaitch remains your precious and beloved friend. I wish you luck, and don't trouble about the galoshes."

The tone was biting, laced with sarcasm, and it carried the unmistakable signature of Ivan Petrovitch's bitterness. The reference to Yevgeny Nikolaitch—casual and dismissive—was like pouring salt on an open wound. The final remark about the galoshes, so flippant and devoid of any real care, struck him as the epitome of disdain.

Pyotr Ivanitch stood motionless for a long time, the two letters now lying side by side on the table. They seemed to glare up at him, the words etched in ink but burning like fire. His mind raced, filled with anger, confusion, and a profound sense of betrayal. What had started as an ordinary day had turned into one that would leave a scar on his heart and pride forever.

Chapter 9

On the seventeenth of November, Ivan Petrovitch received two letters delivered by post. Both were addressed to him, and as he tore open the first envelope, he felt a peculiar sense of foreboding. The note inside was hastily written, its handwriting familiar—his wife's. It bore a date: August the fourth, and it was addressed to none other than Yevgeny Nikolaitch. The envelope contained nothing else, no explanation or additional context, just the note. With a growing sense of unease, Ivan Petrovitch unfolded the paper and read its contents:

"Good-bye, good-bye, Yevgeny Nikolaitch! The Lord reward you for this too. May you be happy, but my lot is bitter, terribly bitter! It is your choice. If it had not been for my aunt I should not have put such trust in you. Do not laugh at me nor at my aunt. To-morrow is our wedding. Aunt is relieved that a good man has been found, and that he will take me without a dowry. I took a good look at him for the first time to-day. He seems good-natured. They are hurrying me. Farewell, farewell.... My darling!! Think of me sometimes; I shall never forget you. Farewell! I sign this last like my first letter, do you remember?

Tatyana."

Ivan Petrovitch stared at the letter, his hands trembling slightly as he held the delicate sheet of paper. The raw emotion in the words hit him like a wave, the references to trust, to bitterness, to farewells—all directed at another man, another name. The tone carried the weight of resignation, of a decision made under duress, of a heart left wounded and longing. The closing line struck him the hardest, the mention of the first letter—something he had no knowledge of, a private exchange between his wife and this man. His mind raced with questions, yet no answers presented themselves.

Unable to linger on the implications of the first note for long, he reached for the second letter, his apprehension mounting. The tone here was starkly different. It was short, almost curt, devoid of the emotional intensity of the first. It read:

"Ivan Petrovitch,

To-morrow you will receive a new pair of galoshes. It is not my habit to filch from other men's pockets, and I am not fond of picking up all sorts of rubbish in the streets.

Yevgeny Nikolaitch is going to Simbirsk in a day or two on his grandfather's business, and he has asked me to find a travelling companion for him; wouldn't you like to take him with you?"

The brevity of the letter, paired with its dismissive tone, added fuel to Ivan Petrovitch's growing turmoil. The pointed remark about not "filching from other men's pockets" and the casual reference to galoshes felt almost mocking. The suggestion of accompanying

Yevgeny Nikolaitch on a journey was the final twist, an absurd invitation in light of what the first letter had revealed.

Ivan Petrovitch sat back, the two letters lying before him on the table. His thoughts were a storm of disbelief, anger, and sorrow. The disparity between the emotional vulnerability of the first note and the dismissive coldness of the second was jarring. The letters seemed to encapsulate a web of deceit, unspoken truths, and relationships he barely understood but was now irreversibly entangled in.

An Unpleasant Predicament

This rather unpleasant and peculiar incident unfolded during a period when the regeneration of our cherished fatherland was taking its first vigorous strides, and the fervent ambitions of her valiant sons were propelling them toward new hopes and grand destinies. The era was marked by a blend of uncontainable enthusiasm and an almost childlike, endearing impulsiveness. It was on one winter evening of that transformative epoch, between the hours of eleven and midnight, that three highly respectable gentlemen found themselves in the elegant drawing room of a handsome, two-storey residence on the Petersburg Side. The setting was one of refinement, with furnishings exuding luxury and taste. These gentlemen, each of whom held the rank of general, were seated comfortably in plush, inviting armchairs around a small table. Their conversation, conducted in low, measured tones, revolved around a most edifying and engaging topic.

As they spoke, they sipped champagne from crystal glasses, the bottle resting nearby in a silver stand encased in ice. The host of the evening, Stepan Nikiforovitch Nikiforov, was a privy councillor and a man of precise habits. He was an old bachelor, sixty-five years of age, who had chosen this occasion to celebrate two milestones: his recent acquisition of a fine house and, somewhat unexpectedly, his birthday— an event he had rarely acknowledged in previous years. The celebration, however, was intentionally modest. Only two guests graced his evening, both of whom were former colleagues and subordinates: Semyon Ivanovitch Shipulenko, an actual civil councillor, and another of the same rank, Ivan Ilyitch Pralinsky.

The evening had commenced with tea at nine, transitioning soon after to wine. The guests, well aware of Stepan Nikiforovitch's preference for punctuality, knew they would be departing precisely at half-past eleven. It was in keeping with the host's lifelong devotion to routine. But before delving into the nuances of the evening, a few words about the host are in order.

Stepan Nikiforovitch's career had begun humbly, as a petty clerk, devoid of connections or privilege. Over forty-five years, he had quietly but determinedly climbed the ranks, always mindful of his limitations and never allowing ambition to blind him to his capacities. His aspirations were measured; he desired neither glory nor monumental achievement, contenting himself instead with a modest accumulation of respect and stability.

In character, he was a man of quiet intellect who shunned displays of wit or brilliance. Honesty was his guiding principle, though it must be said that he had never faced a situation that truly tested his moral fibre. He remained a bachelor, not for lack of opportunity, but because his nature was fundamentally self-contained. Averse to sloppiness of any kind, be it in appearance, habits, or emotion, he had come to regard enthusiasm itself as a form of untidiness. Over the years, this disposition had deepened, leading him to embrace a life of indulgent solitude, punctuated only by the ticking of his dining-room clock—a sound he found both soothing and companionable.

Physically, he was well-preserved, younger in appearance than his age might suggest, and scrupulously proper in his demeanor. His position, though not particularly demanding, allowed him to preside over proceedings and sign important documents, tasks he performed with an air of calm authority. His reputation as a "first-rate man" was unchallenged, and his only indulgence—his one great desire—had been to own a home befitting his station. That dream had recently been realized when he purchased a house on the Petersburg Side, a property complete with a garden and an air of genteel elegance. The distance from the city center suited him; it reduced the likelihood of uninvited guests. For transportation, he relied on his handsome chocolate-colored carriage, driven by Mihey, a coachman of impeccable reliability, and drawn by a pair of sturdy, well-kept horses. All this had been acquired through decades of careful saving, and his heart swelled with pride at the accomplishment.

This sense of contentment inspired him to extend an invitation to his two guests, a rare gesture. Stepan Nikiforovitch had even entertained a practical motive for one of his visitors. The lower floor of his newly purchased home, identical in layout to his own, was unoccupied, and he hoped to persuade Semyon Ivanovitch Shipulenko to rent it. Twice during the evening, he had broached the subject, but Semyon Ivanovitch had remained noncommittal, responding with nothing more than polite indifference.

Semyon Ivanovitch himself was a man of steady temperament and meticulous habits. A long career had honed his skills in navigating bureaucratic complexities. His austere demeanor, complemented by his dark hair and slightly jaundiced complexion, gave him an air of severity. Married and firmly rooted in his domestic life, he ruled his household with an iron hand and approached his professional duties with a similar resolve. Though not particularly moved by the wave of reforms sweeping through the country, he maintained a skeptical detachment, regarding them as distractions to his well-established routines.

The third gentleman, Ivan Ilyitch Pralinsky, was of a different breed altogether. A relatively young general at forty-three, he carried himself with the confidence of a man accustomed to admiration. Tall, impeccably dressed, and bearing a distinguished order on his chest, he exuded charm and vitality. Yet, beneath this polished exterior lay a man of contradictions. Born into privilege and accustomed to luxury, Ivan Ilyitch had navigated his career with a blend of ambition and self-assurance. He dreamed of greatness, of carving out a legacy that would endure, and while he occasionally questioned his own capabilities, he quickly dismissed such doubts, buoyed by an unwavering belief in his potential.

As the evening progressed, Ivan Ilyitch grew increasingly animated. Fuelled by champagne, he launched into a spirited critique of the reforms, directing much of his fervor at Stepan Nikiforovitch, whom he perceived as a symbol of outdated conservatism. The older man listened with a sly smile, allowing Ivan Ilyitch to exhaust himself in rhetoric. Meanwhile, Semyon Ivanovitch observed the exchange with a hint of amusement, his silence a subtle rebuke to Ivan Ilyitch's impassioned outbursts.

By the end of the evening, Ivan Ilyitch felt both exhilarated and unsettled. The sense of being subtly mocked by his companions gnawed at him, fuelling his determination to assert himself further. Yet, as the clock struck eleven-thirty and the guests prepared to leave, a sense of unease lingered, hinting that the evening's dynamics had unsettled more than just the champagne glasses.

"No, it was time, high time," Ivan Ilyitch continued passionately, his voice tinged with righteous conviction. "We have delayed this far too long, and, in my opinion, humanity must be our first priority—humanity toward those beneath us in rank, acknowledging that they, too, are human. It is humanity that will save us, guide us, and draw out the best in everyone."

From the corner of the room came a low, derisive chuckle—"He-he-he-he!"—courtesy of Semyon Ivanovitch.

"But why all this fervent lecturing?" Stepan Nikiforovitch interjected, his tone genial yet slightly bemused. A faint smile played on his lips as he added, "Forgive me, Ivan Ilyitch, but I still fail to grasp the crux of your argument. You are advocating humanity—by which, I take it, you mean love for one's fellow man?"

"Precisely, if you must summarize it that way," Ivan Ilyitch affirmed, though there was a hint of impatience in his voice. "I…"

"One moment!" Stepan Nikiforovitch raised a hand to interrupt him. "Surely, love for one's fellow man has always been a commendable sentiment. But if I understand correctly, what you are proposing goes beyond that. Love alone does not encapsulate the scope of the reform movement. We are confronting a deluge of issues: the peasantry, judicial reform, economic policies, government contracts, morality—the list is endless. These questions have the potential to provoke significant upheavals, so to speak. That, my dear friend, is where our concern lies—not simply with humanity alone."

"Indeed, it's a great deal more complex than that," Semyon Ivanovitch added, with a tone that bordered on condescension.

"I fully comprehend the complexity," Ivan Ilyitch retorted, his sarcasm cutting as he addressed Semyon Ivanovitch directly. "And I assure you, sir, I take great exception to the implication that my understanding of these matters is somehow less profound than yours. Allow me to clarify, Stepan Nikiforovitch, that you, too, have misunderstood me."

"That may very well be," Stepan Nikiforovitch replied mildly, arching his eyebrows in feigned confusion. "Do enlighten us, then."

"I assert, and will continue to assert," Ivan Ilyitch declared, his tone brimming with fiery conviction, "that humanity—extending down the hierarchical ladder, from high-ranking officials to the humblest peasants—should serve as the cornerstone of all forthcoming reforms. It is humanity, in all its forms, that will underpin the transformation of society at large. Allow me to explain: If I, as a human being, treat another with respect and kindness, that generates trust. Trust fosters understanding. Understanding breeds unity, and unity—"

"Breeds love," Semyon Ivanovitch interrupted, his sardonic grin widening. "Or perhaps yet another syllogism?"

Ivan Ilyitch shot him a withering glare. "I fail to see what you find so amusing," he snapped. "What I am advocating is both logical and necessary. If we can build trust among all levels of society, we lay the foundation for progress. But that requires vision and courage— qualities I would not expect everyone to possess."

Stepan Nikiforovitch, who had been silently observing the exchange, finally spoke, his tone deliberately neutral. "I fear we would collapse under the weight of such aspirations," he remarked, almost to himself.

"What precisely do you mean by that?" Ivan Ilyitch asked, his irritation giving way to curiosity.

"I mean," Stepan Nikiforovitch replied slowly, "that the strain might prove too much for the system. It may simply be unsustainable."

"Ah, I see!" Ivan Ilyitch exclaimed, his voice tinged with irony. "You're suggesting, then, that we are like old wineskins trying to contain new wine? Well, I cannot speak for others, but I am confident that I, at least, am up to the challenge."

At that precise moment, the clock chimed half-past eleven. The sound seemed to break the tension in the room, prompting Semyon Ivanovitch to rise from his chair.

"One sits and sits," he remarked dryly, "but at some point, one must leave."

Before he could finish, however, Ivan Ilyitch had already stood, reaching for his elegant sable cap resting on the mantel. There was an air of affront about him, as though he had been slighted.

"And what of the flat, Semyon Ivanovitch?" Stepan Nikiforovitch inquired as he escorted his guests to the door. "Will you give it some thought?"

"I'll think it over," Semyon Ivanovitch replied curtly, adjusting his shabby raccoon coat. "I'll let you know soon."

Meanwhile, Ivan Ilyitch lingered by the doorway, clearly feeling overlooked. "Still discussing business, I see," he remarked in a tone that was meant to sound affable but carried an edge of reproach.

Stepan Nikiforovitch raised his eyebrows again but said nothing, leaving Ivan Ilyitch to interpret the silence as dismissal. They parted with a polite but cool exchange of handshakes.

Once outside, the two men descended the steps in silence. The disparity between Ivan Ilyitch's luxurious fur coat and Semyon Ivanovitch's threadbare attire was glaring, though neither man commented on it. When they reached the street, they discovered that Ivan Ilyitch's carriage was nowhere to be found.

"What is this nonsense?" Ivan Ilyitch exclaimed angrily. "Where is my carriage? What has Trifon done with it?"

The coachman for Semyon Ivanovitch's modest sledge shrugged indifferently. "He said something about attending a wedding nearby, sir," he offered. "But he promised to return quickly."

"That scoundrel!" Ivan Ilyitch fumed. "I'll make him pay for this! What nerve—leaving me stranded on a night like this."

"Would you care for a ride?" Semyon Ivanovitch offered with a smirk, though his tone was anything but sincere.

"Thank you, but no," Ivan Ilyitch replied icily. "Enjoy your journey."

As Semyon Ivanovitch drove off, Ivan Ilyitch set off on foot, his irritation mounting with every step. Yet as he walked, the biting cold and the serene beauty of the moonlit night began to temper his anger. The frost sparkled on the wooden pavement, and the stars seemed to twinkle just for him.

"Perhaps this is for the best," he mused. "A brisk walk will do me good. It serves as a lesson to Trifon, and it's not unpleasant to walk on such a night. How quaint these little houses are—clerks and tradesmen, no doubt, making their humble lives here."

Despite himself, Ivan Ilyitch felt his mood lift. The crisp air seemed to sharpen his thoughts, and he began to reflect again on his earlier argument. "Humanity," he thought. "The key to everything is humanity. Restore a man's dignity, give him a sense of worth, and he will thrive. It's such a simple, clear truth. Why couldn't they see it? Especially that smug Semyon Ivanovitch with his condescending smile."

As he continued down the street, Ivan Ilyitch found himself speaking aloud, weaving grand theories and elaborate arguments to an invisible audience. The night, so silent and vast, seemed to embrace his words, magnifying his conviction and lending a kind of poetic rhythm to his thoughts. By the time he reached the Great Prospect, his earlier frustrations had melted away, leaving only the comforting certainty of his own brilliance.

"'Flog him in the police station,' he said that deliberately, just to provoke me," Ivan Ilyitch muttered to himself, his stride quickening as if to outpace his own irritation. "What utter nonsense! Flogging? No, that's not my way. You can beat a man, but words—words can strike deeper, cut sharper, and linger longer. I'll punish Trifon with words, with reproaches he won't forget. Yes, that's the civilized approach. Flogging, after all, is an archaic method, h'm… though the debate over its morality is ongoing, h'm…"

His thoughts trailed off, distracted by the uneven pavement. "Damn this accursed city!" he exclaimed aloud as he stumbled slightly. "And this is supposed to be the capital? Enlightenment, progress— bah! A man could break his leg here!" He paused, rubbing his shin before continuing. "And as for Semyon Ivanovitch, what a smug, despicable face he has. Laughing at me earlier, mocking me when I said people would embrace one another in a moral sense. Well, why shouldn't they? They will embrace, and what's it to him? I wouldn't embrace him, though—I'd much rather embrace a peasant, someone simple, uncorrupted by pretension."

He stopped briefly to adjust his coat, then resumed his walk. "If I meet a peasant tonight, I shall talk to him," he resolved. "Perhaps I was unclear earlier. Maybe the wine muddled my words, as it often does. Yes, I must stop drinking. In the evening, you babble away, and by morning, you regret every word. Yet here I am, walking steadily enough. No, I'm not drunk; it's just that they're all scoundrels, every last one of them!"

Ivan Ilyitch's thoughts ebbed and flowed in fragments, the cool night air invigorating his mind. Soon, the rhythmic tapping of his boots on the wooden pavement began to calm him. His agitation softened into a reflective haze. Five minutes more, and he might have been entirely at peace—might even have felt drowsy—but then, faint strains of music reached his ears. He stopped abruptly, the lively melody pulling him from his reverie.

Across the street, in a dilapidated one-story wooden house, a celebration was in full swing. Violins scratched out a lively tune, a double bass rumbled steadily, and a flute shrieked its high-pitched contribution to what sounded like a quadrille. From within came the thud of feet on wooden floors, unmistakable evidence of energetic dancing. Outside, a small crowd had gathered—mostly women bundled in wadded pelisses and kerchiefs, craning their necks to peer through a crack in the shutters. The air was alive with the unmistakable hum of festivity.

Curious, Ivan Ilyitch crossed the street, his expensive fur coat catching the moonlight as he approached a policeman stationed nearby. "Whose house is this, brother?" he asked, his tone carrying the authority of his rank. As he spoke, he casually flung open his coat just enough to reveal the glinting decoration pinned to his chest.

The policeman immediately straightened, recognizing the insignia. "This house, your Honour? It belongs to the registration clerk, Pseldonimov."

"Pseldonimov?" Ivan Ilyitch repeated, the name vaguely familiar. "And what's the occasion? A wedding?"

"Yes, your Honour," the policeman confirmed. "He's marrying the daughter of a titular councillor, Mlekopitaev. The house comes with the bride."

"So, it's Pseldonimov's house now, not Mlekopitaev's?"

"Exactly, sir. It was Mlekopitaev's, but now it's Pseldonimov's."

"H'm, interesting." Ivan Ilyitch nodded thoughtfully. "I ask because Pseldonimov is one of my subordinates. I'm a general in his department."

"Indeed, your Excellency," the policeman replied, drawing himself up even straighter, clearly eager to impress.

Ivan Ilyitch stood still, his thoughts swirling. Pseldonimov… yes, the name rang a bell. He pictured a young man—thin, awkward, with tufts of flaxen hair and a nose too large for his face. His uniform had been threadbare, and his trousers so ill-fitting as to verge on indecency. Ivan Ilyitch recalled briefly considering a Christmas bonus for the poor fellow—ten roubles, perhaps, to improve his wardrobe—but something in Pseldonimov's austere, almost repellant demeanor had made him reconsider. Yet here he was now, hosting a wedding in a house of his own, with a dowry of four hundred roubles and property attached. The juxtaposition of the surnames Pseldonimov and Mlekopitaev had even elicited a wry comment from Ivan Ilyitch when he approved the marriage request weeks ago.

Lost in thought, Ivan Ilyitch felt a surge of conflicting emotions. "So here I stand," he mused, "outside the home of my subordinate on the happiest day of his life. And what if I were to go in? What would Pseldonimov think? He'd be terrified at first, of course—frozen with embarrassment. But why should he be? I am no ordinary general. If I entered, it would not be to scold or to intimidate, but to inspire, to demonstrate the principles of humanity I've so fervently advocated."

He began pacing, his thoughts racing. "Yes, humanity! That's the cornerstone of everything. Stepan Nikiforovitch scoffed at me earlier, but here's a chance to prove my point. A gesture like this—stepping into the home of a clerk earning ten roubles a month—would be revolutionary, a true act of moral courage. It would unsettle conventions, challenge the old ways, and yet... it would be beautiful, patriarchal, even sublime. Others might see it as folly, but I would transform it into a noble act, a symbol of progress and unity."

The music swelled again, and Ivan Ilyitch stopped in his tracks. "Shall I go in?" he asked himself. "Shall I show them all what it means to lead by example? Yes, I shall!" His resolve hardened, and with a determined stride, he moved toward the brightly lit house, his mind already composing the magnanimous speech he would deliver to the astonished guests.

"Here I am, standing outside this house, and what if I were to step inside?" Ivan Ilyitch mused, his mind racing ahead of him, building the scenario brick by brick. "Of course, the moment I walk in, they would stop everything. The dancing would halt, the music would falter, and

54

everyone would stare at me in disbelief. It would be like a scene out of a play—the grand general descending into the modest home of his subordinate. Their jaws would drop, their eyes would go wide, and for a moment, they'd all be frozen, unsure whether to bow, to run, or simply faint from shock."

He allowed himself a wry smile at the imagined scene. "But then I'd take charge, wouldn't I? I'd go straight up to Pseldonimov, who'd likely be shaking in his boots, and I'd flash him the warmest, most affable smile. In the simplest, most casual tone, I'd say, 'Well, my dear fellow, I've just come from his Excellency Stepan Nikiforovitch's. You know, just around the corner.' Then, lightly, with a touch of humor, I'd recount my little adventure with Trifon. That would break the ice. From Trifon, I'd segue seamlessly into how I decided to walk here on foot—'And then I heard music,' I'd say. 'So I asked a policeman what the commotion was and learned it was your wedding! Well, how could I not stop by? I thought to myself, let me see how my clerks celebrate such a joyous occasion.'"

He chuckled at his own cleverness, imagining Pseldonimov's reaction. "Would he dare to turn me out? Impossible! The very thought! No, he'd be half out of his mind with joy and terror. He'd rush to find me the best chair in the room, his hands trembling as he struggled to decide whether to bow or salute. Delight would overwhelm him, and for a moment, he'd be completely beside himself.

"And what could be simpler, more elegant than such an action on my part? Why did I go in? Ah, now that's the deeper question. That's the moral crux of the matter, isn't it? The essence of the act."

Ivan Ilyitch paused in his mental rehearsal, savoring the imagined triumph. "Let's see, what would happen next? They'd sit me with their most important guest—a titular councillor, perhaps, or some retired captain with a ruddy nose. I'd make polite conversation, of course.

Compliment the bride, encourage the guests to continue enjoying themselves, urge them not to let my presence disrupt the festivities. I'd crack a few jokes, laugh heartily, and be utterly charming. I'm always charming when I'm in the mood for it. Yes, I'd blend right in, not as a general, but as a gentleman. That's key."

He frowned for a moment, reconsidering. "But then again, I am not just any gentleman. Morally speaking, my presence there carries a different weight. It's symbolic. They'd sense that, of course. They'd understand that this is no ordinary visit. My actions would resonate, would awaken something noble in them. I'd stay, oh, half an hour, perhaps an hour at most. Certainly not long enough to disrupt their supper preparations. I'd have a single glass of wine, toast to their happiness, and politely decline any further hospitality. 'Business,' I'd say. Just that one word. And with it, they'd all straighten their backs, their faces suddenly solemn with respect. They'd be reminded of the vast gulf between us—earth and sky, as it were."

He nodded to himself, satisfied. "Of course, I'd soften it immediately, smiling and joking once more, restoring the easy atmosphere. I might even tease the bride, hinting that in nine months' time I'd be back to stand as godfather to their first child. That would bring a roar of laughter from the guests. The bride would blush, I'd kiss her forehead with a fatherly air, and then, with a final blessing, I'd take my leave."

He pictured the aftermath with growing satisfaction. "The next day, the whole office would be buzzing. They'd whisper about how the general himself attended Pseldonimov's wedding. By then, I'd be my usual stern, exacting self, but they'd see me differently. They'd know my heart, my true nature. 'He's strict, but he's an angel of a man,' they'd say. I'd have won them over, body and soul, with one simple act that none of those old fogies like Stepan Nikiforovitch would ever dream of attempting."

His imagination ran further. "And Pseldonimov! He'd tell the story to his children, who'd tell it to their children. For generations, they'd pass down the tale of how the great general graced their humble wedding with his presence. It would become a family legend, a sacred story. By elevating him in this way, I'd be restoring his dignity, giving him something to hold onto. A man who earns ten roubles a month! To him, this act would be transformative."

He strode forward, his resolve hardening. "If I do this five, ten times—who knows?—my name will be imprinted on their hearts. They'll remember me as a true leader, a man of the people. Popularity like that—why, it could change everything. Who knows where it might lead?" His heart swelled with the possibilities as he approached the house, ready to transform his vision into reality.

The thoughts that had surged through Ivan Ilyitch's mind in mere moments might have remained as harmless musings, and he could have walked home quietly, putting Stepan Nikiforovitch to shame in his imagination alone. Such a course of action would have been prudent, even wise. But unfortunately, fate had conspired against him in this eccentric moment.

As he stood there, the smug, disdainful expressions of Stepan Nikiforovitch and Semyon Ivanovitch seemed to materialize before him, vivid and mocking.

"We shall break down!" Stepan Nikiforovitch had sneered, his voice dripping with condescension.

"He-he-he!" Semyon Ivanovitch had added with his signature sardonic chuckle, the one that grated on Ivan Ilyitch like nails on glass.

"We'll see who breaks down!" Ivan Ilyitch muttered aloud, his face flushing hot with defiance and a sudden surge of adrenaline. Without hesitation, he stepped off the pavement, crossed the street, and made his way toward the house where Pseldonimov's wedding celebration was in full swing.

His decision felt monumental, almost preordained. The stars seemed to carry him forward as he strode through the open gate with resolute purpose. A shaggy little sheepdog barked hoarsely at his legs, more out of duty than conviction, but Ivan Ilyitch dismissed it with an almost contemptuous nudge of his foot. The dog retreated, and he pressed onward, following a wooden plank path to the covered porch. Three creaky wooden steps led him to a narrow entryway, dimly lit by a feeble tallow candle.

The moment he stepped inside, misfortune struck. His left foot, still clad in its galosh, sank into something cold and gelatinous. Glancing down, he realized with horror that he had trampled a beautifully prepared galantine. Around it were other dishes: more jelly, and what appeared to be blancmange, all carefully placed to cool. Ivan Ilyitch froze. For a fleeting moment, he considered retreating, slinking away before anyone noticed. But pride intervened. No, he couldn't stoop to that. Instead, he wiped his galosh on the wooden floorboards, attempting to erase the evidence of his clumsiness.

He fumbled for the felt-covered door and, upon finding it, entered the house. The small anteroom he stepped into was crowded with coats, scarves, and galoshes. On the other side of the room, a makeshift band of street musicians—a quartet consisting of two violins, a flute, and a double bass—were energetically sawing out the final figure of a quadrille. Their unpolished music spilled through an open door into a smoke-filled drawing room, where laughter, shouting, and the rhythmic thud of dancing feet created a cacophony of joyous chaos.

Ivan Ilyitch stood for a moment, taking in the scene. The room, though small and crowded with about thirty guests, pulsed with an exuberant energy. The air was thick with tobacco smoke and the faint odor of wax. Amid the swirling dresses and animated faces, a blue scarf brushed against his nose as a medical student, wild-haired and red-faced with excitement, barreled past, nearly knocking into him. The atmosphere was one of unrestrained revelry, but it felt utterly alien to Ivan Ilyitch, who remained rooted near the door, his cap in hand.

For a few seconds, no one noticed him. Then, as the quadrille ended, the very reaction Ivan Ilyitch had envisioned earlier on the pavement unfolded with uncanny accuracy. A ripple of murmurs spread through the crowd. Faces turned toward him, one by one, eyes wide with surprise. The music stopped; the laughter faded. Gradually, an awkward silence settled over the room as an invisible line seemed to form between the general and the guests. They edged back slightly, creating a widening gap on the floor littered with sweet wrappers and cigarette butts.

From the midst of the gathering, a figure hesitantly emerged—a young man in uniform with a hooked nose and a mop of flaxen hair. It was Pseldonimov, his expression one of pure terror. He shuffled forward with a hunched posture, his every movement radiating uncertainty. His face bore the same look of timid dread one might see on a dog summoned by its master for punishment.

"Good evening, Pseldonimov. Do you know me?" Ivan Ilyitch asked, his voice faltering slightly as he realized how awkward the situation had become. The moment the words left his mouth, he regretted them. The question sounded both unnecessary and clumsy.

"Y-your Excellency!" Pseldonimov stammered, his voice barely audible.

"Indeed. I happened to be in the neighborhood," Ivan Ilyitch began, trying to sound casual. "I thought I'd drop in and congratulate you. I heard the music and realized it must be your wedding. Naturally, I couldn't resist paying my respects."

But Pseldonimov stood frozen, his wide-eyed confusion bordering on panic. His mind seemed incapable of processing what was happening. The sight of his superior at his modest wedding was so incongruous that he appeared to suspect a cruel joke.

"You won't turn me out, I suppose?" Ivan Ilyitch added with a forced laugh, trying to lighten the mood. "Surely, you'd welcome a visitor—even an uninvited one."

Pseldonimov opened his mouth but said nothing, his face a mask of bewilderment. Ivan Ilyitch's discomfort deepened. He could feel the weight of every pair of eyes in the room fixed upon him, scrutinizing his every gesture.

"I'm not in the way, am I?" he ventured, his voice barely above a whisper now. "If so, I can leave...."

A faint tremor appeared at the corner of his mouth, betraying his growing unease. He stood there, a towering figure of authority, reduced to a state of near humiliation by the very people he had intended to inspire.

Pseldonimov, though visibly flustered, began to recover himself. His expression shifted from frozen panic to hurried deference, though his movements were still awkward and jerky.

"Good heavens, your Excellency ... such an honor!" he stammered, bowing repeatedly. "Please, graciously sit down, your Excellency!" He gestured with both hands toward a sofa, hastily shifting a small table away from its front to make room, evidently trying to create an inviting space.

Ivan Ilyitch, inwardly relieved by the semblance of normalcy returning, sank into the sofa. Almost immediately, someone darted forward to push the table back into position before him. As he settled, he became acutely aware of the peculiar dynamic in the room. He was the only one seated; everyone else—guests, musicians, even the servants peering in from the hallway—stood watching him. This silent attention felt suffocating, as though he were on display. The stiffness of the gathering confirmed that his unanticipated arrival had unsettled everyone.

Yet it was not the moment to begin making lighthearted conversation. He could sense the crowd needed reassurance, and he himself was grappling with a growing awkwardness. Pseldonimov stood just a few feet away, still bent at an angle as though perpetually mid-bow, his nervousness rendering him incapable of any expression beyond pure reverence.

Then, suddenly, a small figure emerged from the corner of the room. A wave of relief swept over Ivan Ilyitch as he recognized the individual: Akim Petrovitch Zubikov, the head clerk from his office. Though their relationship had never gone beyond the formalities of a superior and subordinate, Ivan Ilyitch had always considered Zubikov dependable and businesslike. At this moment, Zubikov's presence felt like a godsend—a familiar and steady face in a sea of confusion.

With newfound enthusiasm, Ivan Ilyitch rose from the sofa and extended his hand—not just two fingers, but his entire hand—in a gesture of respect and cordiality. Akim Petrovitch, visibly taken aback but deeply flattered, took his superior's hand in both of his own with almost comical reverence. This small but deliberate act transformed the atmosphere. The tension in the room lessened, and Ivan Ilyitch sensed that he had regained a measure of control over the situation.

"Ah, Akim Petrovitch!" Ivan Ilyitch exclaimed warmly, his voice steadier now. "It is good to see you here."

With Zubikov's presence serving as a stabilizing force, Ivan Ilyitch shifted his focus. Pseldonimov, though still hovering nearby, was effectively sidelined. This allowed the general to direct his remarks primarily toward the head clerk, using him as a bridge to communicate with the room. Pseldonimov, now relegated to the role of an onlooker, continued to stand rigidly, his hands nervously fidgeting with the cuffs of his ill-fitting jacket.

"Imagine my surprise," Ivan Ilyitch began, his tone taking on an almost theatrical quality, "to find myself here tonight. A curious chain of events brought me to your wedding, Pseldonimov. Truly, it seems fate itself intended me to join in your celebration!"

Pseldonimov's mouth opened slightly as though to respond, but no words came out. Ivan Ilyitch pressed on, now addressing Zubikov directly, as if to draw focus away from the groom's evident discomfort.

"I was just at the home of Stepan Nikiforovitch Nikiforov," he explained, leaning back slightly to adopt a more conversational tone. "You know of him, of course—the esteemed privy councillor and a man of no small reputation. Today was both his birthday and a housewarming for his new residence—a splendid property, I must say."

Zubikov nodded vigorously, his entire demeanor one of deferential agreement. The crowd, meanwhile, listened with a mixture of awe and curiosity. Ivan Ilyitch could feel their attention turning toward him, their initial shock gradually morphing into interest.

"I must say, the evening was delightful," he continued, allowing a faint smile to play across his lips. "We had champagne, excellent conversation, and even a bit of friendly debate. But then—" He paused for effect, glancing around the room as though letting the suspense build. "Then, just as I was leaving, I discovered that my coachman, Trifon, had gone missing—along with my carriage!"

A collective gasp rippled through the audience. Even Pseldonimov, despite his wooden demeanor, widened his eyes slightly in surprise.

"Yes, gone without a trace!" Ivan Ilyitch exclaimed, leaning forward slightly to emphasize his words. "And do you know why? The scoundrel had taken the carriage to attend a wedding—this very wedding, as it turns out!"

This revelation elicited murmurs and whispers from the assembled guests. Some exchanged glances, while others looked toward Pseldonimov as though expecting him to offer an explanation. Zubikov chuckled politely, clearly eager to match the general's tone.

"But no matter," Ivan Ilyitch said, waving his hand dismissively. "What better reason could there be for such a breach of duty than to celebrate the union of two fine individuals?" He gestured vaguely toward Pseldonimov, whose face reddened under the scrutiny.

Encouraged by the faint ripple of laughter from the crowd, Ivan Ilyitch pressed forward. "And so, with no carriage to be found, I decided to walk. The night was beautiful, after all—clear skies, crisp air, and the faint sound of music guiding me here. And now that I am here, I must say, the atmosphere is delightful. You've gathered quite the lively company, Pseldonimov!"

"He-he-he! To be sure!" Zubikov chimed in obligingly, his laughter more enthusiastic than the situation warranted.

Ivan Ilyitch smiled, but his eyes flicked briefly to Pseldonimov, who still had not managed even a faint grin. The groom's stony expression grated on his nerves, but he pressed on, determined not to let the moment slip from his control.

"If I may say so," Ivan Ilyitch added, his tone becoming almost paternal, "this is a night to remember, a true testament to joy and the bonds that unite us. Let us raise our spirits and celebrate with the warmth and camaraderie befitting such a momentous occasion."

As he concluded, a faint cheer rose from the crowd. The ice had begun to thaw, though Pseldonimov's rigid posture remained a frustrating reminder of the challenges Ivan Ilyitch faced in fully winning over the room. Still, he felt a growing confidence that his impromptu visit would, in the end, be seen as a gesture of goodwill and magnanimity.

"I thought it would be a pleasant surprise to drop in and see my clerk on this momentous occasion. After all, I'm not one to intrude where I'm not wanted," Ivan Ilyitch began, his tone light but tinged with unease. "If my presence is a disruption, just say the word, and I'll leave. I assure you, I came only to offer my congratulations and see how the celebration was going."

His words seemed to send a ripple through the room. Akim Petrovitch, standing awkwardly nearby, cast him a mawkishly sweet look, as if silently reassuring him, "How could your Excellency ever be in the way?" Around the room, the other guests began to stir, their stiff postures loosening slightly. Almost imperceptibly, the atmosphere shifted. Several women ventured to take their seats, a promising signal of the tension easing. The bolder ones fanned themselves with their handkerchiefs, and one particularly daring woman, clad in a worn velvet dress, made a loud comment, seemingly to assert her ease in the general's presence. Her companion, an officer, attempted to respond in kind but quickly retreated into silence upon realizing their voices were the only ones breaking the quiet.

The men—government clerks and a smattering of students— exchanged glances, as if daring each other to relax. A few cleared their throats, shuffled their feet, and moved hesitantly about the room. Yet, despite the faint thaw, there was a palpable undercurrent of suspicion. The unwelcome guest had disrupted their merriment, and many regarded him with thinly veiled hostility. The officer, perhaps trying to save face, edged closer to the table, his expression a mixture of irritation and curiosity.

"But tell me, my friend," Ivan Ilyitch said, turning to Pseldonimov with what he hoped was an affable smile, "may I have the honor of knowing your full name?"

"Porfiry Petrovitch, your Excellency," Pseldonimov replied stiffly, his posture as straight as if he were standing at attention.

"Well, Porfiry Petrovitch," Ivan Ilyitch continued, his tone growing warmer, "introduce me to your bride, won't you? I'd like to meet the lady of the hour." He began to rise, but Pseldonimov, clearly flustered, darted toward the drawing room.

The bride, who had been standing near the door, quickly slipped out of sight as soon as she heard herself mentioned. Moments later, Pseldonimov reappeared, leading her by the hand. The guests parted like a wave to make room for them, their eyes riveted on the scene. Ivan Ilyitch rose to his feet and greeted her with a polished, aristocratic half-bow, his most charming smile firmly in place.

"Delighted to make your acquaintance," he said, his voice smooth and affable. "And especially on such a joyful occasion as this."

His graciousness elicited a soft murmur from the crowd. A woman in the velvet dress leaned toward her neighbor and whispered audibly, "Charmé!" adding a touch of theatricality to her exclamation.

The bride was a petite, delicate young woman, likely no older than seventeen. Pale, with a sharp little nose and a small, pointed face, she possessed an understated prettiness that contrasted starkly with her thin, almost birdlike frame. Her quick, observant eyes betrayed no shyness; instead, they met Ivan Ilyitch's gaze with a steady, almost defiant stare. Her demeanor suggested that she was not easily overawed, even by the likes of a general.

"She is quite pretty," Ivan Ilyitch remarked in a lower tone, as though confiding to Pseldonimov but ensuring the bride could hear. He hoped the compliment would elicit a blush or a shy smile, but her expression remained impassive. Her only response was a perfunctory nod, and her silence created an awkward void.

"An interesting couple," Ivan Ilyitch thought, glancing from the bride to her groom. "But this silence—it's unbearable." He asked the bride a few polite questions, but her answers were monosyllabic at best. Her reticence, coupled with Pseldonimov's wooden demeanor, left him feeling increasingly out of place.

"My dear friends," he said at last, addressing the entire room in an effort to regain control of the situation, "surely I haven't disrupted your enjoyment? Do let me know if I've been an inconvenience."

Sweat was beginning to bead on his palms, a sensation he found deeply unsettling.

"No, no, your Excellency," the officer spoke up, his tone polite but tinged with defensiveness. "We were just cooling off for a moment. We'll be resuming shortly."

The bride turned toward the officer with evident approval. Ivan Ilyitch noted the exchange with growing irritation. Pseldonimov, meanwhile, stood motionless, his hooked nose and hunched posture giving him the air of a valet awaiting his master's next command. The comparison sprang unbidden to Ivan Ilyitch's mind, and he found it maddening. "Is he truly incapable of even the smallest gesture of warmth?" he thought.

Suddenly, the crowd shifted, and a new figure entered the room. She was a stout, middle-aged woman, plainly dressed in her Sunday best. A large shawl was wrapped snugly around her shoulders, and a slightly crooked cap adorned her head, suggesting she was unaccustomed to wearing such finery. In her hands, she carried a modest tray bearing a single bottle of champagne and two glasses.

"Your Excellency," she began, her voice warm and unpretentious, "we are humbled and honored by your presence at my son's wedding. Please, do us the kindness of toasting the young couple's health. It would mean so much to us."

Her rosy cheeks and kind, unassuming smile were a balm to Ivan Ilyitch's frazzled nerves. The sincerity of her gesture seemed to cut through the awkwardness that had been suffocating the room. He felt a surge of gratitude and relief as he accepted her offering.

"Madam," he said, rising to his feet, "it is I who am honored to share in this joyful occasion. Let us indeed drink to the happiness of this fine young couple."

The room began to stir again, and for the first time that evening, Ivan Ilyitch sensed that he might yet salvage the situation.

"So you are the mo-ther of your so-on?" Ivan Ilyitch inquired, rising from the sofa with exaggerated courtesy, his syllables drawn out in a tone of mock ceremony that barely masked his unease.

"Yes, indeed, your Excellency," Pseldonimov stammered, craning his neck and thrusting forward his long, thin nose in a gesture of eager compliance. His discomfort was palpable, but he tried to compensate with deference.

"Ah! Delighted—truly de-light-ed to make your acquaintance," Ivan Ilyitch replied, bowing slightly toward the woman.

"Please, your Excellency, do not refuse us this honor," the mother entreated, her voice warm and laden with earnest hospitality.

"With the greatest pleasure," Ivan Ilyitch responded, attempting to match her warmth. The tray she carried was carefully placed on the table, and Pseldonimov, in a sudden burst of activity, scrambled to pour the wine. Ivan Ilyitch remained standing as he accepted the glass, lifting it with a ceremonial flourish.

"I am particularly, particularly glad on this special occasion," he began, addressing the bride and groom with a labored air of geniality, "that I have the opportunity ... the privilege ... to testify before all of you my heartfelt wishes. As your chief, I must express my sincerest congratulations. Madam," he said, turning to the bride with a strained smile, "and you, Porfiry, my dear friend, I wish you endless happiness and the fullest blessings for many, many long years."

With an almost theatrical flourish, Ivan Ilyitch drained the glass, his seventh of the evening. The gesture, intended to convey warmth and ease, only underscored the growing tension in the room. Pseldonimov stood motionless, his expression as grave as ever, perhaps even edging toward a faint sullenness. The general felt a wave of irritation rising in him.

"And that officer," Ivan Ilyitch thought bitterly, casting a sideways glance at the man in uniform who stood rigid and silent in the corner, "couldn't even muster a simple 'hurrah!' It would have lightened the mood, it really would have."

At that moment, the old woman turned to Akim Petrovitch, the head clerk, her tone a mix of maternal pride and gentle pleading. "And you too, Akim Petrovitch, drink to their health. You are his superior, after all. He works under you. Look after my boy, I beg you, as a mother would. Please don't forget us in the future, our kind and good friend."

"How charmingly earnest these old Russian women are," Ivan Ilyitch mused, his irritation momentarily displaced by a genuine appreciation for her sincerity. "They have a way of warming the heart. Such a lively spirit she has! I've always admired the simplicity of the people."

At that moment, a second tray appeared, carried in by a young maid whose crisp cotton dress rustled audibly as she moved. She approached with visible effort, balancing an enormous tray laden with plates of apples, sugared sweets, meringues, walnuts, and other confections. Ivan Ilyitch immediately recognized the gesture: the tray, previously enjoyed by all the guests, had now been brought over as a special offering for him.

"Do not disdain our humble fare, your Excellency," the old woman said, bowing low once more. "What little we have, we are pleased to offer you."

"Delighted, truly delighted!" Ivan Ilyitch exclaimed, taking a walnut from the tray with evident pleasure. He cracked it expertly between his fingers, determined to appear approachable and at ease. Internally, he resolved to secure his popularity at all costs.

A sudden giggle interrupted his thoughts. It came from the bride. Ivan Ilyitch turned toward her, a hopeful smile spreading across his face.

"What is it?" he asked, encouraged by this unexpected sign of animation.

"It's Ivan Kostenkinitch," she answered, lowering her gaze with an embarrassed smile. "He's making me laugh."

Following her gaze, Ivan Ilyitch spotted a flaxen-haired young man seated awkwardly at the far end of the sofa, whispering something to the bride. The youth stood up abruptly, clearly flustered but attempting to compose himself.

"I was telling the lady about a 'dream book,' your Excellency," he mumbled, his voice tinged with nervousness, as though apologizing for his very existence.

"A dream book, you say?" Ivan Ilyitch inquired with polite condescension.

"Yes, your Excellency. It's a new literary one. I was explaining to the lady that dreaming of Mr. Panaev supposedly foretells spilling coffee on one's shirtfront."

"How innocent," Ivan Ilyitch thought, suppressing a sigh of annoyance. The young man, oblivious to the general's growing impatience, flushed a deep red, clearly delighted to have spoken.

Before Ivan Ilyitch could respond, another voice chimed in, its tone confident and assertive. "There's something far more amusing than that," said a young man in a white waistcoat, holding his hat with an air of studied nonchalance. "They say Mr. Kraevsky is writing articles for a new encyclopedia. Satirical ones, at that."

This newcomer, evidently a staff writer for the satirical journal The Firebrand, carried himself with an air of superiority that Ivan Ilyitch found particularly irksome. The general noted his casual demeanor and uninvited familiarity with growing disapproval.

The flaxen-haired youth, eager to reclaim attention, added hastily, "The joke is that Mr. Kraevsky supposedly thinks 'satirical' should be spelled with a 'y' instead of an 'i.' That's why it's funny, your Excellency."

But his attempt to amuse fell flat. Ivan Ilyitch's restrained reaction conveyed that he was unimpressed, and the young man, sensing his misstep, blushed furiously and sank into a morose silence for the rest of the evening.

The satirical writer, however, seemed intent on staying close to Ivan Ilyitch, positioning himself with an air of camaraderie that struck the general as unseemly.

Desperate to shift the conversation, Ivan Ilyitch turned to Pseldonimov with a question that had been nagging at him. "Porfiry, tell me—why are you called Pseldonimov instead of Pseudonimov? Surely your name ought to be the latter?"

Pseldonimov looked confused but answered dutifully, "I cannot say for certain, your Excellency."

"It must have been a clerical error," Akim Petrovitch interjected helpfully. "When his father joined the service, the name was likely written down incorrectly in the official documents, and it's remained Pseldonimov ever since."

"Ah, I see," Ivan Ilyitch said, though inwardly he felt more exasperated than ever. "How utterly trivial."

"Un-doubted-ly," Ivan Ilyitch said with deliberate emphasis, letting the word roll off his tongue with the warmth of one offering a sage observation, "un-doubted-ly. Consider, Pseldonimov comes directly from the literary word pseudonym, signifying something, while Pseldonimov—well, it amounts to nothing at all."

"That is due to foolishness," Akim Petrovitch interjected, as though providing a footnote to a lecture.

"What precisely do you mean by 'due to foolishness'?" Ivan Ilyitch asked, raising his eyebrows, though his tone remained indulgent.

"The Russian common folk," Akim Petrovitch elaborated, "often alter letters out of ignorance, and pronounce words in their own peculiar way. For instance, they say nevalid instead of invalid."

"Ah, yes, nevalid! He-he-he!" Ivan Ilyitch chuckled, attempting a jovial tone that felt slightly forced.

"And mumber, your Excellency," boomed the tall officer, seizing his chance to shine, "they say mumber instead of number!"

"Mumber! Oh yes, mumber instead of number!" Ivan Ilyitch echoed, managing another laugh. "To be sure, to be sure.... He-he-he!" The officer, visibly pleased, adjusted his tie with an air of accomplishment.

"And sometimes," interjected the young man from the satirical paper, his voice cutting through the brief lull, "nigh by instead of near."

Ivan Ilyitch, however, chose to ignore this. His chuckles, after all, were not for everyone.

"Nigh by," the young man persisted, his irritation evident. "Nigh by instead of near."

Ivan Ilyitch turned a stern gaze upon him, silencing him effectively. Pseldonimov, noticing the tension, leaned toward the young man and whispered, "Why insist? Let it go."

"But I was only talking. Mayn't one speak?" the young man grumbled under his breath, though he refrained from saying more and soon left the room. His exit was not to sulk but to retreat to the small back room, where refreshments awaited.

In the snug, dimly lit room, the young man poured himself a glass of vodka, his motions sharp with irritation. The medical student, the life of the dancing crowd with his disheveled hair and exuberance, bounded into the room, heading straight for the decanter.

"They're about to start again," the student exclaimed excitedly. "Come and see! I'm going to dance a solo on my head. After supper, I'll attempt the fish dance. It's perfect for a wedding—and a subtle jab at Pseldonimov too. Kleopatra Semyonovna—what a lively one she is! You can try anything with her!"

"He's a reactionary," the young man from the satirical paper muttered gloomily, tossing back his vodka.

"Who's a reactionary?" the student asked, already half out the door.

"That 'personage,' the one they're pampering with sweets. He's a reactionary, I tell you."

"What nonsense," the student dismissed with a wave, rushing back to the dance floor as the music struck up. Left alone, the young man on the satirical paper poured another drink. As the alcohol took hold, his irritation deepened into a simmering resentment against Ivan Ilyitch, who had slighted him so cruelly.

Meanwhile, in the main room, the atmosphere was shifting. Though Ivan Ilyitch had provided what he believed was a sufficient explanation for his presence, the guests had remained uneasy. Then, like magic, a whisper began to circulate: "He's a little … under the influence." What had initially seemed a dreadful imposition now made perfect sense. The guests relaxed, their guarded politeness giving way to unrestrained merriment. Laughter rang out, voices grew louder, and the festivities resumed with renewed vigor.

The quadrille began. Just as Ivan Ilyitch prepared to address the bride with another carefully crafted remark, the tall officer dashed forward, dropped theatrically to one knee, and whisked her away before Ivan Ilyitch could protest. The bride, clearly relieved, didn't even glance back as she joined the dance.

"Well, she has every right to enjoy herself," Ivan Ilyitch mused, though inwardly he bristled. "And yet, it's evident—they simply don't know how to behave."

Turning to Pseldonimov, who hovered nearby with an almost canine devotion, he said, "Don't stand on ceremony, my dear Porfiry. Surely you have arrangements to attend to or something pressing…. Please, don't let me keep you."

Pseldonimov, with his perpetually bent neck and intent gaze, remained unmoving. His presence was becoming unbearable to Ivan

Ilyitch, who thought with growing irritation, "Why is he watching me like that? What does he want?"

Akim Petrovitch, eager to play the dutiful host, seized a bottle of champagne and approached Ivan Ilyitch. "Will you allow me, your Excellency?" he asked, holding the bottle reverently, as though presenting a sacred offering.

"I ... I'm not sure I should...." Ivan Ilyitch began hesitantly.

But Akim Petrovitch, with an almost reverential glow, was already pouring. After filling Ivan Ilyitch's glass, he carefully poured a smaller amount for himself. His deference, bordering on obsequiousness, was both gratifying and irritating.

The general sipped his champagne—tepid and poor in quality— while Akim Petrovitch fidgeted beside him, clearly struggling to find a topic of conversation. Ivan Ilyitch, though frustrated, felt a small, fleeting satisfaction in the quiet acknowledgment of his authority.

Ivan Ilyitch glanced at the bottle and thought, "The old fellow probably wants a drink himself but doesn't dare take one until I do. I shouldn't stop him. Besides, it would look ridiculous to leave the bottle untouched between us." To break the silence, he took a sip, thinking it was better than just sitting there doing nothing.

"I'm here," he said slowly, pausing for emphasis between words, "I'm here, you might say, by chance. And naturally, there are some who might think it's ... inappropriate for someone like me to attend ... an event like this."

Akim Petrovitch, sitting nearby, didn't respond. He merely watched with timid curiosity.

"But I hope," Ivan Ilyitch continued, "you can understand why I've come. It's not just to drink wine ... he-he!" He let out a small laugh, attempting to lighten the mood.

Akim Petrovitch tried to join in with a chuckle of his own, imitating his superior, but the sound barely came out. He remained silent and offered no comforting reply.

"I'm here," Ivan Ilyitch went on, "to encourage you, to show, in a way, a moral purpose." He felt annoyed by Akim Petrovitch's lack of response, but before he could continue, he suddenly fell silent himself. He noticed that Akim Petrovitch had lowered his gaze as though he were guilty of some offense. Feeling slightly awkward, Ivan Ilyitch took another sip from his glass. At the same time, Akim Petrovitch hastily grabbed the bottle and refilled his superior's drink as if it were his only way to escape discomfort.

"You really don't have many ideas, do you?" Ivan Ilyitch thought, glaring at Akim Petrovitch, who, under the weight of that stern gaze, decided it was safer to remain silent and keep his eyes downcast. The two men sat side by side in an oppressive, awkward silence that lasted a couple of painful minutes.

A few words about Akim Petrovitch: he was a man of the old school, humble to the point of obsequiousness. From his earliest years, he had been trained to be meek and subservient, though he was a kind-hearted and honest man. He came from a family that had lived and worked in Petersburg for generations and had never set foot outside the city. This made him a very particular type of Russian, one whose entire world revolved around Petersburg, his workplace, and his modest salary. Russian traditions and songs were foreign to him, except perhaps "Lutchinushka," which he might have heard on a barrel organ.

Petersburg Russians could be recognized by two peculiar habits: first, they always referred to the local newspaper as the "Academic News" instead of the "Petersburg News." Second, they never said "breakfast," preferring the word "Frühstück," pronounced with a distinct emphasis on the first syllable. These traits made them stand out from other Russians. While Akim Petrovitch was no fool and could discuss his field of expertise intelligently, he thought it improper to respond to Ivan Ilyitch's lofty musings, though he was burning with curiosity about his superior's real motives.

Meanwhile, Ivan Ilyitch sank deeper into thought, sipping his drink absentmindedly every few moments. Akim Petrovitch dutifully refilled the glass each time. Both men sat in silence. Ivan Ilyitch's gaze wandered to the dancers, and something suddenly caught his attention.

The dancing was lively, full of unrestrained joy. The guests weren't particularly skilled dancers, but their sheer enthusiasm made up for it. The officer stood out, particularly in solos where he performed exaggerated moves, bending sharply to one side as though he might fall, only to recover with equal vigor in the opposite direction. He maintained a serious expression, fully convinced everyone was watching him.

Another guest, who had clearly had too much to drink, fell asleep beside his partner, leaving her to dance alone. A young clerk, meanwhile, repeatedly kissed the end of his partner's blue scarf as they crossed paths during the quadrille. His partner acted as though she didn't notice and glided along gracefully. The medical student even performed a headstand, earning wild applause and cheers from the crowd.

At first, Ivan Ilyitch found himself smiling at their uninhibited joy. He had hoped for this kind of carefree atmosphere, but as time passed, he began to feel uneasy. The revelry seemed almost disrespectful, as if the guests had forgotten his presence entirely. One woman, wearing a shabby second-hand velvet dress, even pinned her skirt to resemble trousers, to the delight of her dance partner.

"They were so reserved before, and now they're completely uninhibited," Ivan Ilyitch thought. "How did things change so quickly? Have they forgotten I'm here?"

Trying to recover his footing, Ivan Ilyitch turned to the medical student and said, "You dance remarkably well, young man." But deep down, he felt an unsettling doubt gnawing at him. Something had shifted, and he wasn't sure what.

The student suddenly turned toward Ivan Ilyitch, made a ridiculous face, and, leaning in so close that his breath could be felt, let out a loud, pitch-perfect imitation of a rooster's crow. It was so unexpected and absurd that the room erupted in raucous laughter. Despite his bewilderment, Ivan Ilyitch stood up, clutching his hat. The imitation was undeniably good, but the sheer brazenness of it was intolerable.

Just as Ivan Ilyitch was debating how to handle the situation, Pseldonimov appeared, bowing nervously, and invited him to join them for supper. His mother followed closely behind, adding her own earnest plea.

"Your Excellency," she said with a deep bow, "please, honor us. Don't disdain our humble offering."

"I… I'm not sure," Ivan Ilyitch stammered, still clutching his hat. "I didn't come here with that intention… I really should be going…."

At that very moment, he resolved internally to leave immediately, to escape the increasingly awkward situation. But somehow, despite his resolve, he found himself staying. A minute later, he was leading the group to the supper table. Pseldonimov and his mother cleared the way for him, treating him with exaggerated reverence, and seated him in the place of honor. A freshly opened bottle of champagne was placed beside his plate. Hors d'oeuvres—salt herring and vodka—were arranged before him.

Mechanically, Ivan Ilyitch reached for the vodka, poured himself a large glass, and downed it in one gulp. He had never drunk vodka before, and the sharp burn was overwhelming. He felt as though he were tumbling uncontrollably down a hill, unable to stop himself or grab hold of anything solid.

His situation had taken an undeniably bizarre turn. It felt as though fate itself were mocking him. How had things spiraled so far out of control in just an hour? He had entered the house with noble intentions, full of warmth and goodwill toward all humanity, eager to connect with his subordinates on a deeper level. Yet now, an hour later, he felt nothing but resentment. His heart ached with irritation toward Pseldonimov, his wife, and even the entire wedding itself.

Worse still, he could sense Pseldonimov's own disdain. The young clerk's expression seemed to say, "Why don't you leave already? Curse you for imposing yourself on us!" Ivan Ilyitch had read this silent plea in Pseldonimov's eyes for some time now.

Still, he could never have admitted—either to himself or aloud—that this interpretation might be accurate. His pride wouldn't allow it. Instead, he tried to convince himself that the night could still be salvaged. Yet, deep down, he felt suffocated and yearned for freedom, for air, for peace. He was too kind-hearted to cause a scene, too bound by the weight of social expectations to leave abruptly.

He chastised himself silently. "Why am I still here? Did I come to eat and drink?" As he tasted the herring, he felt a flicker of doubt, even skepticism, about the grand purpose of his visit. The lofty ideals that had driven him to enter the house now seemed faint and far away.

But leaving without a proper conclusion felt impossible. What would people think? Rumors would spread by morning—at the office, at social gatherings, at the homes of acquaintances like the Shembels and the Shubins. Stepan Nikiforovitch and Semyon Ivanovitch would undoubtedly hear of it. If he left now, he would seem like someone who frequented lowly company, someone who had lost his sense of decorum. No, he needed to find a way to make his moral purpose clear. He had to end the evening on a note of dignity.

Yet the right moment for such an exit refused to present itself. He felt increasingly alienated. "They don't even respect me," he thought bitterly. "What are they laughing at? They're so carefree, so lacking in decency. The younger generation is completely devoid of feeling!" Still, he resolved to stay. "Now that they're all gathered at the table, I'll seize the moment. I'll talk to them about serious matters—reforms, the greatness of Russia. I can still win them over. Perhaps it's not too late."

But his confidence wavered. "How should I begin? What approach should I take to capture their attention? I'm floundering here. They're laughing over there—are they laughing at me? Oh, heavens, what am I even doing here? Why don't I just leave? Why do I keep forcing myself to stay?"

These thoughts tormented him, and a deep, unbearable shame began to settle over him. He felt trapped, his dignity eroding with every passing moment. Yet despite his internal turmoil, the evening carried on, one awkward moment following another. It seemed there was no escape from this slow, painful unraveling of his intentions.

Within two minutes of sitting at the table, an alarming realization struck Ivan Ilyitch like a thunderbolt. He was dreadfully drunk—not just slightly intoxicated as he had been before, but completely and irredeemably so. The culprit was the glass of vodka he had consumed after the champagne, which had taken hold of him with alarming speed. Every fiber of his being was now overwhelmed by a creeping sense of weakness and instability. Though his confidence seemed to swell, a persistent, gnawing voice inside him cried out, "This is bad—terribly bad—and utterly inappropriate!"

His inebriated mind began to oscillate between two opposing states. On one side, he felt a swaggering self-assurance, a daring disregard for obstacles, and an almost reckless belief that he would achieve whatever goal he had in mind. But on the other side, a dull ache in his chest gnawed at him, whispering fears about the consequences. "What will they think? How will this end? What will happen tomorrow—tomorrow—tomorrow?" These thoughts tormented him.

Before, he had vaguely sensed that there might be enemies among the guests. Now, with a heart-sinking clarity, he became convinced of it. The signs were unmistakable, he thought. But why? What had he done to provoke such hostility? His bewilderment was as painful as his growing unease.

The table was crowded with thirty guests, many of whom had clearly had too much to drink. Some were behaving with unsettling boldness, shouting over one another, bawling out toasts out of turn, and even pelting the ladies with wads of bread. One particularly unkempt man, dressed in a greasy coat, had fallen off his chair the moment he sat down and remained sprawled on the floor for the entirety of supper. Another guest repeatedly attempted to stand on the table to deliver a toast, only to be restrained by the officer, who firmly grabbed his coat-tails and pulled him down each time.

The supper itself was chaotic, despite the supposed credentials of the hired cook, who had once worked for a general. The dishes included galantine, tongue with potatoes, rissoles with peas, a goose, and, finally, blancmange. As for drinks, there was beer, vodka, and sherry, though the only champagne was the bottle placed beside Ivan Ilyitch. This arrangement required him to pour for both himself and Akim Petrovitch, who lacked the nerve to help himself without explicit permission. The rest of the guests were left to make do with whatever alcohol they could find—be it Caucasian wine or something else.

The table itself was an awkward assembly of mismatched furniture, including a card table, all covered with an assortment of tablecloths, one of which was a brightly colored Yaroslav cloth. Guests were seated haphazardly, with men and women alternating in a disorganized manner. Pseldonimov's mother chose not to sit down, bustling around to supervise instead. However, another figure made her entrance during the meal—a woman in a faded reddish silk dress, wearing a high cap and a bandage around her face for toothache. This was the bride's mother, who had only emerged from a back room for supper, her appearance underscoring her hostility toward Pseldonimov's mother. This enmity would warrant further explanation later, but for now, her presence unsettled Ivan Ilyitch. She shot him spiteful, almost sarcastic glances and made no effort to be introduced to him. Her demeanor struck him as deeply suspicious.

But she wasn't the only one who put him on edge. As Ivan Ilyitch scanned the table, he found himself growing increasingly wary of several other guests. He couldn't shake the impression that some of them were conspiring against him. One man, a bearded artist of some kind, seemed especially ominous, frequently glancing at Ivan Ilyitch and whispering to the person beside him. Another guest, visibly drunk, nevertheless exuded a certain suspicious energy. The medical student, whose antics had already been questionable, now seemed to carry an undercurrent of unpredictability. Even the officer, though previously a source of mild annoyance, now struck Ivan Ilyitch as potentially unreliable.

The young man from the satirical paper, however, was the most aggravating presence at the table. Reclining insolently in his chair, he radiated arrogance and contempt. His loud snorting and smug expression were impossible to ignore. Although the other guests seemed to disregard him entirely—likely because his contributions to the literary world amounted to just four subpar poems published in

The Firebrand—Ivan Ilyitch felt a burning irritation toward him. When a bread pellet landed suspiciously close to Ivan Ilyitch, he was convinced it had been hurled by none other than this insolent journalist.

All of this—the drunken disorder, the perceived hostility, the young journalist's defiance—deepened Ivan Ilyitch's sense of despair. The evening, which he had envisioned as a triumph of goodwill and moral purpose, had descended into a grotesque farce. The bitterness of his predicament settled heavily in his chest, leaving him to wonder how everything had gone so disastrously wrong.

Ivan Ilyitch was suddenly overtaken by a particularly troubling realization. He noticed that his speech had become slurred and that forming words required far more effort than usual. He had so much he wanted to say, but his tongue seemed to rebel against him. Even worse, he occasionally burst into loud, inexplicable laughter that caught everyone off guard, and there was no real reason for it. This embarrassing habit seemed to vanish for a moment after he accidentally drank another glass of champagne—one he hadn't even meant to pour, let alone consume. But the drink brought an entirely different sensation: an unexpected wave of sentimentality that washed over him.

In this state, Ivan Ilyitch was overcome with an immense, inexplicable affection for everyone around him. He felt a sudden desire to embrace them all—yes, even Pseldonimov and that irritating young man from the satirical paper. He wanted to pour his heart out, confess everything, and bask in the unity and understanding he believed his honesty would inspire. He imagined telling them, without holding back, what a good and remarkable man he was. He would talk about his extraordinary talents, the significant contributions he had made to society, and his unique ability to charm women with his wit and intellect. Above all, he would showcase his progressive nature and readiness to show kindness and leniency even to the humblest of people. He even fantasized about explaining why he had come to Pseldonimov's wedding uninvited, drunk so much champagne, and offered his presence as a form of magnanimity.

"The truth! Absolute, unvarnished truth!" he thought fervently. "I'll capture their hearts with my sincerity. They'll see me for who I truly am, and their hostility will melt away. They'll fill their glasses, raise them to me with cheers, and drink my health. Perhaps the officer will break his glass on his spur in celebration. They might even shout hurrah! And if they want to toss me into the air like the Hussars do, I won't resist—it would actually be rather fun! I'll kiss the bride on her forehead; she's quite charming. Akim Petrovitch is a decent fellow, too. Pseldonimov? Well, he'll polish himself up eventually. These young people may lack refinement, but I can inspire them! I'll talk to them about Russia's place in Europe, about the peasant question, about reform. They'll adore me, and I'll leave this gathering as a hero!"

These lofty dreams filled Ivan Ilyitch with a temporary warmth, but soon a less pleasant realization crept in. Something strange and undignified was happening to him—he was drooling. Saliva escaped his mouth uncontrollably, and he caught himself spitting unintentionally. Worse still, he noticed that a spray of spit had landed on Akim Petrovitch's cheek. Poor Akim Petrovitch, too polite to wipe it away, sat rigidly in discomfort. Embarrassed, Ivan Ilyitch hastily took a napkin and wiped it himself, but this action struck him as so absurd and inappropriate that he froze in mortification.

As he looked at Akim Petrovitch, Ivan Ilyitch realized something else: for the past fifteen minutes, he had been speaking animatedly about some important subject, yet Akim Petrovitch seemed more nervous and frightened than engaged. Pseldonimov, sitting just one chair away, leaned in with a peculiar, almost watchful air, his head tilted slightly to one side as though scrutinizing Ivan Ilyitch. It was as if he were waiting for something specific, something unsettling. Glancing around the room, Ivan Ilyitch noticed that several guests were openly staring at him, and some were even laughing. Yet, oddly enough, he didn't feel embarrassed—in fact, he doubled down.

Taking another sip from his glass, he suddenly raised his voice to ensure everyone could hear him. "I was just saying," he began, loudly and deliberately, "I was just saying to Akim Petrovitch here, ladies and gentlemen, that Russia... yes, Russia... in my view, is currently experiencing a significant period of hu-hu-manity."

From the far end of the table came a mocking echo: "Hu-hu-manity!"

"Hu-hu!"

"Tu-tu!"

Ivan Ilyitch stopped mid-sentence, startled. Pseldonimov stood abruptly, craning his neck to locate the source of the interruptions, while Akim Petrovitch subtly shook his head, as though scolding the unruly guests. Ivan Ilyitch saw the gesture but was too flustered to respond. Instead, he resumed, his voice firmer but tinged with desperation: "Humanity! Yes, that is what I meant! And just this evening, I was telling Stepan Niki-ki-foro-vitch... yes, I told him... that we are on the brink of a great regeneration, so to speak, of everything..."

But his words began to trail off as his confidence wavered. He couldn't shake the sensation that the room, once so full of possibility, now felt unwelcoming, even hostile. Still, he pressed on, as though sheer determination might salvage his dignity.

"Your Excellency!" came a loud exclamation from the far end of the table.

"What is it you want?" Ivan Ilyitch asked, halting his speech and trying to identify the speaker.

"Nothing at all, your Excellency. I got carried away. Please, continue! Continue!" the voice called out again.

Ivan Ilyitch felt a pang of irritation. "The regeneration, so to speak, of those same things..." he began again, only to be interrupted once more.

"Your Excellency!" the voice shouted louder.

"What now?"

"How do you do!"

Ivan Ilyitch could no longer suppress his frustration. He broke off entirely and turned toward the source of the disruption. It was a very young man, still a schoolboy, who was evidently quite drunk and had already drawn suspicion. This boy had been causing disturbances throughout the evening, breaking glasses and plates in his misguided belief that such antics were appropriate for a wedding. At the very moment Ivan Ilyitch fixed his gaze on him, the officer at the table had already begun reprimanding the unruly lad.

"What do you think you're doing? Why are you yelling? If you don't behave, we'll throw you out!" the officer barked.

"I didn't mean you, Your Excellency! I didn't mean you. Please, continue!" the drunken schoolboy slurred, slouching in his chair. "I'm listening. I'm ve-ry, ve-ry, ve-ry much enjoying it! Praiseworthy, praiseworthy!"

"The boy is drunk," Pseldonimov whispered anxiously to Ivan Ilyitch.

"I can see that, but..."

"I was just telling a very amusing story, Your Excellency!" the officer interjected, trying to redirect attention. "It's about a lieutenant in our company who used to behave just like that with his superiors, always saying 'praiseworthy, praiseworthy' to everything. He ended up being dismissed from the army ten years ago."

"What kind of lieutenant was that?" Ivan Ilyitch asked, attempting to reestablish some order.

"He was in our company, Your Excellency. The poor man went completely mad over the word 'praiseworthy.' At first, they tried gentle methods to address it, but eventually, he was put under arrest. His commanding officer even tried to counsel him like a father, but he just kept repeating, 'praiseworthy, praiseworthy.' Strangely enough, he was a tall, imposing man—over six feet! They were considering a court-martial when they realized he was genuinely insane."

"So... a schoolboy's antics should not be taken too seriously," Ivan Ilyitch said, attempting to smooth things over. "For my part, I am prepared to overlook this."

"They conducted a medical inquiry into the lieutenant's condition, Your Excellency," the officer continued.

"Good heavens, but the man was alive, wasn't he?" Ivan Ilyitch asked, perplexed.

"What? Did they dissect him?" someone quipped loudly, triggering a wave of laughter from the guests.

The laughter grew louder and more raucous. It spread across the table, infecting nearly everyone present, many of whom had otherwise behaved with restraint until that moment. Ivan Ilyitch felt a hot flush of anger and humiliation rise within him.

"Ladies and gentlemen!" he shouted, struggling to maintain his composure but stumbling over his words, "I am perfectly capable of comprehending that a man is not dissected while alive. What I meant to say was... I assumed he had died as a result of his condition... or that he ceased to exist in some way... I mean to say that you don't like me, but I... I like all of you... yes, even Por... Porfiry! And yet, here I am, lowering myself to explain myself to you!"

At that moment, Ivan Ilyitch unintentionally spat on the tablecloth in the middle of his impassioned outburst. A large, conspicuous spot of saliva landed directly in front of him. Pseldonimov leapt forward, snatching up a napkin to wipe it clean, but the incident only deepened Ivan Ilyitch's despair.

"My friends, this is too much!" he cried out in frustration.

"The man is drunk, Your Excellency," Pseldonimov whispered again, visibly trembling.

"Porfiry, I see what's happening here... yes, I see it. But I must ask you all, in what way have I lowered myself?" Ivan Ilyitch implored, his voice cracking with emotion.

His plea was met with a chilling silence. It was a silence so absolute, so damning, that it crushed Ivan Ilyitch's last shred of hope. "At least someone could shout something at this moment!" he thought bitterly. But the guests exchanged only awkward glances, leaving him adrift. Akim Petrovitch sat frozen, as though petrified, while Pseldonimov's pale, stricken face betrayed a single haunting thought: What will this cost me tomorrow?

At last, breaking the unbearable tension, the young man from the satirical paper—now thoroughly drunk but seething with pent-up animosity—spoke up with piercing clarity.

"Yes," he said, his voice loud and accusatory. "Yes, you have lowered yourself. You're a reactionary... a re-ac-tion-ary!"

"Young man, mind your manners! To whom do you think you're speaking?" Ivan Ilyitch roared, springing to his feet in indignation.

"To you! And I am not a young man!" the journalist retorted, his eyes blazing. "You came here to show off, to pretend at being humane, and to win applause. But all you've done is ruin the evening for everyone. You've been guzzling champagne without a second thought, knowing it's far beyond the means of a clerk who earns ten roubles a month. And let's not overlook the fact that you high-ranking officials are often far too fond of the young wives of your subordinates. Yes, I said it! And I'll add this: you support state monopolies!"

Pandemonium erupted. Ivan Ilyitch turned to Pseldonimov, his face a mixture of fury and disbelief. "Pseldonimov, what does this mean?" he demanded.

But Pseldonimov stood paralyzed, his face drained of all color, utterly incapable of offering an explanation. The other guests remained in stunned silence, save for the artist and the schoolboy, who clapped and shouted, "Bravo, bravo!" The young journalist, emboldened by the chaos, continued his tirade with unrestrained venom. Ivan Ilyitch, shaken to his core, realized he had lost all control of the situation.

"Pseldonimov! Pseldonimov!" Ivan Ilyitch called out desperately, reaching his hands toward him. Every word from the sarcastic young man felt like a sharp dagger piercing his heart, twisting deeper with each phrase.

"Right away, Your Excellency! Please, don't trouble yourself!" Pseldonimov responded quickly, darting toward the offending young man. He grabbed him firmly by the collar and yanked him away from the table. It was surprising to see such strength from someone as frail-looking as Pseldonimov, but the young man, being heavily drunk, was in no condition to resist. Pseldonimov landed a few firm slaps on the man's back and shoved him out through the door.

"You're all a bunch of scoundrels!" the young man shouted as he stumbled out. "I'll draw caricatures of every one of you in The Firebrand tomorrow!"

The remaining guests jumped from their seats in shock.

"Your Excellency! Please, don't be upset!" Pseldonimov's mother, along with several others, hurried over to calm Ivan Ilyitch. "Everything is fine, Your Excellency!" they pleaded.

"No, no!" Ivan Ilyitch cried out, his voice trembling with anguish. "I am destroyed! I came here with nothing but good intentions. I wanted to bless you, to give you my best wishes, and this—this is the thanks I get? For everything I've done?"

He collapsed into a chair as if his strength had completely left him. Resting both arms on the table, he buried his face in them, right into a plate of blancmange. A wave of horror rippled through the room, leaving everyone frozen in stunned silence.

Moments later, Ivan Ilyitch stirred, seemingly trying to get up. He wavered unsteadily, then staggered forward, tripping over a chair leg. With a heavy thud, he fell flat onto the floor. Almost immediately, a loud snore escaped from him.

This is often what happens to those unaccustomed to alcohol when they overindulge. They remain conscious until the very last moment, only to collapse as if struck down. Ivan Ilyitch now lay on the floor, completely unconscious. Pseldonimov stood over him, clutching at his hair in utter despair, frozen as if he had turned to stone.

Meanwhile, the guests began leaving hurriedly, each offering their own whispered remarks about the night's dramatic turn of events as they departed. By then, it was close to three in the morning.

Yet, as chaotic as the scene was, Pseldonimov's situation was far graver than it appeared at first glance. His circumstances were much worse than anyone could imagine, given the already dismal surroundings. While Ivan Ilyitch lay unconscious on the floor and Pseldonimov wrestled with his growing panic, we must pause the story for a moment to provide some background on the life of Porfiry Petrovitch Pseldonimov.

Less than a month before his wedding, Pseldonimov had been living in desperate poverty. He came from a provincial town where his father had worked in some government office but died while awaiting trial for unspecified charges. Five months before the wedding, Pseldonimov had been enduring terrible hardship in Petersburg for a year. When he finally secured a position paying ten roubles a month, it briefly lifted his spirits and improved his health. However, this small improvement did not last, and harsh circumstances soon crushed him again.

The only family he had left in the world was his mother, who had moved to Petersburg with him after his father's death. Together, they lived in freezing conditions and survived on the most meager and questionable food. There were days when Pseldonimov himself walked to the Fontanka River with a jug to fetch drinking water. When he finally got his job, he managed to rent a small corner of a room for himself and his mother. She began taking in laundry to help make ends meet, while he saved every penny over four months to buy himself a pair of boots and an overcoat.

At work, he faced endless difficulties. His superiors openly ridiculed him, asking, "When was the last time you had a bath?" Rumors circulated that his uniform collar harbored nests of bugs. Despite this, Pseldonimov was a man of remarkable inner strength. Outwardly, he was mild and unassuming, with only the barest hint of education, and he rarely spoke about anything. Whether he had dreams, plans, or deep thoughts remained uncertain, but within him grew an unshakable, instinctive resolve to escape his miserable circumstances. He was persistent, like an ant that rebuilds its nest no matter how many times it is destroyed. Pseldonimov was determined to carve out a better life, build his own home, and perhaps even save money for the future.

His mother was the one person who loved him unconditionally, and her love was unwavering. She was a hardworking and tireless woman, full of resolve yet kindhearted. Together, they might have managed to scrape by in their tiny corner for five or six years, waiting for their luck to change. But their lives took a different turn when they crossed paths with a retired titular councillor named Mlekopitaev.

Mlekopitaev had once been a clerk in the treasury and served in the provinces but had since settled in Petersburg with his family. He had known Pseldonimov's father and owed him a favor. Although Mlekopitaev had some money, no one—not even his wife, eldest daughter, or relatives—knew exactly how much he possessed. He had two daughters and was known for being a cruel bully, a heavy drinker, and a domestic tyrant. Adding to this, he was also an invalid, confined to a chair due to a disease that didn't stop him from drinking vodka.

Mlekopitaev spent his days drinking and swearing, finding amusement in tormenting those around him. His household was a collection of relatives he could endlessly bully. Among them were his sickly sister, two of his wife's ill-natured sisters, an elderly aunt with a broken rib, and even a German woman who entertained him with stories from The Arabian Nights. These women, along with his long-suffering wife—who had suffered from chronic toothache since birth—were all subjected to his relentless verbal abuse. He delighted in stirring up quarrels among them, encouraging spiteful gossip and discord, only to laugh at their misery.

His joy reached new heights when his widowed eldest daughter, along with her three sickly children, moved in after years of living in poverty with her late husband. Though he hated her children, he relished the opportunity to use them as more fodder for his cruel amusement. All of these unfortunate women and children, along with their tormentor, were crammed into a small wooden house on the Petersburg Side. They were constantly hungry because Mlekopitaev was miserly, doling out money in tiny amounts, although he spared no expense on vodka for himself. They also suffered from lack of sleep, as the old man's insomnia demanded constant entertainment.

Amid this chaos, Mlekopitaev noticed Pseldonimov. Something about his long nose and submissive demeanor appealed to him. His younger daughter, weak and unattractive, had just turned seventeen. Though she had attended a German school, she had learned little more than the alphabet. She grew up sickly, anemic, and perpetually terrified of her drunken, crippled father. Her home life was a toxic environment of bickering, eavesdropping, and constant scolding. With no friends and limited intelligence, she had long been eager to marry. While she remained silent in public, at home, she was spiteful and quarrelsome, often pinching and scolding her sister's children. This behavior led to constant fights with her elder sister.

One day, Mlekopitaev decided to offer this younger daughter to Pseldonimov as a bride. Despite Pseldonimov's miserable state, he hesitated, asking for time to think it over. Both he and his mother were torn. The young woman's dowry included a house—small, wooden, and unimpressive, but still a property—and four hundred roubles, a sum it would take Pseldonimov years to save on his own.

Mlekopitaev, drunk and domineering, declared his intentions loudly. "What am I taking this man into my house for?" he bellowed. "First, because I'm surrounded by women, and I'm sick of it! I want Pseldonimov to dance to my tune because I'm his benefactor. And second, I'll do it to spite all of you since you don't want it to happen. I've made my decision! And you, Porfiry, you'll beat her when she's your wife. She's had seven devils in her since the day she was born. Beat them out of her, and I'll have the stick ready for you."

Pseldonimov said nothing, but he had already made up his mind. Before the wedding, both he and his mother were brought into the household, cleaned up, given proper clothes, boots, and even some money for the upcoming celebration. The old man took them under his wing, perhaps precisely because the rest of the family disliked them. Oddly enough, he seemed to genuinely like Pseldonimov's mother, so much so that he refrained from mocking her. However, his attitude toward Pseldonimov was different. A week before the wedding, he made Pseldonimov perform a Cossack dance in front of him.

"That's enough," he said when the dance ended. "I just wanted to see if you still remembered your place with me."

He allowed just enough money to cover the cost of the wedding, with not a single kopek to spare. He invited all his relatives and acquaintances, ensuring a full house. On Pseldonimov's side, however, the only attendees were the young man who wrote for The Firebrand and Akim Petrovitch, who was considered the guest of honor. Pseldonimov was painfully aware that his bride disliked him and had desperately hoped to marry the officer instead. Still, he endured it all because he had made a pact with his mother to go through with it.

The wedding day was a nightmare. The old man spent the entire day drunk, shouting insults, and using foul language. The rest of the family fled to the back rooms, cramming together in suffocating quarters, while the front rooms were reserved for dancing and supper. At last, the old man passed out, completely drunk, at around eleven o'clock. It was then that the bride's mother, who had been especially displeased with Pseldonimov's mother that day, decided to bury her grudge, adopt a gracious demeanor, and join the gathering. But everything turned upside down with Ivan Ilyitch's unexpected arrival.

Madame Mlekopitaev, overwhelmed with embarrassment, began complaining that she hadn't been informed about the general's attendance. She was assured that he had come uninvited, but her stubborn nature refused to believe it. Champagne had to be found immediately. Pseldonimov's mother only had one rouble, while

Pseldonimov himself didn't even have a single kopek. He was forced to beg his ill-tempered mother-in-law for the money to buy not just one bottle but two. They pleaded with her, citing his future career prospects and the need to maintain appearances for the sake of his professional life. After much persuasion, she finally gave them the money, but not without subjecting Pseldonimov to a torrent of bitter insults. The humiliation was so overwhelming that, several times, he ran into the room where the bridal bed had been prepared. There, shaking with anger and frustration, he buried his head in the bedding meant for his wedding night, unable to contain his despair.

Ivan Ilyitch, of course, had no idea about the price Pseldonimov had paid—both financially and emotionally—for the two bottles of Jackson champagne he had consumed that evening. And when the general's visit ended in such an unfortunate way, Pseldonimov's horror and misery only deepened. He faced the prospect of endless complaints and recriminations from his peevish new bride and her unreasonable relatives. His head was already pounding, his vision blurred, and he felt dizzy with exhaustion. On top of that, Ivan Ilyitch now needed someone to take care of him. At three o'clock in the morning, Pseldonimov had to find a doctor or a carriage to take him home. And not just any carriage—it had to be a proper one, as letting an ordinary cabman drive him in his condition was unthinkable. But where could Pseldonimov find the money for even that?

Madame Mlekopitaev, still furious that the general hadn't said a single word to her or even acknowledged her presence at supper, declared she didn't have a single kopek. Perhaps she truly didn't. But that left Pseldonimov at a complete loss. Where could he get the money? What could he possibly do? No wonder he felt like tearing his hair out in frustration.

Meanwhile, Ivan Ilyitch was moved to a small leather sofa in the dining room while the tables were cleared away. Pseldonimov ran frantically from one person to another, desperately trying to borrow money. He even asked the servants, but none of them had anything to spare. In his desperation, he approached Akim Petrovitch, who had lingered after the other guests had left. But although Akim Petrovitch was kind-hearted, the mere mention of money seemed to alarm him. He stammered, his face filled with confusion and embarrassment.

"Another time, with pleasure," he muttered, "but now ... you must really excuse me...."

Taking his cap, Pseldonimov ran out of the house as quickly as he could. Only the kind young man who had talked about the dream book stayed behind to help, though even his assistance didn't lead to much. He sincerely sympathized with Pseldonimov's troubles and stayed to offer his support. After much discussion, Pseldonimov, his mother, and the young man decided not to call a doctor. Instead, they agreed to get a carriage to take the sick man home and to use home remedies in the meantime. They applied cold water to his head and temples, placed ice on his forehead, and tried other similar measures while waiting for the carriage. Pseldonimov's mother took charge of these tasks, while the young man dashed out in search of a carriage.

Finding transportation at that hour on the Petersburg Side proved difficult. The young man had to go to distant livery stables, wake up the coachmen, and begin bargaining. They initially demanded five roubles, claiming it was reasonable for the time of night. Finally, they agreed to come for three roubles. However, by the time the carriage arrived—just before five o'clock—the plan had changed. Ivan Ilyitch's condition had worsened. He was still unconscious, moaning and tossing so violently that moving him had become dangerous and unsafe.

"What's next?" Pseldonimov exclaimed in utter despair. The new problem was where to put the ailing man if he stayed in the house.

There were only two proper beds: a large double bed where old Mlekopitaev and his wife slept and a newly purchased walnut bed meant for the newlyweds. Everyone else in the house slept on makeshift feather beds laid out on the floor, most of which were in poor condition and unsuitable for a guest of Ivan Ilyitch's status. Even these were insufficient, and there wasn't a single extra one available.

The most suitable spot seemed to be the drawing room, as it was farthest from the family's living quarters and had a door leading to the passage. But how could they make up a proper bed in there? Certainly not on chairs—that was only suitable for schoolboys visiting home for a weekend, and it would be deeply disrespectful to put someone like Ivan Ilyitch on such an arrangement. The only remaining option was the bridal bed.

This bed was in a small room adjoining the dining room. It was furnished with a brand-new double mattress, pristine sheets, and four pillows covered in frilled muslin cases. The satin quilt was pink and beautifully quilted with patterns, and muslin curtains hung from a golden ring above the bed. Everything had been carefully arranged, and the guests had admired the charming decor. Although the bride harbored a strong dislike for Pseldonimov, she had sneaked in several times during the evening to admire the room. When she learned that Ivan Ilyitch—suffering from what seemed to be mild cholera—was to be placed on her bridal bed, her indignation and fury were boundless.

Her mother sided with her, launching into a tirade and threatening to complain to her husband the next day. But Pseldonimov stood firm and insisted. Ivan Ilyitch was moved to the bridal chamber, and the newlyweds had to make do with a bed improvised from chairs. The bride whimpered and felt like pinching her husband in frustration but dared not disobey. She knew her father's temper too well—his crutch was a constant reminder of his authority—and feared the consequences of defying Pseldonimov. As a small consolation, the pink satin quilt and the decorative pillows were taken to the drawing room.

At that moment, the young man returned with the carriage, only to find it was no longer needed. Horrified, he realized he would have to pay for it himself, even though he didn't have a single coin to his name. Pseldonimov, explaining he was completely broke, tried to reason with the driver. The driver, however, grew noisy and began pounding on the shutters. The situation escalated, and in the end, the young man was taken as a sort of hostage to Peski. He hoped to wake a student friend staying on Fourth Rozhdensky Street and borrow some money from him.

By six in the morning, the newlyweds were finally left alone in the drawing room. Pseldonimov's mother, however, spent the entire night by Ivan Ilyitch's side. She lay on a rug on the floor, covered with an old coat, and couldn't sleep because she had to tend to him constantly. Ivan Ilyitch suffered from severe colic, and Madame Pseldonimov—a woman of remarkable courage and dedication—personally undressed him, took care of his needs as if he were her own child, and tirelessly carried basins across the passage all night long. Yet, even with all this, the disasters of that fateful night were far from over.

Just ten minutes after the young couple had been left alone in the drawing room, a piercing scream echoed through the house. It wasn't a joyful cry but a sharp, alarming shriek that sent chills through the air. The scream was quickly followed by a crash, the sound of chairs collapsing, and the unmistakable clamor of chaos. A flood of shouting, frightened women, dressed in all sorts of disheveled nightwear, burst into the dark room. Among them were the bride's mother, her elder sister who had momentarily abandoned her sick children, and three aunts—one of whom, despite her broken rib, had managed to join the commotion. Even the cook and the German storyteller, whose prized feather bed had been confiscated for the young couple's use, trailed in with the others.

These women, driven by insatiable curiosity, had tiptoed out of the kitchen a quarter of an hour earlier and had been eavesdropping in the anteroom. When someone lit a candle, the scene that greeted them was shocking. The chairs that had supported the edges of the feather bed had given way, causing the bed to collapse onto the floor. The bride was sobbing in frustration, deeply offended by the incident. Pseldonimov stood there like a criminal caught red-handed, too humiliated to defend himself. Cries and accusations erupted from all sides. Pseldonimov's mother rushed in at the sound of the commotion, but the bride's mother immediately took control of the situation. She unleashed a storm of accusations, many of them exaggerated or entirely undeserved, saying things like, "What kind of husband are you after this? What good are you now after such a disgrace?"

Eventually, she took her daughter away, declaring she would take full responsibility when her fearsome husband demanded an explanation. The other women followed, shaking their heads and voicing their disapproval. Left alone, Pseldonimov's mother tried to console her son, but he quickly sent her away. He was beyond comfort.

Pseldonimov sank onto the sofa, barefoot and still in his nightclothes, utterly overwhelmed. His thoughts spiraled in all directions. Occasionally, his eyes wandered around the room, which not long ago had been filled with dancing and celebration. Now, the lingering smoke of cigarettes, scattered sweet wrappers, and the wreckage of the bridal bed told a grim story of how quickly joyful dreams could turn to dust. He sat there for nearly an hour, consumed by oppressive thoughts. One particularly painful realization was that he would have to transfer to a different office. There was no way he could stay where he was after everything that had happened. He also dreaded what Mlekopitaev might do, imagining the old man forcing him to dance the Cossack dance again to prove his obedience.

He thought bitterly about the fifty roubles Mlekopitaev had contributed to the wedding, all of which had been spent, and the fact that no one had mentioned the promised four hundred roubles—or even formally transferring the house to him. His thoughts wandered to his new wife, who had abandoned him at such a critical moment, and to the tall officer who had knelt before her during the wedding festivities. He recalled the seven devils her father claimed she had and the crutch supposedly ready to drive them out. Although Pseldonimov believed himself capable of enduring much, the unrelenting barrage of hardships made him doubt his resilience.

As these thoughts tormented him, the flickering candle cast his distorted shadow on the wall. His elongated neck, hooked nose, and tufts of hair created a surreal and haunting image. At last, chilled by the early morning air, he dragged himself to the collapsed feather bed. Without fixing anything or even extinguishing the dying candle, he lay down, too drained to care, and fell into a deep, almost lifeless sleep, the kind of sleep a man might have before facing a flogging.

Meanwhile, Ivan Ilyitch Pralinsky was enduring his own private torment on the now-desecrated bridal bed. His suffering was relentless—headaches, nausea, and a string of other unbearable symptoms kept him in constant agony. When fleeting moments of clarity did come, they brought visions so dreadful that unconsciousness seemed preferable. His mind was a jumbled mess. He vaguely recognized Pseldonimov's mother, who tended to him with gentle reassurances like, "Be patient, dear sir. It will pass soon." Although he recognized her, he couldn't make sense of her presence. Grotesque images haunted him, including visions of Semyon Ivanitch, who, upon closer inspection, seemed to morph into Pseldonimov's nose.

Other unsettling figures appeared in his fevered mind: the flamboyant artist, the officer, and the old woman with her face wrapped in cloth. Strangely, he found himself fixated on the golden ring from which the curtains above the bed hung. In the dim candlelight, it seemed to glow, and he became obsessed with its purpose. He asked the old woman about it several times but couldn't make himself understood, nor could she grasp what he wanted to know. Finally, by morning, the worst of his symptoms subsided, and he slipped into a deep, dreamless sleep.

When he awoke an hour later, his headache was excruciating, and his mouth felt unbearably dry and foul. As he sat up, the pale morning light streamed through the cracks in the shutters, casting a thin beam on the wall. It was seven o'clock. With horrifying clarity, he recalled the events of the previous night—his failed speech, his grand gesture gone awry, and the utter humiliation that awaited him in the eyes of others. Looking around the room, he saw the chaotic state of the bridal chamber and realized how thoroughly he had ruined it. Overwhelmed with shame and despair, he let out a cry, buried his face in his hands, and collapsed back onto the pillow.

A minute later, he jumped out of bed and noticed his clothes neatly folded and brushed on a chair. In a frenzy, he began dressing as quickly as he could, throwing panicked glances around the room as if expecting something dreadful to happen. On another chair nearby lay his greatcoat, fur cap, and yellow gloves. Intent on sneaking away unnoticed, he reached for his belongings. Just then, the door opened, and Pseldonimov's mother walked in, carrying an earthenware jug and basin. With a towel slung over her shoulder, she set the jug down and, without saying much, firmly informed him that he needed to wash.

"Come on, dear sir, wash yourself; you can't leave without freshening up," said the old woman.

At that moment, Ivan Ilyitch realized that if there was anyone in the world he didn't need to fear or feel embarrassed around, it was this old lady. He complied and washed. Later in his life, during moments of deep regret, he often recalled this scene vividly—the earthenware basin, the porcelain jug filled with icy water that still had floating ice chunks, and the oval soap wrapped in pink paper embossed with letters, clearly bought for the newlyweds but used by him instead. He remembered the old lady standing there with a linen towel draped over her shoulder. The cold water revived him, and after drying his face, he grabbed his hat, flung on the coat Pseldonimov handed him, and dashed across the hallway and through the kitchen. The cat was meowing, and the cook, still sitting on her bed, watched him leave with wide, curious eyes. Ivan Ilyitch hurried outside to the yard and then into the street, where he jumped into the first sledge he could find.

The morning was frosty, wrapped in a yellowish fog that blurred the surroundings. He turned up his coat collar, convinced that everyone he passed was staring at him, recognizing him.

For eight days, he stayed home, avoiding both the office and the outside world. He was ill, though more from emotional distress than physical sickness. Those days were like living in a personal hell, and he often thought they might count against him in the afterlife. At times, he even considered becoming a monk and retreating to a monastery. His imagination wandered during those days, conjuring images of mournful chanting, open coffins, solitary cells, dense forests, and dark caves. But when he snapped back to reality, he quickly dismissed these thoughts as absurd and felt ashamed of himself for entertaining such fantasies.

Then came waves of moral torment about his failed life. Shame would engulf him, burning through his soul like fire and reopening his inner wounds. He cringed at the thought of what people might say about him, how they would react when he returned to the office. He pictured whispers trailing him for years, perhaps even his whole life. His story, he feared, would become infamous. At times, he sank into such despair that he imagined going to Semyon Ivanovitch to ask for forgiveness and friendship. He didn't even try to justify his actions; instead, he blamed himself entirely, finding no excuse or defense for what had happened.

He also thought about resigning from his position and dedicating himself to living humbly, contributing to humanity as an ordinary citizen. At the very least, he considered cutting ties with everyone he knew, erasing all memory of himself. But this plan, too, felt unrealistic. Then he wondered if adopting a stricter demeanor at work might restore order and respect. This gave him moments of renewed hope and determination. Finally, after eight days of inner turmoil, he decided he couldn't bear the uncertainty any longer and resolved to return to the office.

For days, he had rehearsed this moment in his mind, imagining every detail of his return. He was certain he would be met with whispers, knowing glances, and smirks. Yet to his astonishment, none of that happened. His colleagues greeted him with respect, bowing politely and maintaining a professional demeanor. Everyone seemed busy with their work, and no one acted out of the ordinary. His heart filled with relief as he walked to his office.

He immediately threw himself into his tasks with seriousness. He reviewed reports, answered questions, and resolved issues with a sharpness and clarity he hadn't felt in a long time. He noticed that his colleagues seemed satisfied with his decisions and treated him with the same respect as always. Even the most sensitive observer wouldn't have found a trace of mockery or disrespect.

Eventually, Akim Petrovitch entered with some paperwork. Seeing him gave Ivan Ilyitch a brief pang of unease, but he quickly recovered.

They discussed the matter at hand, and Ivan Ilyitch explained things with his usual authority. The only thing he noticed was that Akim Petrovitch avoided meeting his eyes, and Ivan Ilyitch found himself doing the same. When they finished, Akim Petrovitch began gathering his papers.

"There's one more thing," Akim Petrovitch said in a dry tone. "The clerk Pseldonimov has submitted a request to transfer to another department. His Excellency Semyon Ivanovitch Shipulenko has offered him a position. He asks for your approval."

"Oh, so he's transferring," Ivan Ilyitch replied, feeling as though a heavy burden had been lifted from his chest. He glanced at Akim Petrovitch, and for a moment, their eyes met. "Of course, I have no objection. I approve," he said.

Akim Petrovitch appeared eager to leave as quickly as possible. But in a surge of emotion, Ivan Ilyitch decided to speak further. Inspiration seemed to strike him.

"Tell him," Ivan Ilyitch began, fixing Akim Petrovitch with a look of sincerity, "tell Pseldonimov that I hold no grudge. None at all! On the contrary, I am willing to forget everything that happened, completely forget it…"

But Ivan Ilyitch stopped mid-sentence, startled by Akim Petrovitch's odd reaction. Instead of listening attentively, Akim Petrovitch blushed deeply, made hurried little bows, and edged toward the door as if desperate to escape. His awkward behavior made him seem almost foolish, as though he couldn't wait to get back to his desk.

Left alone, Ivan Ilyitch rose from his chair, feeling unsettled. He glanced at himself in the mirror without really noticing his reflection.

"No, strictness—strictness and nothing else," he muttered under his breath. But suddenly, his face flushed deeply, and a fresh wave of shame overwhelmed him. The weight of it felt even heavier than during his most agonizing days at home. "I broke down," he thought bitterly and sank back into his chair, utterly defeated.

Another Man's Wife Or
The Husband Under the Bed

An Extraordinary Adventure

Chapter 1

"Excuse me, sir... may I ask you something?"

The man who was addressed stopped and turned, looking a bit startled and uneasy at the man in the raccoon fur coat who had approached him so suddenly at eight o'clock in the evening on the street. It's a known fact that in Petersburg, if a stranger starts speaking to you in the street, your first reaction is almost always alarm.

And so, the man who was spoken to was indeed startled and slightly alarmed.

"Forgive me for troubling you," said the man in the raccoon coat. "I... I'm not sure how to put this... please excuse me; I seem to be a little flustered."

At that moment, the young man in the quilted overcoat noticed that the man in the raccoon coat truly seemed distressed. His wrinkled face was pale, and his voice trembled as he spoke. He was clearly struggling to maintain his composure, and it was obvious that it took a great deal of effort for him to make this request—especially to someone who might be of lower rank or social standing. But it was clear that he was compelled by some urgent need to ask for help.

Still, the nature of his request seemed odd and inappropriate, especially for a man wearing such a fine coat, such a distinguished dark green jacket, and impressive decorations on his chest. The man in the raccoon coat appeared just as uncomfortable about the situation as he was determined to see it through. Finally, unable to handle the tension any longer, he decided to put an end to it with a polite retreat.

"Forgive me. I am not myself right now," he said hurriedly. "You don't know me, and I'm sorry for disturbing you. I've changed my mind."

With that, he lifted his hat in a courteous gesture and disappeared into the shadows.

"But wait..."

Before the young man could respond, the man in the raccoon coat had vanished, leaving him frozen in confusion.

"What a strange fellow," thought the young man in the quilted coat. After a brief moment of puzzlement, he shook off his surprise and turned back to his original task. He began pacing back and forth, watching the gate of a large, multi-story building. A thick fog was beginning to settle over the street, which made him feel a little better. The fog helped conceal his pacing, though there was no one around to notice him except perhaps a cab driver waiting hopelessly for a passenger.

"Excuse me!"

Once again, the young man jumped. The man in the raccoon coat was back, standing right in front of him.

"Forgive me for disturbing you again," the man began, his voice trembling as before. "But you... you seem like an honorable person! Please don't think about my position or rank... just see me as one man speaking to another. I... I am so flustered. I am here to ask for a simple favor."

"If I can help," said the young man cautiously. "What do you need?"

"Perhaps you think I'm asking for money," said the man in the raccoon coat with a bitter smile, his laughter turning almost hysterical as his face grew even paler.

"Oh, no, not at all," the young man assured him.

"No, I can see that I'm bothering you! Forgive me; I can't stand myself right now. Please understand that I am in a state of extreme agitation, almost madness. Don't judge me by this moment..."

"Get to the point, please," the young man interrupted, nodding as though trying to encourage him to speak but showing some impatience.

"I am not acting for myself, believe me. This concerns another man's wife! Her husband is standing over there on the Voznesensky Bridge, trying to catch her in the act but hesitating, as any husband would. He's still clinging to some hope." The gentleman in the raccoon coat tried to force a smile, but it was strained and bitter. "I'm merely a friend of his. You can see for yourself that I'm a respectable person. I could never be what you might think I am."

"Oh, of course, of course. Go on."

"You see, I've been tasked with watching out for her. The poor husband entrusted me with this duty. But let me tell you, the young lady is cunning—she hides Paul de Kock novels under her pillow, you know! I've long suspected her of sneaking off somewhere. As soon as the cook let slip that she comes to this building, I dashed over here like a madman. I wanted to catch her in the act. And now, seeing you here, walking back and forth... you—you must understand why I'm asking."

"All right, but what exactly do you want from me?"

"Yes, yes, I don't know you, and I have no right to ask, but still... allow me to introduce myself. Pleased to meet you!" The gentleman, visibly agitated, grabbed the young man's hand and shook it vigorously.

"I should have done that from the start," he admitted. "But I've been so flustered that I've forgotten all manners."

As he spoke, the man in the raccoon coat couldn't keep still. He looked around nervously, shuffled his feet, and clung to the young man's hand like a drowning man clutching a lifeline.

"Here's what I had in mind," he continued. "Excuse my forwardness, but I wanted to ask if you could walk around to the side street where the back entrance is. Meanwhile, I'll stay here near the front entrance. That way, we won't miss her if she leaves. If you see her, just stop her and call for me. But... oh, what nonsense I'm spouting! What an absurd plan this is!"

"No, no, it's not absurd at all," the young man reassured him.

"Don't make excuses for me. I've never been in such a state before. I feel like a man on trial for his life! I must confess something to you—something shameful. At first, I thought... I thought you might be the lover."

"You mean to say you suspect me of being here for her?"

"No, no! Please don't think that! You are an honorable man, and I'd never insult you with such an accusation. But... please, give me your word of honor that you are not her lover."

"Fine. I give you my word of honor that I am a lover—but not of your lady. If I were, I wouldn't be standing here in the street—I'd be with her now!"

"Wife! Who said she was my wife? I never said that. I'm not married—I'm a bachelor. I—well, I'm a lover too."

"But you just mentioned a husband standing on the Voznesensky Bridge!"

"Ah, yes, that's true, but the ties... the situation is complicated. You understand, don't you?"

"Yes, yes, of course."

"Let me be clear—I am not her husband."

"Fine, but let me tell you, I'm growing impatient. You're upsetting me, and you're getting in my way. I'll call you if I see anything, but please, I beg you to step back and leave me alone. I'm waiting for someone too."

"Of course, of course, I'll move away. I respect the passionate urgency in your heart. How well I understand it!"

"All right, thank you."

"Until we meet again! But... excuse me, just one more thing. Please, once more, give me your word of honor that you are not her lover."

"Good grief!"

"One last question. Do you know the name of the husband of... I mean, the lady you are waiting for?"

"Of course I do. It's not your name—that's all you need to know."

"How do you even know my name?"

"Look, you're wasting time. She could leave any moment! You're looking for someone in a fox cape and hood, while my lady is in a plaid cloak and a pale blue velvet hat. What else do you want?"

"A pale blue velvet hat? A plaid cloak and a pale blue velvet hat?" The man's eyes widened, and he turned back quickly.

"Oh, for heaven's sake! It could very well be. But my lady doesn't even come to this building!"

"Then where is she?"

"Why do you care? What difference does it make to you?"

"I must admit, I'm still uncertain..."

"Oh, this is ridiculous! All right, fine. My lady has friends on the third floor, the side facing the street. Do you want their names too?"

"The third floor? Friends? But I also know people on the third floor, facing the street. A general lives there!"

"A general?"

"Yes, General Polovitsyn."

"That can't be! No, it's not the same!"

"Not the same?"

"No, not at all."

They both stood in silence, staring at each other in confusion.

"Why are you looking at me like that?" the young man snapped, shaking off his uncertainty.

The older man stammered, "I must admit..."

"Enough! Let's talk sensibly. Who do you know in that building?"

"My friends, you mean?"

"Yes, your friends."

"Well, you see..."

"Oh, never mind! I don't care anymore," the young man shouted, turning away in frustration.

"Wait, please! I'll tell you everything. At first, my wife—no, I mean, not my wife but someone else's—used to visit this building alone. Her relatives live here. I never suspected anything. But yesterday, I found out that his Excellency moved out three weeks ago, yet she told me she visited him here just two days ago! And now I've heard that a young man named Bobynitsyn has taken over the flat."

"Oh, enough! This is madness!"

"My dear sir, I'm terrified! I'm desperate!"

"Well, good luck to you! Oh, wait—someone just passed by over there!"

"Where? Where? Call for me—shout 'Ivan Andreyitch!' I'll run!"

"All right. Ivan Andreyitch!"

"Here I am!" the man cried, breathless. "What is it? Where?"

"Oh, nothing. I just wanted to know the lady's name."

"Glaf..."

"Glafira?"

"No, not Glafira. I can't tell you her name."

As he spoke, the man's face turned pale as a sheet.

"Oh, of course, it's not Glafira! I know it's not Glafira, and mine's not Glafira! But then, who could she be with?"

"Where?"

"There! Oh, damn it, damn it!" The young man was so furious that he couldn't stand still.

"There, you see! How did you know her name was Glafira?"

"Oh, for heaven's sake! Really! Now I've got to deal with you too? You said it yourself—that yours isn't called Glafira!"

"My dear sir, is that any way to talk?"

"Oh, the devil! Like that matters now! Who is she? Your wife?"

"No, that is—I'm not married. But still, I wouldn't go around flinging curses at a respectable man who's already in trouble. Maybe I'm not exactly worthy of admiration, but at least I'm an educated man. Yet you keep shouting, 'The devil, the devil!'"

"Fine, to hell with it! There you are—do you understand?"

"You're blinded by anger, and I say nothing. Oh, dear, who's that?"

"Where?"

There was a noise followed by laughter, and two pretty young women ran down the steps. Both men rushed toward them.

"Oh, how rude! What do you want?"

"Why are you pushing?"

"They're not the right ones!"

"Aha, so you've got the wrong people! Cab!"

"Where do you want to go, mademoiselle?"

"To Pokrov. Get in, Annushka; I'll take you."

"Oh, I'll sit on the other side. Off we go! And drive quickly!"

The cab sped off.

"Where did they come from?"

"Oh, dear, oh, dear! Shouldn't we go there?"

"Where?"

"Why, to Bobynitsyn's...."

"No, that's not an option."

"Why not?"

"I'd go, sure, but then she'd come up with another story. She'd twist it around. She'd say she came there just to catch me with someone else, and then I'd be in hot water."

"But what if she really is there? I don't know why, but maybe you could go to the general's...."

"But you know he's moved!"

"That doesn't matter. She could've gone there. So you go too—just act like you didn't know the general had moved. Pretend you came to pick up your wife, or something like that."

"And then?"

"Well, then you can find the person you're looking for at Bobynitsyn's. Tfoo, damn it all, what a ridiculous idea!"

"Well, what's it to you, me finding her? You see, you see!"

"What? What? You're going on about the same thing again. Oh, for heaven's sake! You're such a fool, such an absurd fool!"

"Yes, but why are you so interested? Do you want to figure out...."

"Figure out what? What? Oh, forget it, damn you! I don't have time for this now. I'll go on my own. Get lost; leave me alone; just go away!"

"My dear sir, you're really starting to lose control of yourself!" the man in the raccoon coat cried out in despair.

"Well, so what if I am? What does it matter if I lose control?" shouted the young man, his teeth clenched in anger as he stepped toward the man in the raccoon coat. "What does it matter? Lose control in front of who?" he bellowed, fists clenched tight.

"But allow me, sir..."

"Well, who are you that I should mind myself in front of you? What's your name?"

"I don't see why you need to know my name, young man. Why does it matter? I'd rather not tell you... but I'll come with you instead. Let's go; I won't hold back. I'm ready for anything. But I do think I deserve more politeness and respect! You should never lose your composure, even if you're upset—I can guess why—but that's no excuse to forget yourself. You're still so very young!"

"What do I care if you're old? There's nothing special about that! Now go away. Why are you still hanging around here?"

"Old? In status, maybe. But I'm not dancing around here..."

"I can see that. Now leave me alone."

"No, I'm staying with you. You can't stop me. I'm part of this too, and I'll go with you."

"Fine, then, but keep quiet. Be quiet and hold your tongue."

They went up the steps and climbed the stairs to the third floor. It was dimly lit.

"Wait—do you have matches?"

"Matches? What matches?"

"Do you smoke cigars?"

"Oh yes, I do, I do! Here they are, here they are... wait a second." The man in the raccoon coat fumbled around nervously.

"Ugh, what nonsense! Damn it, I think this is the door."

"This one? This one?"

"This one! Stop shouting! Be quiet!"

"My dear sir, I'm holding back my feelings, but... you are a reckless young man, that's what you are!"

A match flared.

"Yes, this is it. Look, there's the brass plate. This is Bobynitsyn's. Do you see it?"

"I see it. I see it."

"Shhh!"

"What happened? Did it go out?"

"Yes, it's out."

"Should we knock?"

"Yes, we should," said the man in the raccoon coat.

"Then knock."

"No, why should I? You knock first."

"Coward!"

"You're the coward!"

"Get out of here!"

"I almost regret sharing my secret with you. You're..."

"I'm what?"

"You're taking advantage of my distress. You see I'm upset..."

"So what? I just think this whole thing is ridiculous!"

"Then why are you here?"

"Why are you here?"

"Great sense of morality!" said the man in the raccoon coat indignantly.

"What are you even saying about morality? And who are you?"

"It's immoral!"

"What?"

"You think every husband who's been cheated on is a fool!"

"Wait, are you the husband? I thought the husband was on Voznesensky Bridge! What does this have to do with you? Why are you even involved?"

"I think you're the lover!"

"Listen, if you keep talking like this, I'll have to think you're a fool. And by fool, you know exactly what I mean!"

"Are you trying to say I'm the husband?" asked the man in the raccoon coat, stepping back as if he'd been burned by boiling water.

"Quiet, hold your tongue. Do you hear me?"

"It's her."

"No!"

"Damn, it's so dark!"

They both fell silent. A faint noise could be heard from inside Bobynitsyn's apartment.

"Why are we even arguing, sir?" whispered the man in the raccoon coat.

"You were the one who got offended, damn it!"

"Well, you pushed me past my limit."

"Just be quiet!"

"You have to admit, you're still very young."

"Quiet, I said!"

"Of course, I agree with you that a husband in this situation looks like a fool."

"Oh, will you just shut up already?!"

"But why torment the poor husband like this?"

"It's her!"

At that moment, the noise stopped.

"Is it her?"

"It is, it is, it is! But why are you so worried about it? This isn't your problem!"

"My dear sir," muttered the man in the raccoon coat, turning pale and gulping nervously, "I admit I'm very shaken up... you can see for yourself how pitiful my situation is. It's late now, of course, but tomorrow... although we're probably not going to meet tomorrow. Not that I'm afraid to meet you! And besides, it's not me—it's my friend on Voznesensky Bridge. Yes, it's him! It's his wife—it's someone else's wife. Poor fellow! I know him very well, I assure you. If you'll let me, I'll explain everything. I'm one of his closest friends; otherwise, I wouldn't be so upset about this, as you can plainly see. I've told him many times, 'Why are you getting married, my friend? You have status, money, and respect. Why risk it all for some flirtation?' But he said, 'No, I want a happy home life.' Well, here's your happy home life! In the past, he fooled around with other men's wives, and now he's getting his share of misery... you'll have to excuse me, but this explanation was absolutely necessary. He's an unlucky man, and now he's paying the price!"

At this point, the man in the raccoon coat let out such a loud gulp it sounded like he was about to cry.

"Ah, damn them all! There are so many fools. But who are you?"

The young man clenched his teeth in frustration.

"At least admit that I've been honest and civil with you... and this is how you respond?"

"No, wait a minute... what's your name?"

"Why do you need to know my name?"

"Ah!"

"I'm not going to tell you my name."

"Do you know Shabrin?" the young man asked quickly.

"Shabrin!!!"

"Yes, Shabrin! Ah!!!" (As he said this, the man in the padded overcoat imitated the man in the raccoon coat.) "Do you get it?"

"No, what Shabrin?" replied the man in the raccoon coat, flustered. "He's not Shabrin; he's a very respectable man! I can overlook your rudeness—it's the jealousy talking."

"He's a crook, a greedy scoundrel, and a thief! He's been stealing government funds, and he'll be caught soon enough!"

"Excuse me," said the man in the raccoon coat, his face pale, "you clearly don't know him. I can see that you don't know him at all."

"No, I don't know him personally, but I've heard about him from people who are very familiar with him."

"From what people, sir? I'm clearly upset, as you can see..."

"A fool! A jealous fool! He doesn't even look after his own wife—that's what he is, if you really want to know!"

"Excuse me, young man, but you're gravely mistaken."

"Oh!"

"Oh!"

A noise came from inside Bobynitsyn's apartment. A door opened, and voices were heard.

"That's not her! I recognize her voice now. I understand everything—this isn't her!" said the man in the raccoon coat, his face turning white as a sheet.

"Quiet!"

The young man leaned against the wall.

"My dear sir, I'm leaving. It's not her, thank goodness."

"All right! Go, then!"

"Why are you staying here, then?"

"What's it to you?"

The door opened, and the man in the raccoon coat couldn't stop himself from rushing downstairs. A man and a woman walked past the young man, and his heart stopped for a moment. He heard a familiar woman's voice, followed by a deep, unfamiliar male voice.

"Don't worry, I'll call for the carriage," said the husky voice.

"Oh, yes, yes, please do."

"It will be here soon."

The woman was left alone.

"Glafira! What happened to your promises?" cried the young man in the padded coat, grabbing her arm.

"Oh, who is that? Is it you, Tvorogov? My goodness! What are you doing here?"

"Who were you just with?"

"My husband. Now go away, go away! He'll be coming out any moment... from... from in there... from the Polovitsyns'. Please, just go!"

"The Polovitsyns moved three weeks ago! I know all about it!"

"Aïe!" The woman bolted down the stairs, but the young man caught up to her.

"Who told you that?" she asked.

"Your husband, Madam—Ivan Andreyitch. He's already here, Madam."

Indeed, Ivan Andreyitch was standing at the front door.

"Aïe, it's you," exclaimed the man in the raccoon coat.

"Ah! C'est vous," cried Glafira Petrovna, running up to him with genuine delight. "Oh, you can't imagine what's happened to me! I went to visit the Polovitsyns. Just think… you know they're living near Izmailovsky Bridge now, right? I told you that, remember? I took a sledge there, but the horses got spooked and ran off. The sledge broke, and I was thrown out not far from here. The coachman was taken away, and I was in such despair. Luckily, Monsieur Tvorogov…"

"What?!"

Monsieur Tvorogov stood frozen, looking more like a statue than himself.

"Monsieur Tvorogov saw me and kindly offered to escort me. But now that you're here, Ivan Ilyitch, I can only express my deepest gratitude."

She extended her hand to the stunned Ivan Ilyitch and gave it a quick squeeze that was almost a pinch.

"Monsieur Tvorogov is an acquaintance of mine. We met at the Skorlupovs' ball—I'm sure I told you about it. Don't you remember, Koko?"

"Oh, of course, of course! Yes, I remember now," said the man in the raccoon coat, who was apparently called Koko. "Very pleased, very pleased!" He warmly shook Monsieur Tvorogov's hand.

"Who is that? What's going on? I'm waiting," said a deep voice.

A very tall man stepped forward, raising a lorgnette to inspect the man in the raccoon coat closely.

"Ah, Monsieur Bobynitsyn!" chirped the woman. "Where did you come from? What a coincidence! I just had an accident in a sledge, but here is my husband! Jean, this is Monsieur Bobynitsyn—from the Karpovs' ball."

"Ah, delighted, absolutely delighted! But I'll go get a carriage for you right away, my dear."

"Yes, please, Jean, do that. I'm still shaken up—I'm trembling and feel a bit faint."

She leaned toward Tvorogov and whispered, "At the masquerade tonight."

"Goodbye, goodbye, Monsieur Bobynitsyn! We'll probably see you tomorrow at the Karpovs' ball."

"No, excuse me, I won't be there tomorrow. Honestly, after this, I don't even know about tomorrow…" muttered Bobynitsyn, before mumbling something else under his breath. He scuffed his boot against the ground, got into his sledge, and left.

A carriage arrived, and the woman climbed in. The man in the raccoon coat hesitated, standing frozen as he stared blankly at the young man in the padded coat. The young man smiled awkwardly.

"I don't know…"

"Excuse me, pleased to meet you," said the young man, bowing with a mix of curiosity and nervousness.

"Likewise, likewise!"

"I think you've lost your overshoe…"

"Ah—oh yes, thank you, thank you. I've been meaning to buy rubber ones."

"Rubber ones make your feet too warm," the young man said with sudden interest.

"Jean! Are you coming?"

"They do make them warm. Coming, darling! We're having such an interesting conversation! You're absolutely right, though—they do make your feet hot. But excuse me, I…"

"Oh, of course."

"Delighted, very delighted to have met you!"

The man in the raccoon coat climbed into the carriage, which drove away, leaving the young man standing there, staring after it in astonishment.

Chapter 2

The next evening, there was a performance at the Italian opera. Ivan Andreyitch stormed into the theater like a whirlwind. No one had ever seen such excitement or passion for music in him before. It was well-known, in fact, that Ivan Andreyitch used to enjoy a good nap during the Italian opera. He had even mentioned more than once how soothing it was. "The prima donna," he would tell his friends, "sings you to sleep like a little white kitten purring a lullaby." But that had been last season. Now, poor Ivan Andreyitch couldn't even sleep at home.

Still, he charged into the packed opera house like an unstoppable force. Even the conductor glanced at him nervously, as though expecting to see the hilt of a dagger sticking out of his coat pocket. At that time, there were two rival groups of opera fans, each fiercely loyal to a favorite prima donna. They were called the ——sists and the ——nists. Their passion for music was so intense that the conductors began to worry about potential outbursts in support of "the good and the beautiful" embodied by their respective stars.

So, when this older man, though not quite elderly—about fifty, slightly bald, and generally respectable-looking—charged into the parterre with such youthful energy, the conductor couldn't help but think of Hamlet's words about the poor example age sets for youth. And yes, he kept glancing sideways at the man's pocket, half-expecting to see a weapon. But there was only a pocketbook, nothing more.

The moment he entered, Ivan Andreyitch scanned the second-tier boxes. And then—oh, horror! His heart stopped. She was there! Sitting in one of the boxes! General Polovitsyn was with her, along with his wife and sister-in-law. The general's adjutant—a sharp, energetic young man—was also there, as well as a civilian. Ivan Andreyitch strained his eyes, desperate to see, but—oh, horror again!—the civilian was hiding behind the adjutant, cloaked in shadows.

She was there, even though she had sworn she wouldn't be! It was this constant deceit in Glafira Petrovna's every action that was destroying Ivan Andreyitch. And now, this mysterious young civilian pushed him to the brink of despair. He collapsed into his seat, completely overwhelmed. Why, you might ask? It was really quite simple.

His seat happened to be right under the box in the second tier where she was sitting. To make matters worse, this meant he couldn't see what was happening above him, no matter how much he tried. This drove him into a fury, making him as hot as a boiling samovar. He didn't hear a single note of the first act. It's often said that music can suit any mood—bringing joy to the happy and comfort to the sorrowful. But to Ivan Andreyitch, it felt like a storm was raging in his ears.

Adding to his frustration, people all around him were shouting and talking loudly. Their voices came from behind him, in front of him, and on either side. It tore at his already fragile nerves. Finally, the act ended. But just as the curtain began to fall, something happened— something no words can truly capture.

Sometimes, during a dull performance, a playbill will flutter down from the upper boxes. It becomes an event for the audience, who watch with great interest as the soft paper zigzags down to the stalls, inevitably landing on someone's unsuspecting head. The embarrassment of the person it lands on always seems to entertain the crowd.

I often worry about opera glasses perched on the edges of boxes. I constantly imagine them falling on someone's head. But perhaps that's a story for another time—a detail better suited for the advice columns of newspapers filled with tips on avoiding scams, dealing with household pests, or using the latest inventions like Mr. Princhipi's remarkable anti-cockroach formula. For now, let's return to the opera.

But Ivan Andreyitch had an experience unlike any other, one that had never been described before. Instead of a playbill landing on his partially bald head, something far more unexpected and shocking fell upon him—a scented love letter. It feels almost shameful to mention it, but there it was, settling on his respectable and partly hairless head: an undeniably improper object. Poor Ivan Andreyitch, completely unprepared for such a bizarre and humiliating event, reacted as if a mouse or some other wild creature had fallen on him.

That it was a love letter was beyond doubt. It was written on perfumed paper, folded as small as possible, clearly meant to slip discreetly into a lady's glove. It must have been dropped by accident, perhaps as it was being handed to her. The playbill might have been requested at the same moment, and the note, cleverly tucked into it, was probably about to be passed along. But then, perhaps due to an accidental nudge from the adjutant—a man quick with his apologies for any clumsiness—the note slipped from the trembling hand of the lady. The eager young civilian, reaching out in anticipation, ended up with the empty playbill instead, left puzzled and unsure of what to do.

This incident must have been quite unpleasant for him, but for Ivan Andreyitch, it was infinitely worse.

"Predestined," he whispered to himself, breaking into a cold sweat as he clutched the note tightly in his hand. "Predestined! The guilty are always found." The thought flashed through his mind, but he quickly corrected himself: "No, that's not it! How am I guilty in any way? But then there's another saying: 'When bad luck starts, it never ends.'"

But this wasn't the end of his troubles. The ringing in his ears and the dizziness in his head were nothing compared to the shame he felt. Ivan Andreyitch sat frozen in his chair, barely alive, convinced that everyone around him had witnessed his embarrassing moment. To make things worse, the entire theater was now filled with shouts and applause calling for an encore. Overwhelmed and blushing furiously, he didn't dare lift his eyes, as if something terribly improper had just happened to him in front of the sophisticated audience. Finally, he mustered the courage to look up.

"Beautifully sung," he remarked to the stylish man seated on his left.

The man, deeply engrossed in the performance and still clapping enthusiastically while stomping his feet, gave Ivan Andreyitch a quick, distracted glance. Then, cupping his hands around his mouth like a megaphone, he shouted the prima donna's name at the top of his lungs. Ivan Andreyitch, startled by the roar, felt relieved. "He didn't notice anything," he thought and turned to look behind him. The large gentleman sitting there had also turned away, busy scanning the boxes through his opera glasses. "He didn't see it either!" Ivan Andreyitch thought with growing hope.

In front of him, of course, no one could have seen anything. With cautious optimism, he glanced toward the nearby baignoire where he had first noticed her presence. But his heart sank. A beautiful woman sitting there was leaning back in her chair, holding a handkerchief to her mouth, laughing hysterically.

"Ugh, these women!" Ivan Andreyitch muttered angrily. Stepping on people's feet as he went, he made his way toward the exit.

Now, I must ask you, dear readers, to consider this carefully: was Ivan Andreyitch justified in his assumptions? The Grand Theatre, as we all know, has four tiers of boxes and an additional row above the gallery. Why did he assume the note came from that particular box and not, for example, from the gallery, where ladies also sit? But passion knows no reason, and jealousy is the most irrational passion of them all.

Ivan Andreyitch hurried into the foyer. Standing near a lamp, he tore open the seal of the letter and read:

"Tonight, immediately after the performance, on G. Street at the corner of X. Lane, K. Buildings, third floor, first door on the right from the stairs. Use the front entrance. Be there without fail, for God's sake."

Ivan Andreyitch didn't recognize the handwriting, but he was certain the note was about a secret meeting. His first thought was to uncover the truth, stop it, and put an end to the mischief before it escalated. He even considered exposing the scandal immediately but quickly realized he had no idea how to go about it. At one point, he rushed up to the second tier of boxes but thought better of it and returned to his seat. He was paralyzed by indecision, not knowing where to go or what to do.

With nothing clear in mind, he ran to the opposite side of the theater and peeked through the open door of another person's box, trying to get a better view of the other side. But it was useless. Young men and women were sitting in rows above one another in all five tiers. The note could have fallen from anywhere, and in his jealousy, Ivan

Andreyitch began to suspect everyone was somehow involved in a plot against him.

This frantic suspicion gave him no peace. For the rest of the second act, he paced the corridors, unable to calm down or think straight. At one point, he even thought about rushing to the box office to demand the names of everyone who had reserved boxes in all four tiers. But the box office was already closed.

Finally, loud applause and shouts erupted as the performance ended. The singers were being called back to the stage, with two particularly loud voices competing from the top gallery. But this didn't matter to Ivan Andreyitch. His mind was racing with plans for what he should do next. Determined, he put on his overcoat and rushed off to G. Street to catch the culprits in the act, confront them, and act more decisively than he had the day before.

It didn't take him long to find the house. Just as he was about to enter through the front door, a well-dressed young man in an overcoat darted past him and headed up the stairs to the third floor. Though Ivan Andreyitch hadn't been able to clearly see the man's face at the theater, he was convinced it was the same person. His heart stopped. The young man was already two flights of stairs ahead of him.

Ivan Andreyitch heard the sound of a door opening on the third floor—without a bell ringing, as if the visitor had been expected. The young man disappeared inside. Ivan Andreyitch climbed the stairs quickly and reached the door before it could close. He paused, trying to collect himself, thinking he should proceed carefully and decide his next move. But just then, a carriage rumbled up outside. The front doors banged open, and the sound of heavy footsteps and coughing echoed up the stairs toward the third floor.

Unable to hold back any longer, Ivan Andreyitch strode into the apartment with all the dignity of a wronged husband. A startled maid rushed to meet him, followed by a manservant. But there was no stopping Ivan Andreyitch. He charged through two dark rooms and suddenly found himself face-to-face with a beautiful young woman in a bedroom. She was trembling with fear and staring at him in complete shock, as though she couldn't comprehend what was happening.

In that moment, heavy footsteps approached the bedroom from the adjoining room. They were the same footsteps Ivan Andreyitch had heard coming up the stairs.

"My God! It's my husband!" the woman cried, clasping her hands and turning even paler than her white dressing gown.

Ivan Andreyitch immediately realized his mistake. He had barged into the wrong place, made a foolish, childish blunder, and acted recklessly without thinking things through. But it was too late. The door was already opening, and the husband—if his footsteps were anything to go by—was about to enter the room.

I cannot say what Ivan Andreyitch thought of himself at that moment or why he didn't simply face the husband, explain that he had made an honest mistake, apologize for the intrusion, and leave. It wouldn't have been a graceful exit, but at least it would have been straightforward and respectful.

Instead, Ivan Andreyitch panicked. Acting as though he were some kind of Don Juan or romantic rogue, he first tried to hide behind the bed curtains. When that failed, he collapsed to the floor in despair and senselessly crawled under the bed. Fear had completely overpowered his reason. Even though he himself considered himself a wronged husband, he couldn't bring himself to face another husband, let alone risk upsetting him with his presence.

And so, before he even realized what had happened, Ivan Andreyitch found himself lying under the bed. What's most surprising is that the lady didn't try to stop him. She didn't scream or call for help when she saw a complete stranger—a middle-aged man no less—hide under her bed. She was probably too terrified to react at all, completely frozen by the shock of the situation.

The husband entered, gasping and clearing his throat. In a singsong, elderly voice, he greeted his wife and dropped heavily into an armchair, as though he'd just carried a load of wood up the stairs. A hollow, drawn-out cough followed.

Meanwhile, Ivan Andreyitch, who had been a ferocious tiger just moments ago, now felt like a timid lamb. He hardly dared to breathe, paralyzed by fear, even though he should have known from his own experience that not every wronged husband is dangerous. But he wasn't thinking clearly. Carefully, trying not to make a sound, he shifted under the bed to make himself more comfortable.

To his shock, his hand brushed against something—or someone. The object moved, and then it seized his hand! Ivan Andreyitch was stunned. Someone else was already under the bed.

"Who are you?" whispered Ivan Andreyitch.

"I'm not about to tell you who I am," the stranger whispered back. "Lie still and be quiet if you've gotten yourself into trouble!"

"But I—"

"Shut up!"

The other man squeezed Ivan Andreyitch's hand so hard that he nearly cried out in pain.

"My good sir…" Ivan began.

"Sh!"

"Then stop pinching me, or I'll scream."

"Go ahead, try it," said the stranger with a challenge.

Ivan Andreyitch flushed with embarrassment. The stranger sounded irritable and short-tempered, perhaps someone who had endured his fair share of misfortune and tight spots before. Ivan Andreyitch, however, was a novice at this sort of predicament. The cramped space made it hard for him to breathe, and the blood rushed to his head. But there was nothing to be done. Lying flat on his face, Ivan Andreyitch resigned himself to silence.

"I was visiting Pavel Ivanitch, my dear," the husband said, addressing his wife. "We played a few rounds of preference. Khee-khee-khee!" He broke into a fit of coughing. "Yes... khee! My back... khee! Bother it all... khee-khee-khee!"

The old man seemed completely absorbed in his coughing.

"My back," he finally managed to say through tears, "my spine started aching. Damn these hemorrhoids—I can't stand, I can't sit. Akkhee-khee-khee!"

The coughing fit resumed, seemingly endless, punctuated by occasional mumbled grumbling, though it was impossible to make out any of the words.

"Please, sir, for heaven's sake, could you move a little?" whispered Ivan Andreyitch, utterly miserable.

"I can't. There's no room," the stranger replied.

"But surely you can see this is unbearable for me! I've never been in such an awful situation before."

"And I've never had such unpleasant company before."

"But, young man..."

"Shut up!"

"Shut up? That's very rude of you, young man. If I'm not mistaken, I'm older than you."

"Shut up!"

"My dear sir! You're forgetting yourself. Do you even know who you're speaking to?"

"A gentleman hiding under the bed," the stranger replied bluntly.

"But this is all a mistake! I was caught off guard, while in your case, if I'm not mistaken, this is…" Ivan hesitated, lowering his voice. "Immorality."

"You're mistaken."

"My dear sir, I'm older than you—"

"Listen, we're both in the same situation. Don't grab at my face!"

"Sir, I can't tell what I'm touching. I apologize, but I have no space!"

"Well, you shouldn't be so fat!"

"Good heavens! I've never been in such a degrading position."

"You couldn't sink much lower."

"Sir, I don't know who you are or how this happened, but I'm here by mistake. I'm not what you think!"

"I wouldn't think anything about you if you didn't keep shoving. Now shut up!"

"Sir, if you don't move a little, I'll have a stroke. You'll be responsible for my death! I assure you, I'm a respectable man, a father of a family. I can't endure this!"

"You put yourself in this situation. Move over! I've made room for you; that's all I can do."

"Thank you, noble young man! Dear sir, I was mistaken about you," Ivan Andreyitch said gratefully as he stretched his cramped limbs. "I understand your position, though it's awful for both of us. I see you've formed a poor opinion of me. Allow me to explain myself, to clear my name in your eyes. I didn't come here by choice—I swear it! I'm terrified out of my wits."

"Oh, just be quiet! Don't you understand that if we're overheard, things will only get worse for us? Shh! He's talking."

The old man's coughing finally seemed to subside.

"I'll tell you something, my dear," he wheezed in a long, mournful tone. "I'll tell you what... khee-khee! Oh, what a misery! Fedosey Ivanovitch told me, 'You should try drinking yarrow tea,' he said. Do you hear me, my dear?"

"Yes, dear."

"Yes, that's what he said: 'Try yarrow tea.' I told him I'd already used leeches. But he said, 'No, Alexandr Demyanovitch, yarrow tea is better. It's a laxative, I tell you.' Khee-khee! Oh dear! What do you think, my dear? Khee! Should I try yarrow tea? Khee-khee-khee! Oh... khee!"

"I think it would be a good idea to try it," his wife replied.

"Yes, I should! 'You might have consumption,' he said. Khee-khee! But I told him it was just gout and stomach trouble. Khee-khee! But he still insisted it could be consumption. What do you think? Khee-khee! Do you think it's consumption?"

"My goodness, what are you talking about?"

"Consumption! You should get undressed and go to bed now, my dear. Khee-khee! I've caught a chill today."

"Ouf!" whispered Ivan Andreyitch. "For God's sake, can't you move over a little?"

"I really don't understand what's wrong with you. Can't you just lie still?"

"You're angry with me, young man. You want to upset me—I can see that. Are you this lady's lover?"

"Shut up!"

"I will not shut up! I won't let you order me around! You must be her lover. If we're discovered, I won't be to blame. I know nothing about this."

"If you don't shut up," the young man hissed through clenched teeth, "I'll say that you brought me here. I'll claim you're my uncle, a man who squandered his fortune. Then no one will think I'm her lover."

"Sir, you're mocking me! You're testing my patience."

"Be quiet, or I'll make you be quiet! You're nothing but a burden to me. Now tell me—why are you even here? If it weren't for you, I could manage to stay hidden until morning and then sneak out."

"But I can't stay here until morning! I'm a respectable man with a family. Surely... surely this old gentleman isn't planning to spend the whole night here?"

"Who?"

"Why, this husband, of course!"

"Naturally, he is. Not all husbands are like you. Some actually sleep at home."

"My dear sir, I assure you, I sleep at home too! This is the first time—oh, my God! Wait, you know who I am, don't you? Who are you? Please, tell me who you are. I'm begging you!"

"Keep it up, and I'll use force."

"But please, sir, let me explain. Let me tell you how all of this happened—"

"I don't want to hear any explanations. I don't care how it happened. Be silent, or else—"

"But I can't—"

A brief scuffle broke out under the bed, and Ivan Andreyitch quickly gave up.

"My dear," said the husband, "it sounds like cats hissing."

"Cats? What will you imagine next?"

The wife was clearly at a loss for words. She was so upset that she couldn't seem to gather her thoughts. Every now and then, she startled, straining her ears.

"What cats?"

"Cats, my dear. The other day, I went into my study, and there was the tomcat, hissing, shoo-shoo-shoo! I said to him, 'What's wrong, kitty?' and he just kept going, shoo-shoo-shoo, like he was whispering something. I thought, 'Good heavens! Is he hissing as a sign of my death?'"

"What nonsense you're talking today! You should be ashamed of yourself!"

"Don't be angry, my love. I see you don't like me talking about dying. I didn't mean it. But you'd better get undressed and go to bed, my dear, and I'll sit here while you do."

"For goodness' sake, stop it already. We'll talk later."

"All right, don't be upset, don't be upset. But really, I think there might be mice here."

"First cats, and now mice? I don't know what's gotten into you."

"Oh, I'm fine... khee... khee-khee-khee! Oh, Lord have mercy on me... khee."

"You're making such a commotion he can hear you," the young man whispered.

"But if only you knew what's happening to me! My nose is bleeding."

"Let it bleed! Be quiet and wait for him to leave."

"Young man, try to imagine yourself in my position. I don't even know who I'm lying next to!"

"Would it make any difference if you did? For that matter, I don't want to know your name either. What's your name, by the way?"

"No, why do you want to know my name? I just want to explain the ridiculous way—"

"Shh! He's talking again."

"My dear, there's definitely whispering," said the old man.

"Oh no, it's just the cotton in your ears slipping out of place."

"Oh, speaking of the cotton, did I tell you about what's happening upstairs? Khee-khee… upstairs… khee-khee…"

"Upstairs?" the young man whispered. "Oh, hell! I thought this was the top floor. Could there be another level?"

"Young man," Ivan Andreyitch whispered back, "what did you say? For God's sake, why does this concern you? I thought this was the top floor too. Tell me, is there another floor?"

"Someone's moving," the old man said, finally stopping his coughing fit.

"Hush! Do you hear that?" the young man whispered, gripping Ivan Andreyitch's hands.

"Sir, you're holding my hands too tightly! Let go!"

"Shh!"

A brief struggle followed, then silence.

"So, I met a pretty woman…" the old man began.

"A pretty woman!" his wife interrupted.

"Yes. I thought I told you about her—maybe I didn't mention it? My memory isn't what it used to be. Yes, St. John's wort… khee!"

"What?"

"I should drink St. John's wort. They say it's good… khee-khee-khee! It's good!"

"You interrupted him," the young man said through clenched teeth.

"You said you met a pretty woman today?" the wife continued.

"Eh?"

"You met a pretty woman?"

"Who did?"

"Why, you!"

"Me? When?"

"Oh, yes!"

"Finally! What a rambling old man!" the young man muttered in frustration.

"My dear sir, I'm trembling with fear. My God, what am I hearing? This is just like yesterday—all over again!" Ivan Andreyitch whispered.

"Quiet!"

"Yes, I remember now! A sly one, with such eyes… and a blue hat."

"A blue hat! Aïe, aïe!"

"It's her! She wears a blue hat! My God!" Ivan Andreyitch cried softly.

"Her? Who is she?" whispered the young man, tightening his grip on Ivan Andreyitch's hands.

"Shh!" Ivan Andreyitch hissed back. "He's still talking."

"My God, my God!"

"Then again, who doesn't own a blue hat?"

"And such a sly little rogue," the old man continued. "She visits friends here and is always making eyes. And other friends come to see her friends too…"

"Ugh, how boring!" the wife interrupted. "Why are you even interested in that?"

"Fine, fine, I'll stop if you don't want to hear it. You seem a bit out of sorts tonight," the old man said soothingly.

"But how did you end up here?" the young man asked.

"Ah, now you're interested! Before, you wouldn't listen!"

"Never mind, I don't care anymore. Just stop telling me. What a mess this is!"

"Don't be upset, young man. I don't even know what I'm saying. I didn't mean anything by it—I just wondered why you're so interested. But who are you? You seem like a stranger. Who are you? Oh dear, I don't even know what I'm saying anymore!"

"Ugh, stop it, will you!" the young man interrupted, sounding as though he was deep in thought.

"But I will tell you everything! You probably think I won't. That I'm angry at you. But no! Here, take my hand. I'm just feeling down, that's all. But for God's sake, first tell me how you got here. What brought you here? As for me, I bear no grudge; really, I don't. Here's my hand. It's a bit dirty—this place is so dusty—but that doesn't matter when the sentiment is genuine."

"Ugh, keep your hand away! There's barely any room, and now you're sticking your hand in my face!"

"My dear sir, you treat me as if I were nothing but an old shoe," Ivan Andreyitch said in a tone of despair, his voice pleading. "Show me just a little civility—a little! And I'll tell you everything! We might even become friends. I'd gladly invite you to dinner. But lying here like this, side by side? It's unbearable. You misunderstand me, young man, you truly do...."

"When did he meet her?" the young man muttered, clearly agitated. "Maybe she's waiting for me right now.... I've got to get out of here!"

"Her? Who is she? My God, who are you talking about? Do you think someone upstairs—Oh, my God! Why am I being punished like this?" Ivan Andreyitch tried to roll onto his back in desperation.

"Why do you care who she is? Oh, to hell with whether it's her or not—I'm getting out of here!"

"My dear sir, what are you thinking? What about me?" Ivan Andreyitch whispered frantically, grabbing at the tails of the young man's coat.

"What's that to me? You can stay here by yourself. If not, I'll just tell them you're my uncle who wasted all his money. That way, the old man won't think I'm his wife's lover."

"That's ridiculous! No one would believe you! Not even a child would buy such a story," Ivan Andreyitch whispered in despair.

"Then stop talking and lie flat like a pancake! You'll probably have to stay the night here and sneak out in the morning. No one will notice. If one of us leaves, they won't expect another person to be here. Unless there's a dozen of us—and you're big enough to count as a dozen. Now move over, or I'm getting out!"

"You're hurting me, young man. What if I start coughing? You have to consider everything."

"Shh!"

"What's that? I think I hear something upstairs again," the old man said, his nap apparently over.

"Upstairs?"

"Do you hear that, young man? I'm leaving."

"Yeah, I hear it."

"My goodness! I'm going."

"Well, I'm staying. I don't care if there's trouble! But you know what I think? You must be an injured husband—that's what you are."

"Good heavens, how cynical! How could you even think that? A husband? No, I'm not married."

"Not married? Nonsense!"

"I could be a lover myself!"

"Some lover!"

"My dear sir, let me explain! Very well, I'll tell you the truth. Listen to my miserable story. I'm not married—I'm a bachelor, like you. It's my friend, my childhood companion. He's a lover. He told me he's a miserable man. 'I'm drinking the cup of bitterness,' he said. 'I suspect my wife.' I asked him, reasonably, 'Why do you suspect her?' But you're not even listening! Listen, listen! I told him, 'Jealousy is absurd. It's a vice!' But he said, 'I'm a miserable man. I'm drinking... I mean, I suspect my wife.' I told him, 'You're my friend, the companion of my youth. Together we embraced the joys of life, rolling in beds of pleasure.' Oh, my God, I don't even know what I'm saying anymore. And you, young man, you're laughing! You'll drive me mad!"

"But you're already mad!"

"I knew you'd say that! Laugh all you want, young man. I laughed too, once upon a time. I made mistakes! Oh, I'm going to have a breakdown!"

"What is it, my dear? I thought I heard someone sneeze," the old man said in his singsong voice. "Was that you sneezing?"

"Oh, goodness!" his wife replied.

"Tch!" came a faint noise from under the bed.

"They must be making a noise upstairs," she said nervously, clearly alarmed.

"Yes, upstairs! I told you earlier—I met a young man with a moustache. Oh, my back!"

"A young man with a moustache? My goodness, that must've been you!" Ivan Andreyitch whispered.

"Good heavens, what are you saying? I'm here with you under this bed! How could he have met me? And stop grabbing my face!"

"My goodness, I'm going to faint any second!"

At that moment, a loud noise echoed from above.

"What's going on up there?" the young man whispered.

"My dear sir, I'm terrified! Help me!"

"Quiet!"

"There really is a commotion upstairs," the old man said. "It's right above your bedroom. Should I send someone to check it out?"

"What will you think of next?" his wife replied.

"Oh, fine, I won't! But really, you're so irritable today!"

"Oh, dear, you'd better just go to bed."

"Liza, you don't love me at all."

"Oh yes, I do! For goodness' sake, I'm so tired."

"All right, all right, I'm going!"

"Oh no, no, don't go!" his wife cried. "Or… no, better go!"

"What's wrong with you? One minute I should go, the next I shouldn't! Khee-khee! It really is time for bed. Khee-khee! The Panafidins' little girl… khee-khee… I saw her Nuremberg doll… khee-khee."

"Now it's dolls!"

"Khee-khee… a lovely doll… khee-khee."

"He's saying goodbye," whispered the young man. "He's going, and we can leave right away. Do you hear me? You can celebrate!"

"Oh, I hope so! God grant it!"

"Let this be a lesson for you."

"A lesson? For what? I understand… but you're young—you can't teach me anything."

"Oh, I will. Listen."

"Oh dear, I'm about to sneeze!"

"Hush, don't you dare!"

"But I can't help it! There's such a smell of mice here. Take my handkerchief from my pocket—I can't move. Oh my God, why am I being punished like this?"

"Here's your handkerchief. I'll tell you why you're being punished. You're jealous. For no reason, you run around like a madman, barging into other people's homes, causing chaos—"

"Young man, I haven't caused any chaos!"

"Quiet!"

"You can't lecture me about morals! I'm more moral than you."

"Quiet!"

"Oh my God—oh my God!"

"You cause trouble, you terrify a young lady—a timid woman— who doesn't know what to do and might even fall ill from fright. You disturb a sick old man who desperately needs rest. And for what? All because of some nonsense you imagined, chasing after shadows! Do you realize how ridiculous your situation is now?"

"I do, young man! I understand it fully, but you have no right—"

"Stop talking! What does 'right' have to do with it? Don't you see this could end tragically? That poor old man, devoted to his wife, could lose his mind if he saw you crawling out from under the bed. But no, I doubt it would even be tragic! When you crawl out, I'm sure everyone will just laugh. I'd love to see how ridiculous you look in the light."

"And you must look ridiculous too. I'd like to see you as well."

"Oh, I'm sure you would!"

"You carry the mark of immorality, young man."

"Morality? How do you know why I'm here? It was a mistake—I came to the wrong floor. Who knows why they let me in? Maybe she was expecting someone else—not you, obviously. When I heard your heavy footsteps and saw how scared she was, I hid under the bed. It was dark, and there was no time. And why should I explain myself to you? You're nothing but a jealous old fool. Do you know why I haven't come out yet? You probably think I'm scared. No, I'm staying here for your sake. What would you do if I weren't here? You'd stand there like a statue, completely lost."

"Why a statue? Couldn't you choose something better to compare me to? Why wouldn't I know what to do? I'd figure it out."

"Oh, my goodness, that dog keeps barking!"

"Hush! That's because you won't stop talking. You've woken it up—now we're in trouble."

The lady's small dog, which had been sleeping peacefully on a pillow, suddenly woke up. It sniffed the air, sensed the strangers, and darted under the bed, barking loudly.

"Oh my God, what a stupid dog!" Ivan Andreyitch whispered. "It's going to ruin everything! Another disaster!"

"Well, you're such a coward, I wouldn't be surprised," the young man replied.

"Ami, Ami, come here," the lady called. "Ici, ici." But the dog ignored her, charging straight for Ivan Andreyitch.

"Why is Amishka barking?" asked the old gentleman. "There must be mice or the cat under there. I think I even heard sneezing. Poor kitty had a cold this morning."

"Stay still," the young man whispered. "Don't move! Maybe it'll stop."

"Let go of my hands, sir! Why are you holding them?"

"Quiet! Don't make a sound!"

"Good heavens, young man, it's going to bite my nose! Do you want me to lose my nose?"

A brief struggle ensued, and Ivan Andreyitch managed to free his hands. The dog's barking grew louder and more frantic—until suddenly it yelped and fell silent.

"Aïe!" cried the lady.

"Monster! What are you doing?" the young man hissed. "You're going to ruin us both! Why are you holding it? My God, he's strangling it! Let go, you brute! Don't you understand anything about women? She'll betray us both if you kill her dog!"

But Ivan Andreyitch couldn't hear a word. Gripped by panic, he had caught the dog and, in a desperate act of self-preservation, squeezed its throat. The dog let out a final yelp before going limp.

"We're doomed!" whispered the young man.

"Amishka! Amishka!" cried the lady. "My God, what are they doing to my Amishka? Amishka! Amishka! Ici! Oh, those monsters! Barbarians! Oh dear, I feel faint!"

"What is it? What is it?" exclaimed the old gentleman, jumping up from his chair. "What's wrong, my dear? Amishka! Here, Amishka! Amishka! Amishka!" he called, snapping his fingers and clicking his tongue. "Amishka, ici, ici! The cat can't have eaten him! That cat needs a beating. He hasn't been punished for a whole month, the rascal. What do you think? I'll have to speak to Praskovya Zaharyevna. But my goodness, what's wrong, my love? Oh, you're so pale! Servants, servants!" he shouted, rushing about the room.

"Villains! Monsters!" cried the lady as she collapsed onto the sofa.

"Who? Who?" the old gentleman demanded.

"There are people under the bed! Strangers! Oh my God, Amishka! Amishka! What have they done to you?"

"Good heavens! Strangers? Amishka... Servants, come here! Who's there? Who is it?" yelled the old gentleman, grabbing a candle and bending down to look under the bed. "Who's under there?"

Ivan Andreyitch lay there, frozen with fear beside Amishka's lifeless body, while the young man watched the old gentleman's every move. Suddenly, the old man moved to the other side of the bed, closer to the wall, to look there. In that instant, the young man crawled out from under the bed and bolted for the door before the husband could notice.

"Good gracious!" the lady exclaimed, staring at the young man. "Who are you? I thought…"

"That monster's still there," the young man whispered. "He's the one responsible for Amishka's death!"

"Aïe!" screamed the lady, but by then, the young man had vanished from the room.

"Aïe! There's someone here! Look, there are boots under the bed!" cried the husband, grabbing Ivan Andreyitch by the leg.

"Murderer! Murderer!" screamed the lady. "Oh, Ami! Ami!"

"Come out! Come out!" shouted the old gentleman, stomping on the carpet. "Who are you? Tell me who you are! What a strange man!"

"It's a thief!" exclaimed the lady.

"For God's sake, for God's sake!" Ivan Andreyitch cried, crawling out. "Please, your Excellency, don't call the servants! There's no need! You don't have to throw me out. I'm not that kind of person. It's all a misunderstanding! I'll explain everything, your Excellency," he said, sobbing and gasping. "It's all because of my wife—well, not my wife, someone else's wife. I'm not even married! It's my friend… a companion from my youth!"

"What companion from your youth?" the old man roared, stamping his feet. "You're a thief! You came here to steal, not to meet some friend from your youth!"

"No, I'm not a thief, your Excellency! I swear I'm a friend from his youth! I just made a mistake. I ended up in the wrong place."

"Yes, I can see where you crawled out from!"

"Your Excellency, you've got it all wrong! Please, just look at me. One glance, and you'll see that I couldn't possibly be a thief. I swear it! Your Excellency!" Ivan Andreyitch pleaded, turning to the lady. "You're a lady; you'll understand. It's true, I'm the one who killed Amishka—but it wasn't my fault! It's all my wife's fault… or someone else's wife. I'm a miserable man, drinking the cup of bitterness!"

"And what does it matter to me that you're drinking the cup of bitterness?" the old man retorted. "It's probably not the first one you've drunk either, judging by your state! But how did you get here, sir?" the old man demanded, his voice trembling with rage. "You've broken in like a thief!"

"I'm not a thief, your Excellency! I simply came to the wrong place. It's all because I was jealous. I'll explain everything, your Excellency. I'll confess everything to you, as if you were my own father—because at your venerable age, I might well take you for a father."

"What do you mean by venerable age?"

"Your Excellency, have I offended you? I meant no disrespect. Of course, such a young lady… and your years… it's a beautiful sight, your Excellency. Truly, such a wonderful union… in the prime of life! But please, don't call the servants. They'll only laugh at us! I know how they are. Not that I only know servants—I have a footman of my own, your Excellency. But they're always laughing, those fools! Your Highness, I'm sorry—your Excellency, I believe I'm speaking to a prince?"

"No, sir, I'm not a prince," the old man snapped. "I'm an independent gentleman. And stop flattering me with titles! How did you get here? Tell me!"

"Your Highness—excuse me, your Excellency. Forgive me, I thought… it happens, you look like Prince Korotkouhov, whom I've had the honor of meeting at my friend Mr. Pusyrev's. You see, I've met princes, too! I'm not what you think I am. I'm not a thief! Please, don't call the servants. What good would it do?"

"But how did you get here?" the lady demanded. "Who are you?"

"Yes, who are you?" the husband echoed. "And to think, my love, I thought it was the cat sneezing under the bed. But it was him! You vagabond! Who are you? Speak!" The old man stamped his feet on the carpet again.

"I can't speak yet, your Excellency. I'm waiting for you to finish— I'm enjoying your witty remarks. As for me, this is an absurd situation, your Excellency. I'll explain everything. It can all be cleared up right away. But please, don't call the servants, your Excellency! Treat me as a gentleman. Just because I was under the bed doesn't mean I've lost my dignity. This is a ridiculous story, your Excellency!" cried Ivan Andreyitch, glancing imploringly at the lady. "You, especially, your Excellency, will laugh! What you see here is a jealous husband— nothing more. Look at me! I humiliate myself willingly. Yes, I killed Amishka, but... my God, I don't even know what I'm saying!"

"But how? How did you get here?"

"Under cover of night, your Excellency. Under cover of night. Forgive me, please forgive me! I'm just an injured husband, nothing else! Don't think I'm a lover—I am not! Your wife is virtuous, your Excellency. She's pure and innocent!"

"What? What did you just say?" roared the old gentleman, stamping his foot. "Are you out of your mind? How dare you talk about my wife like that?"

"He's a villain! A murderer! He killed Amishka!" wailed the lady, breaking into sobs. "And then he dares...!"

"Your Excellency, your Excellency! I spoke foolishly," stammered Ivan Andreyitch, flustered. "I wasn't thinking. Please, think of me as out of my mind... yes, as completely out of my mind! That would be the greatest favor you could do for me. I'd offer you my hand, but I don't dare. I wasn't alone under the bed—I was... well, I mean, I wasn't what you think. Oh dear, I've said something wrong again. Don't be offended, your Excellency," he pleaded to the lady. "You're a lady; you understand love—it's such a delicate feeling. Oh no, there I go again, talking nonsense! I'm just a middle-aged man—an older man, but not that old. I couldn't possibly be your lover! A lover is someone like Lovelace from Richardson's novels. Oh, what am I saying? I'm talking nonsense again. But you see, your Excellency, I'm an educated man— I've read literature. You're laughing, your Excellency. I'm delighted! Truly delighted to see you laugh!"

"My goodness, what a funny man!" cried the lady, bursting into laughter.

"Yes, he's very funny—and in such a mess," said the old gentleman, clearly amused now that his wife was laughing. "He can't be a thief, my dear. But how on earth did he end up here?"

"It's strange, so strange! Like something out of a novel! A man under the bed in the middle of the night, in a big city—it's bizarre! It's funny! Like a Rinaldo-Rinaldini kind of thing. But never mind, your Excellency, never mind. I'll explain everything. And I'll buy you a new lapdog, your Excellency. A wonderful little lapdog with a long coat and short little legs. It can barely walk two steps without tripping over itself. You'll only need to feed it sugar! I'll bring it to you, I promise!"

"Ha-ha-ha-ha-ha!" The lady was laughing so hard she could barely sit up. "Oh, I'm going to have hysterics! Oh, he's so funny!"

"Yes, yes! Ha-ha-ha! Khee-khee-khee! He's funny and in such a ridiculous situation—khee-khee-khee!"

"Your Excellency, I'm so happy now. I would offer you my hand, but I don't dare. I see now that I was wrong. My wife is innocent! Completely innocent! I was wrong to suspect her!"

"His wife?" exclaimed the lady through tears of laughter. "He's married? Impossible! I never would have guessed."

"Your Excellency, it's all my fault. I was jealous. I thought she had arranged an assignation—upstairs. I intercepted a letter, got the floor wrong, and ended up under the bed."

"He-he-he-he!"

"Ha-ha-ha-ha!"

"Ha-ha-ha-ha!" Ivan Andreyitch joined in, laughing at last. "Oh, how happy I am! It's wonderful to see everyone so cheerful and at peace. My wife is entirely innocent—that's certain now, your Excellency!"

"He-he-he! Khee-khee! Do you know who it must have been, my dear?" the old gentleman asked, catching his breath.

"Who? Ha-ha-ha!"

"The pretty woman who makes eyes at everyone—the one with the dandy! It must be her! That's his wife!"

"No, your Excellency, I'm sure it's not her! She's at home right now—I know it! It's all my fault, all because of my jealousy. Do you really think I'd find them upstairs, your Excellency?"

"Ha-ha-ha!"

"He-he-he! Khee-khee!"

"You must go, you must go! And when you come back, come and tell us what happened!" cried the lady. "Or better yet, come tomorrow morning—and bring your wife! I'd love to meet her."

"Goodbye, your Excellency. Goodbye! I will bring her, I promise. I'll be so happy to introduce her to you. I'm so glad everything turned out well!"

"And don't forget the lapdog! Be sure to bring the lapdog!"

"I'll bring it, your Excellency, I'll definitely bring it," said Ivan Andreyitch, darting back into the room even though he had already bowed and stepped out. "I'll absolutely bring it. It's such a sweet little thing, almost as if a confectioner had made it out of candy. It's so funny—it gets tangled up in its own fur and tumbles over. It's a real lapdog! I said to my wife, 'Why does it keep falling over?' She said, 'It's just so tiny.' Honestly, it's like it's made of sugar! Goodbye, your Excellency, so glad to have made your acquaintance. Very glad indeed!"

Ivan Andreyitch bowed again and made his way out.

"Hey, sir! Wait a moment, come back!" called the old gentleman.

Ivan Andreyitch returned for the third time.

"I still can't find the cat. Didn't you see him while you were under the bed?"

"No, your Excellency, I didn't. But I'd be honored to meet him someday."

"He's got a cold and keeps sneezing and sneezing. That cat needs a good thrashing."

"Yes, your Excellency, of course. Corrective measures are essential with pets."

"What?"

"I mean, discipline is necessary to keep domestic animals obedient, your Excellency."

"Ah… Well, goodbye, goodbye—that's all I needed to say."

Once outside, Ivan Andreyitch stood still, his expression suggesting he was on the verge of fainting. He removed his hat, wiped the cold sweat from his brow, squinted at nothing in particular, and after a moment of thought, set off toward home.

Imagine his shock when he arrived to find out that Glafira Petrovna had returned from the theater hours earlier. She was in bed with a toothache, had sent for the doctor, requested leeches, and had been waiting for Ivan Andreyitch.

He slapped his forehead, asked the servant to help him clean up and brush his clothes, and finally gathered the courage to go into his wife's room.

"Where have you been all this time? Just look at yourself—what a mess you are!" Glafira Petrovna scolded him. "While I'm lying here dying, you're nowhere to be found! The whole town could be out looking for you! What were you doing? Don't tell me you've been out tracking me, imagining I arranged some kind of rendezvous with… with who even? Shame on you! You're my husband, and people will start pointing fingers at you in the street!"

"My love…" Ivan Andreyitch began, but he was so flustered that he fumbled for his handkerchief and broke off. He had neither the words nor the composure to explain himself.

To his horror, when he pulled out his handkerchief, something else fell from his pocket—the lifeless body of Amishka. In his blind panic earlier, when he had scrambled out from under the bed, Ivan Andreyitch had stuffed the dog's body into his pocket, vaguely thinking he would bury it later to hide the evidence of his misdeed.

"What is this?" cried Glafira Petrovna. "A dead dog? Where did it come from? What on earth have you been doing? Where have you been? Tell me immediately!"

"My love," Ivan Andreyitch stammered, as pale as Amishka himself. "My love..."

But here, we must leave our unfortunate hero. His story takes a turn into yet another adventure, which we will recount another time. For now, let us agree on one thing: jealousy is not only an unforgivable fault—it is also a terrible misfortune.

The Heavenly Christmas Tree

I am a novelist, and I suppose I've made up this story. I say "I suppose" even though I know for certain that I created it. Yet, somehow, I can't help imagining that it must have happened somewhere, sometime— perhaps on Christmas Eve, in a large city, during a bitterly cold winter night.

I picture a boy, a little boy, maybe six years old or even younger. That morning, he woke up in a cold, damp cellar. He was wearing a small dressing gown and shivering from the chill. Clouds of white breath puffed out of his mouth as he sat on a box in the corner, amusing himself by watching the steam float away. But he was terribly hungry.

Several times that morning, he went over to the plank bed where his sick mother lay. She was stretched out on a mattress so thin it felt like a pancake, with some sort of bundle under her head for a pillow. How had she ended up here? It seemed she had come to this place with her son from another town, only to suddenly fall ill.

The landlady, who rented out "corners" to tenants, had been taken to the police station two days earlier. The other lodgers were out, likely preparing for the holiday, and the only one left had spent the last twenty-four hours dead drunk, too far gone to care about Christmas. In another corner of the room, a miserable old woman, almost eighty years old and once a children's nurse, lay groaning with rheumatism. She grumbled and scolded the boy so much that he was too afraid to go near her.

The boy had managed to find some water in the outer room, but there wasn't even a crumb of bread to be found. He'd thought about

153

waking his mother a dozen times, but each time, something stopped him. As darkness fell and no light was lit, he began to feel frightened.

He touched his mother's face and was startled when she didn't move. Her skin was as cold as the walls of the cellar. "It's very cold here," he thought to himself. He stood there for a moment, his small hands resting on her lifeless shoulders. Then he blew on his fingers to warm them and, fumbling for his cap on the bed, quietly slipped out of the cellar.

He had wanted to leave earlier but was afraid of the large dog that had been howling all day outside the neighbor's door at the top of the stairs. But now the dog was gone, so he stepped out into the street.

What a strange and overwhelming place this town was! He had never seen anything like it before. In his old town, it was always pitch-black at night. There was only one street lamp, the low wooden houses were shut tight with shutters, and the streets were empty after dark. People stayed inside, and the only sounds were the barking and howling of packs of dogs—hundreds of them—all night long. But it had been warm there, and he was fed. Here, though—oh, how he wished he had something to eat!

The noise and commotion were deafening. Lights shone everywhere. People bustled past, horses trotted, and carriages clattered along the streets. The frost was biting. Clouds of frozen steam hung in the air over the horses, puffing from their warm breaths, and their hooves clanged against the cobblestones, kicking up powdery snow.

He tried to navigate through the crowd, but he was starving, and the cold only made him feel worse. A wave of sadness washed over him, and his misery grew unbearable. A policeman walked by but quickly turned his head away, pretending not to see the boy.

Here was another street—so wide, it seemed impossible not to get run over here. Everyone was shouting, rushing, and driving by so fast, and the lights were dazzling! And what was this? A massive glass window, and inside, a tree that stretched all the way to the ceiling. It was a fir tree, covered with so many lights, shiny gold papers, apples, little dolls, and toy horses. Children, clean and dressed in their best clothes, were running around the room, laughing, playing, eating, and drinking something. Then a little girl started dancing with a boy. What a beautiful little girl she was! Through the window, the boy could even hear the music.

He stared in amazement, smiling despite the aching pain in his frozen toes and his fingers, which were red and stiff, hurting whenever he tried to move them. But suddenly, as he remembered the cold biting into him, he began to cry and ran on.

Through another window, he saw another Christmas tree. On a table nearby were all kinds of cakes—almond cakes, red cakes, yellow cakes—and three elegant young ladies were sitting there, handing the cakes to anyone who came up to them. The door kept opening as gentlemen and ladies entered from the street.

The boy crept closer, then suddenly opened the door and stepped inside. Oh, how they shouted at him and waved him away! One lady rushed up to him, slipped a kopeck into his hand, and quickly pushed him back out the door. Terrified, he stumbled out. The coin rolled from his numb fingers and clinked on the steps—he couldn't bend his stiff hands to hold it properly. Frightened, he ran off again, not knowing where he was going. He was on the verge of tears, but fear kept him moving. He blew on his hands to warm them, feeling utterly alone and scared.

And then—what was this? Another crowd was gathered, watching something through a large glass window. Inside were three little dolls dressed in red and green, and they looked so lifelike. One was an old man sitting and playing a big violin, while the other two stood nearby, playing smaller violins. They nodded in time with the music, looked at each other, and even moved their lips as though they were speaking, though no sound came through the glass.

At first, the boy thought they were real people. When he realized they were dolls, he laughed. He had never seen such lifelike dolls before and had no idea they existed. For a moment, he forgot his misery, amused by the dolls.

But suddenly, he felt a tug on his smock. A mean older boy was standing next to him. Before he could react, the boy hit him on the head, snatched his cap, and tripped him. The little boy fell to the ground, stunned and terrified. Hearing shouts around him, he jumped up and ran away as fast as he could.

He ran blindly until he found a courtyard and slipped through its gate. Behind a stack of wood, he crouched down to hide. "They won't find me here," he thought. "Besides, it's dark."

As he sat huddled in the shadows, breathless from fear, he suddenly felt a strange warmth. His aching hands and feet no longer hurt, and they grew as warm as if he were sitting on a stove. A shiver ran through him, and then he felt calm. "Did I fall asleep?" he wondered. "It feels so nice to sleep here." He smiled, thinking of the dolls again. "I'll sit here a little longer and then go back to see the dolls," he thought. "They looked so real!"

Then, out of nowhere, he heard his mother singing softly. "Mama, I'm asleep," he murmured. "It's so nice to sleep here."

"Come to my Christmas tree, little one," a gentle voice whispered above him.

He thought it was his mother, but when he opened his eyes, he realized it wasn't her. Someone he couldn't see bent down and

embraced him in the dark. He reached out his hands, and suddenly—
oh, what a bright light! What a Christmas tree!

But it wasn't a fir tree like the ones he had seen before. This tree
was unlike anything he had ever imagined. Where was he now?
Everything around him sparkled and glowed. Bright, shining children
surrounded him—not dolls, but real boys and girls.

They flew around him, kissed him, took his hands, and carried him
along with them. He felt himself flying, and as he soared, he saw his
mother looking at him and laughing joyfully.

"Mama, Mama!" he cried. "Oh, it's so nice here, Mama!"

He kissed the children around him, eager to tell them about the
dolls in the shop window. "Who are you, boys? Who are you, girls?"
he asked, laughing and filled with wonder.

"This is Christ's Christmas tree," they told him. "Christ always has
a Christmas tree on this day for little children who don't have one of
their own."

And then he realized that all these boys and girls were children just
like him. Some had frozen to death in the baskets where they'd been
left as babies on the doorsteps of wealthy families in Petersburg.
Others had been sent to live with Finnish foster mothers and had
suffocated. Some had died at their starving mothers' breasts during the
Samara famine, and others had passed away in the foul air of third-class
railway carriages.

Yet, here they all were, gathered together, shining like angels
around Christ. He stood in their midst, stretching out His hands to
bless them and their sorrowful mothers.

The mothers of these children stood to one side, weeping quietly.
Each mother recognized her own child, and the children flew to them,
kissing them, wiping away their tears with their tiny hands, and begging

them not to cry. "Don't be sad," the children said, "because we are so happy now."

Meanwhile, down below, as the morning dawned, the porter found the frozen body of the little boy on the woodstack. They discovered his mother too—she had died before him. In heaven, they met again before the Lord God.

Why have I written such a story, one so unlike the usual content of a diary, especially a writer's diary? And I had promised two stories based on real events! But that's just it—I keep imagining that all of this could have truly happened.

The part about the cellar and the woodstack—I believe that might have been real. But Christ's Christmas tree? That, I cannot say for certain.

The Peasant Marey

It was the second day in Easter week. The air was warm, the sky was blue, the sun was high, warm, bright, but my soul was very gloomy. I sauntered behind the prison barracks. I stared at the palings of the stout prison fence, counting the movers; but I had no inclination to count them, though it was my habit to do so. This was the second day of the "holidays" in the prison; the convicts were not taken out to work, there were numbers of men drunk, loud abuse and quarrelling was springing up continually in every corner. There were hideous, disgusting songs and card-parties installed beside the platform-beds. Several of the convicts who had been sentenced by their comrades, for special violence, to be beaten till they were half dead, were lying on the platform-bed, covered with sheepskins till they should recover and come to themselves again; knives had already been drawn several times. For these two days of holiday all this had been torturing me till it made me ill. And indeed I could never endure without repulsion the noise and disorder of drunken people, and especially in this place. On these days even the prison officials did not look into the prison, made no searches, did not look for vodka, understanding that they must allow even these outcasts to enjoy themselves once a year, and that things would be even worse if they did not. At last a sudden fury flamed up in my heart. A political prisoner called M. met me; he looked at me gloomily, his eyes flashed and his lips quivered. "Je haïs ces brigands!" he hissed to me through his teeth, and walked on. I returned to the prison ward, though only a quarter of an hour before I had rushed out of it, as though I were crazy, when six stalwart fellows had all together flung themselves upon the drunken Tatar Gazin to suppress him and had begun beating him; they beat him stupidly, a camel might have been killed by such blows, but they knew that this Hercules was not

159

easy to kill, and so they beat him without uneasiness. Now on returning I noticed on the bed in the furthest corner of the room Gazin lying unconscious, almost without sign of life. He lay covered with a sheepskin, and every one walked round him, without speaking; though they confidently hoped that he would come to himself next morning, yet if luck was against him, maybe from a beating like that, the man would die. I made my way to my own place opposite the window with the iron grating, and lay on my back with my hands behind my head and my eyes shut. I liked to lie like that; a sleeping man is not molested, and meanwhile one can dream and think. But I could not dream, my heart was beating uneasily, and M.'s words, "Je haïs ces brigands!" were echoing in my ears. But why describe my impressions; I sometimes dream even now of those times at night, and I have no dreams more agonising. Perhaps it will be noticed that even to this day I have scarcely once spoken in print of my life in prison. The House of the Dead I wrote fifteen years ago in the character of an imaginary person, a criminal who had killed his wife. I may add by the way that since then, very many persons have supposed, and even now maintain, that I was sent to penal servitude for the murder of my wife.

Gradually I sank into forgetfulness and by degrees was lost in memories. During the whole course of my four years in prison I was continually recalling all my past, and seemed to live over again the whole of my life in recollection. These memories rose up of themselves, it was not often that of my own will I summoned them. It would begin from some point, some little thing, at times unnoticed, and then by degrees there would rise up a complete picture, some vivid and complete impression. I used to analyse these impressions, give new features to what had happened long ago, and best of all, I used to correct it, correct it continually, that was my great amusement. On this occasion, I suddenly for some reason remembered an unnoticed moment in my early childhood when I was only nine years old—a moment which I should have thought I had utterly forgotten; but at that time I was particularly fond of memories of my early childhood. I remembered the month of August in our country house: a dry bright day but rather cold and windy; summer was waning and soon we should have to go to Moscow to be bored all the winter over French lessons, and I was so sorry to leave the country. I walked past the threshing-floor and, going down the ravine, I went up to the dense thicket of bushes that covered the further side of the ravine as far as the copse. And I plunged right into the midst of the bushes, and heard a peasant ploughing alone on the clearing about thirty paces away. I knew that he was ploughing up the steep hill and the horse was moving with effort, and from time to time the peasant's call "come up!" floated upwards to me. I knew almost all our peasants, but I did not know which it was ploughing now, and I did not care who it was, I was absorbed in my own affairs. I was busy, too; I was breaking off switches from the nut trees to whip the frogs with. Nut sticks make such fine whips, but they do not last; while birch twigs are just the opposite. I was interested, too, in beetles and other insects; I used to collect them, some were very ornamental. I was very fond, too, of the little nimble red and yellow lizards with black spots on them, but I was afraid of snakes. Snakes, however, were much more rare than lizards. There were not many mushrooms there. To get mushrooms one had to go to the birch wood, and I was about to set off there. And there was nothing in the world that I loved so much as the wood with its mushrooms and wild berries, with its beetles and its birds, its hedgehogs and squirrels, with its damp smell of dead leaves which I loved so much, and even as I write I smell the fragrance of our birch wood: these impressions will remain for my whole life. Suddenly in the midst of the profound stillness I heard a clear and distinct shout, "Wolf!" I shrieked and, beside myself with terror, calling out at the top of my voice, ran out into the clearing and straight to the peasant who was ploughing.

It was our peasant Marey. I don't know if there is such a name, but every one called him Marey—a thick-set, rather well-grown peasant of fifty, with a good many grey hairs in his dark brown, spreading beard. I knew him, but had scarcely ever happened to speak to him till then. He stopped his horse on hearing my cry, and when, breathless, I caught with one hand at his plough and with the other at his sleeve, he saw how frightened I was.

"There is a wolf!" I cried, panting.

He flung up his head, and could not help looking round for an instant, almost believing me.

"Where is the wolf?"

"A shout ... some one shouted: 'wolf' ..." I faltered out.

"Nonsense, nonsense! A wolf? Why, it was your fancy! How could there be a wolf?" he muttered, reassuring me. But I was trembling all over, and still kept tight hold of his smock frock, and I must have been quite pale. He looked at me with an uneasy smile, evidently anxious and troubled over me.

"Why, you have had a fright, aïe, aïe!" He shook his head. "There, dear.... Come, little one, aïe!"

He stretched out his hand, and all at once stroked my cheek.

"Come, come, there; Christ be with you! Cross yourself!"

But I did not cross myself. The corners of my mouth were twitching, and I think that struck him particularly. He put out his thick, black-nailed, earth-stained finger and softly touched my twitching lips.

"Aïe, there, there," he said to me with a slow, almost motherly smile. "Dear, dear, what is the matter? There; come, come!"

I grasped at last that there was no wolf, and that the shout that I had heard was my fancy. Yet that shout had been so clear and distinct, but such shouts (not only about wolves) I had imagined once or twice before, and I was aware of that. (These hallucinations passed away later as I grew older.)

"Well, I will go then," I said, looking at him timidly and inquiringly.

"Well, do, and I'll keep watch on you as you go. I won't let the wolf get at you," he added, still smiling at me with the same motherly expression. "Well, Christ be with you! Come, run along then," and he made the sign of the cross over me and then over himself. I walked away, looking back almost at every tenth step. Marey stood still with his mare as I walked away, and looked after me and nodded to me every time I looked round. I must own I felt a little ashamed at having let him see me so frightened, but I was still very much afraid of the wolf as I walked away, until I reached the first barn half-way up the slope of the ravine; there my fright vanished completely, and all at once our yard-dog Voltchok flew to meet me. With Voltchok I felt quite safe, and I turned round to Marey for the last time; I could not see his face distinctly, but I felt that he was still nodding and smiling affectionately to me. I waved to him; he waved back to me and started his little mare. "Come up!" I heard his call in the distance again, and the little mare pulled at the plough again.

All this I recalled all at once, I don't know why, but with extraordinary minuteness of detail. I suddenly roused myself and sat up on the platform-bed, and, I remember, found myself still smiling quietly at my memories. I brooded over them for another minute.

When I got home that day I told no one of my "adventure" with Marey. And indeed it was hardly an adventure. And in fact I soon forgot Marey. When I met him now and then afterwards, I never even spoke to him about the wolf or anything else; and all at once now, twenty years afterwards in Siberia, I remembered this meeting with such distinctness to the smallest detail. So it must have lain hidden in my soul, though I knew nothing of it, and rose suddenly to my memory when it was wanted; I remembered the soft motherly smile of the poor serf, the way he signed me with the cross and shook his head. "There, there, you have had a fright, little one!" And I remembered particularly the thick earth-stained finger with which he softly and with timid tenderness touched my quivering lips. Of course any one would have reassured a child, but something quite different seemed to have happened in that solitary meeting; and if I had been his own son, he could not have looked at me with eyes shining with greater love. And what made him like that? He was our serf and I was his little master, after all. No one would know that he had been kind to me and reward him for it. Was he, perhaps, very fond of little children? Some people are. It was a solitary meeting in the deserted fields, and only God, perhaps, may have seen from above with what deep and humane civilised feeling, and with what delicate, almost feminine tenderness, the heart of a coarse, brutally ignorant Russian serf, who had as yet no expectation, no idea even of his freedom, may be filled. Was not this, perhaps, what Konstantin Aksakov meant when he spoke of the high degree of culture of our peasantry?

And when I got down off the bed and looked around me, I remember I suddenly felt that I could look at these unhappy creatures with quite different eyes, and that suddenly by some miracle all hatred and anger had vanished utterly from my heart. I walked about, looking into the faces that I met. That shaven peasant, branded on his face as a criminal, bawling his hoarse, drunken song, may be that very Marey; I cannot look into his heart.

I met M. again that evening. Poor fellow! he could have no memories of Russian peasants, and no other view of these people but: "Je haïs ces brigands!" Yes, the Polish prisoners had more to bear than I.

The Crocodile

An Extraordinary Incident

A true account of how a well-dressed, middle-aged gentleman was swallowed whole by a crocodile in the Arcade and the events that unfolded afterward.

Ohé Lambert! Where is Lambert?

Have you seen Lambert?

Chapter 1

On January 13 of this year, 1865, at about half-past twelve in the afternoon, Elena Ivanovna, the wife of my cultured friend Ivan Matveitch, who works in the same department as I do and is also a distant relative, expressed a desire to see the crocodile being exhibited in the Arcade for an admission fee. Since Ivan Matveitch already had his ticket for a trip abroad, not so much for health reasons as to broaden his mind, he was free from official duties that morning and had nothing else to do. He readily agreed to his wife's whim and was, in fact, curious himself.

"Great idea!" he said cheerfully. "Let's go see the crocodile! Before we head to Europe, it's good to get acquainted with its native creatures." With that, he took his wife's arm, and off they went to the Arcade. As their close family friend, I joined them, as I often did. I had never seen Ivan Matveitch in such a lively and agreeable mood before. It's strange how unaware we are of what fate has in store for us.

As we entered the Arcade, Ivan Matveitch was immediately impressed by the grandeur of the building. When we reached the shop where the recently arrived crocodile was on display, he even offered to pay the small admission fee for me—a gesture that had never happened before. Inside the small room, alongside the crocodile, there were cockatoo parrots and a group of monkeys kept in a separate case. Near the entrance, on the left wall, there was a large tin tank resembling a shallow bath. The tank, covered with a thin iron grating, held a few inches of water, and in it lay a massive crocodile. The creature was completely still, looking more like a log than a living animal, seemingly dulled by the damp climate, which clearly didn't suit it. At first, none of us found the crocodile particularly interesting.

"So, this is the crocodile," said Elena Ivanovna with a tone of disappointment. "I thought it would be... something different."

She had likely imagined something more dazzling, perhaps made of jewels. The crocodile's owner, a German man, emerged and looked at us with pride.

"He has every reason to be proud," Ivan Matveitch whispered to me. "He knows he's the only person in Russia exhibiting a crocodile."

This odd remark reflected Ivan Matveitch's unusually cheerful mood, quite different from his usual envious nature.

"I don't think your crocodile is alive," said Elena Ivanovna, irritated by the owner's indifference. Flashing a charming smile to soften her words, she added, "Are you sure it's not stuffed?"

"Oh, no, madam," replied the German in broken Russian. He slid the grate off the tank halfway and poked the crocodile's snout with a stick. The beast stirred faintly, moving its paws and tail slightly, raising its head, and letting out a low snuffle.

"Don't be upset, Karlchen," the German said soothingly, clearly pleased with the attention his pet was getting.

"How horrible that crocodile is! It's really frightening," Elena Ivanovna exclaimed, shuddering dramatically. "I know I'm going to dream about it tonight."

"But it won't bite you in your dreams," the German joked, laughing at his own humor. However, none of us joined in.

"Come on, Semyon Semyonitch," Elena Ivanovna said, turning to me, "let's go look at the monkeys. I love monkeys—they're so adorable! The crocodile is awful."

"Don't worry, my dear!" Ivan Matveitch called out, putting on a show of bravery for his wife. "This lazy relic of the Pharaohs' time won't hurt us." He stayed by the tank, even removing his glove to tickle the crocodile's nose, hoping to make it snort. The German, showing politeness to Elena Ivanovna, followed her to the monkey enclosure.

Everything seemed perfectly normal. Elena Ivanovna was laughing and making jokes about how much the monkeys resembled some of her friends, pointing this out to me and laughing heartily. I couldn't help but laugh too—the resemblance was uncanny. The German wasn't sure whether to laugh or take offense, so he simply frowned. It was then that we heard a terrible, unnatural scream that filled the room. For a moment, I stood frozen, but when I saw Elena Ivanovna screaming as well, I turned around.

What I saw left me paralyzed. Ivan Matveitch was in the crocodile's jaws, caught around the waist. The enormous creature had lifted him off the ground, and Ivan Matveitch was frantically kicking. In one horrifying instant, he was gone—swallowed whole. I stood rooted to the spot, watching the entire process with a strange, detached interest. My only thought in that moment was, "What if it had been me instead of Ivan Matveitch? How unpleasant that would have been!"

The crocodile began by clamping Ivan Matveitch in its jaws and positioning him so it could swallow his legs first. It lifted him up, then pulled him down into its mouth up to his waist. Ivan Matveitch struggled, trying to grab the sides of the tank to escape, but the crocodile kept lifting and swallowing him repeatedly. Little by little, he was disappearing right before our eyes. Finally, with one last gulp, the crocodile swallowed him completely, leaving no trace of him outside its body.

From the crocodile's exterior, we could still see the outline of Ivan Matveitch's form moving inside. I was about to scream when something even more shocking happened. The crocodile, seemingly overwhelmed by the size of its meal, opened its jaws wide once more. With a tremendous hiccup, it briefly allowed Ivan Matveitch's head to pop out, his face filled with despair. For a fleeting moment, his spectacles fell from his nose to the bottom of the tank. It felt as though his face had appeared only to take one last look at the world, to bid farewell to life. But the crocodile made another effort, gave a forceful gulp, and the head vanished—this time for good.

The brief appearance and disappearance of Ivan Matveitch's head was horrifying, but at the same time, there was something absurdly comical about it—perhaps due to its unexpectedness or the falling of the spectacles. I couldn't help myself and burst out laughing. Realizing how inappropriate it was to laugh at such a moment, especially as a close family friend, I quickly composed myself. Turning to Elena Ivanovna with an air of sympathy, I said, "Well, that's the end of poor Ivan Matveitch!"

I can hardly describe how distraught Elena Ivanovna was during the entire ordeal. After her initial scream, she stood frozen, staring at the scene as though in a trance. Her eyes seemed ready to pop out of her head. Then, she let out a piercing wail. I grabbed her hands to calm her. At the same time, the crocodile's owner, who had also been frozen in shock, suddenly clasped his hands and cried out, "Oh, my crocodile! Oh, mein allerliebster Karlchen! Mutter, Mutter, Mutter!"

At his cries, a door at the back of the room flew open, and a rosy-faced, disheveled woman in a cap, clearly the Mutter, rushed in, shrieking and running to the German. Chaos erupted. Elena Ivanovna continued to scream, repeatedly yelling, "Flay him! Flay him!" in a frenzy, as though pleading for someone to skin the crocodile or take revenge.

Meanwhile, the German and his wife were wailing uncontrollably over the crocodile. "He's done for!" the man shouted. "He'll burst any moment; he swallowed an entire government official!"

"Our Karlchen, our dear Karlchen, will die!" sobbed his wife.

"We'll be ruined and left without a livelihood!" the man added.

"Flay him! Flay him! Flay him!" Elena Ivanovna kept shouting, tugging at the German's coat.

"He provoked the crocodile! Why did your man tease my crocodile?" the German shouted back, pulling himself free from her grasp. "If Karlchen bursts, you'll have to pay! Das war mein Sohn, das war mein einziger Sohn!" he cried, as though the crocodile were his only child.

I was deeply annoyed by the selfishness of the German and the cold attitude of his disheveled wife, the Mutter. But what alarmed me even more was Elena Ivanovna's repeated cry of "Flay him! Flay him!" I completely misunderstood her strange outburst. I thought, in her grief over the loss of her beloved Ivan Matveitch, she had momentarily lost her senses and was demanding the crocodile be punished by being skinned. But, as I later discovered, she meant something entirely different.

Embarrassed and glancing uneasily toward the door, I began to beg Elena Ivanovna to calm down and, most importantly, to stop using such a shocking word as "flay." Such a reactionary statement, here in the cultured surroundings of the Arcade—mere steps from the lecture hall where Mr. Lavrov might at that moment be delivering a public address—was both inappropriate and unthinkable. It could easily provoke the scorn of sophisticated society or even inspire ridicule in the satirical cartoons of Mr. Stepanov.

To my horror, my fears were quickly realized. The curtain dividing the crocodile room from the entryway where admission was collected suddenly parted. A man with a mustache and beard appeared in the doorway, leaning far forward but keeping his feet carefully outside the room to avoid paying the entrance fee.

"Such a backward and uncultured demand, madam," the stranger declared, trying to balance precariously while staying outside the room, "shows a lack of proper development. It is a result of insufficient phosphorus in your brain. You will surely be ridiculed in the Chronicle of Progress and mocked in satirical illustrations…."

The man couldn't finish his remarks. The proprietor, realizing in horror that someone was speaking in the crocodile room without paying, rushed at the progressive stranger and punched him. Both vanished behind the curtain for a moment, leaving only muffled sounds of scuffling.

It was then I realized the entire commotion was unnecessary. Elena Ivanovna, as it turned out, was completely innocent. She hadn't been calling for the crocodile to be punished. Instead, she simply wanted the crocodile cut open so her husband could be freed.

"What? You want my crocodile destroyed?" the proprietor yelled, storming back into the room. "No! Let your husband perish before my crocodile does! My father showed crocodiles, my grandfather showed crocodiles, my son will show crocodiles, and I will show crocodiles! Everyone will show crocodiles! I am known throughout Europe, and you are known nowhere! You must pay me a fine!"

"Yes, yes!" added the spiteful German woman. "You will pay since Karlchen is ruined!"

"It's pointless to flay the crocodile," I interjected calmly, eager to take Elena Ivanovna home as soon as possible. "Our dear Ivan Matveitch is probably already in heaven."

"My dear," we suddenly heard a voice say, shocking us all. "My advice is to go straight to the superintendent's office. Without the police, you'll never make this German see reason."

The voice was so unexpected and calm that for a moment we couldn't believe our ears. But we quickly rushed to the crocodile's tank, listening with amazement and disbelief to the muffled words of Ivan Matveitch. His voice was faint, high-pitched, and squeaky, as though it were coming from far away. It sounded like someone trying to shout through a pillow from another room, mimicking distant calls across a plain.

"Ivan Matveitch, my dear, you're alive!" Elena Ivanovna stammered in shock.

Ivan Matveitch's voice came through, faint but steady. "Yes, I'm alive and well," he said, "and thankfully, I've been swallowed without harm. My only worry is how my superiors will view this incident. After all, I got permission to travel abroad and ended up inside a crocodile. It's not exactly clever."

"But, my dear, forget about being clever right now," interrupted Elena Ivanovna. "The first thing we need to do is figure out how to get you out of there."

"Excavate!" the German proprietor cried out. "I won't allow my crocodile to be cut open! Now the public will come in greater numbers, and I will charge fifty kopecks, and Karlchen won't burst anymore."

"Thank God!" his wife added.

"They're right," Ivan Matveitch said calmly. "Economic principles come before anything else."

"My dear, I'm going straight to the authorities to file a complaint. We can't handle this on our own."

"I think that's wise," Ivan Matveitch agreed. "But in these times of economic hardship, cutting open a crocodile without compensation isn't simple. The question is: What will the German take for his crocodile? And how will it be paid? As you know, I don't have the funds."

"Maybe from your salary?" I suggested timidly, but the proprietor immediately cut me off.

"I will not sell the crocodile! For three thousand, maybe I sell! For four thousand, perhaps! Now the public will come even more. I will sell for five thousand!"

His greedy eyes sparkled as he spoke, and his arrogance was insufferable.

"I'm leaving!" I exclaimed, irritated.

"And I will go too! I'll go straight to Andrey Osipitch and beg him," cried Elena Ivanovna.

"Don't do that, my dear," Ivan Matveitch said quickly. He had always been jealous of Andrey Osipitch's refined manners and knew Elena would enjoy pleading with him. "And you," he added, turning to me, "shouldn't rush off in such a reckless way either. Go to Timofey Semyonitch today as if it were just a normal visit. He's old-fashioned and not particularly brilliant, but he's honest and dependable. Send him my regards and explain the situation. Oh, and since I owe him seven roubles from our last card game, pay him back. That will help soften him. His advice might guide us. In the meantime, take Elena Ivanovna home."

"Calm yourself, my dear," he continued, addressing his wife. "All this shouting and fussing has worn me out. I'd like to rest. It's soft and warm in here, though it's still dark."

"Dark? Then how can you look around?" Elena Ivanovna asked hopefully.

"It's pitch black," Ivan Matveitch replied, "but I can feel my surroundings with my hands. Now, goodbye, and don't worry. Take care of yourself. And you, Semyon Semyonitch, come see me tonight. Tie a knot in your handkerchief to remind yourself."

I was relieved to leave, feeling both tired and bored. Offering my arm to the distraught but still radiant Elena Ivanovna, I hurried her out of the crocodile room.

"The next visit will cost another quarter-rouble," the proprietor called after us.

"They're so greedy!" Elena Ivanovna muttered, glancing at herself in every mirror in the Arcade. She was clearly aware that her distress had only enhanced her beauty.

"It's the principles of economics," I said, proud that passersby could see her on my arm.

"The principles of economics," she repeated, her voice soft and curious. "I didn't really understand what Ivan Matveitch was saying about economics."

"I'll explain," I replied and began recounting an article I had read that morning about the benefits of foreign investment in our country.

"How strange," she interrupted after a while. "But stop, you awful man. What nonsense! Do I look flushed?"

"You look perfect, not flushed at all," I said, using the chance to pay her a compliment.

"Naughty man," she said with a playful smile. Then, after a pause, she added, "Poor Ivan Matveitch. I do feel sorry for him. But how will he eat? And... what if he needs something?"

It was a practical question that hadn't even crossed my mind. Women are often more attentive to such details.

"Poor thing! He's stuck in there with nothing to do, and it's so dark. Oh, how I wish I had a photograph of him! I suppose I'm a kind of widow now," she added with a flirtatious smile. "Hm... I do feel sorry for him."

Her remarks were a natural expression of a young wife's grief, tinged with her usual charm. I finally escorted her home, comforted her, and stayed for dinner. After enjoying a cup of aromatic coffee, I set out for Timofey Semyonitch's house, timing my visit for the evening when most settled families would be at home.

Chapter 2

Timofey Semyonitch greeted me with a hint of nervousness, as though he was slightly uneasy. He led me into his small study and carefully shut the door behind him. "So the children don't disturb us," he explained, clearly a bit flustered. He gestured for me to sit in a chair by his desk, while he settled into an armchair, wrapping the worn edges of his quilted dressing gown around himself. His expression turned serious, almost official, despite the fact that he wasn't my superior or Ivan Matveitch's. Until now, we had regarded him as more of a colleague, even a friend.

"First of all," he began, "let me make it clear that I hold no position of authority here. I'm just another subordinate official, like you and Ivan Matveitch. I have no intention of getting involved in this matter."

I was surprised he seemed to already know what had happened. Nevertheless, I explained the situation in full detail, speaking with genuine concern, as I felt I was fulfilling my duty as a loyal friend. He listened without much surprise but with an air of suspicion.

"You know," he said, "I always thought something like this would happen to him."

"Why, Timofey Semyonitch? This is such an unusual and unexpected event."

"I admit that it's unusual, but his entire career has been leading to this. He was always a bit too reckless, too full of himself—always talking about 'progress' and big ideas. And look where that's gotten him."

"But this is hardly a reflection of progress in general. Surely it's just an unfortunate accident."

"No, it's over-education, I tell you," he said firmly. "Over-education leads people to stick their noses where they don't belong. That's what happened here. But maybe you know better," he added, sounding a bit offended. "I'm just an old man with little education. I started out as a soldier's son, and this year marks my service jubilee."

"Oh no, Timofey Semyonitch, not at all," I replied quickly. "Ivan Matveitch values your guidance greatly. He's eager for your advice, almost pleading for it."

"Pleading for it, is he? Hmph. Crocodile tears, I'd say. I can't believe them. And what was he thinking, planning a trip abroad? He has no money for that sort of thing."

"He saved up from his last bonus," I explained earnestly. "It was only supposed to be a three-month trip—to Switzerland, to see the Alps and maybe visit Naples for spring."

"Naples? Hmph. And for what? Museums? Animals?" Timofey Semyonitch scoffed. "We've got animals here. Bears not far from Petersburg! And now he's become part of a crocodile exhibit himself."

"Please, Timofey Semyonitch, the man is in trouble. He's appealing to you as a friend and elder. Show some compassion—for Elena Ivanovna's sake, at least."

"Ah, his wife?" Timofey Semyonitch's tone softened as he reached for his snuffbox. "A delightful lady. So charming, always tilting her head like that. And such a figure—Andrey Osipitch was praising her just the other day."

"He was praising her?" I asked, a bit startled.

"Yes, and quite enthusiastically. Such eyes, such hair, he said. A real gem, not a lady. And he laughed, of course. He's still young."

"That's a different matter entirely, Timofey Semyonitch."

"Of course, of course. Well then, what do you want me to do?"

Timofey Semyonitch met my request with a measured tone. "Give advice, guidance, as a man of experience, a relative! What are we to do? What steps are we to take? Should we go to the authorities?"

"To the authorities? Absolutely not," Timofey Semyonitch quickly replied. "If you want my advice, the best thing is to keep this quiet and handle it privately. This incident is strange, unheard of, and not at all something to be proud of. Discretion is key here. Let him stay where he is for a while. We need to wait and see."

"But how can we just wait? What if he suffocates in there?"

"Why should he? Didn't you say he seemed relatively comfortable?"

I recounted the entire story again, and Timofey Semyonitch considered it carefully.

"Hm," he murmured, twisting his snuffbox in his hands. "In a way, it's probably good for him to stay there instead of going abroad. Let him reflect on things. Of course, we don't want him to suffocate, so he'll need to take precautions—avoid catching a cough, for example. And as for the German, I believe he's within his rights. After all, it wasn't the German who climbed into Ivan Matveitch's crocodile uninvited. Besides, a crocodile is private property, so we can't simply cut it open without compensation."

"But surely saving a human life matters more than property, Timofey Semyonitch."

"Well, that's a matter for the police. You'll need to involve them."

"But Ivan Matveitch is an important member of the department. What if he's needed?"

"Needed? Ha! Besides, he's on leave. For now, he can 'inspect the countries of Europe' from his current situation. If he doesn't show up when his leave ends, then we'll start asking questions."

"Three months, Timofey Semyonitch! Surely you can see how serious this is?"

"It's his own doing. No one forced him into that crocodile. Are we supposed to assign him a government-paid nurse now? That's not in the regulations. The main issue here is that the crocodile is private property, so the principles of economics apply. And economic principles are essential. Just the other evening, Ignaty Prokofyitch was talking about this at Luka Andreitch's place. Do you know Ignaty Prokofyitch? He's a prominent businessman, very eloquent."

"What was he saying?"

"He was talking about the need for industrial development in our country. According to him, we have too little of it, and to fix that, we need to attract foreign capital. He argued that foreign companies should be encouraged to buy land in Russia, just as they do abroad. Communal landholding, he said, is ruining us. He was passionate about it. He insisted that foreign companies should divide large tracts of land into smaller plots to lease them out. This way, the peasants would have to work harder, knowing they could be evicted. That would supposedly make them more productive and disciplined. In turn, this would bring more money into Russia, create capital, and establish a middle class. He even quoted an article in The Times, which said Russia's finances were weak because we lacked a bourgeoisie, big fortunes, and a compliant working class."

"He certainly sounds convincing," I said.

"He is! He's an orator and plans to present his ideas to the authorities. He even wants to publish them in The News. That's far more substantial than any poetry Ivan Matveitch could write."

Timofey Semyonitch listened as I asked, "But what about Ivan Matveitch?"

He seemed eager to continue his own thoughts, enjoying the chance to show he was well-informed about current issues. "About Ivan Matveitch? I was just getting to that. Here we are, trying to attract foreign capital, and what happens? The moment a foreigner's investment—this crocodile—is doubled in value because of Ivan Matveitch, instead of protecting this capitalist, we're talking about cutting open the source of that capital! Does that make any sense? To me, Ivan Matveitch, as a patriot, should be proud that he's helped double or even triple the crocodile's worth. That's exactly what's needed to bring more capital here. If one crocodile does well, another foreigner might bring one, and then another might bring several. Capital will grow around them—that's how you create a middle class. It must be encouraged."

"Timofey Semyonitch," I exclaimed, "you're asking for an almost superhuman level of sacrifice from poor Ivan Matveitch!"

"I'm asking nothing," he replied firmly. "And let me remind you, I'm not in a position of authority, so I can't demand anything. I'm speaking as a patriot, not as a government official. But let's be honest—why did he get into the crocodile in the first place? A respectable man, married, and in government service—then he does something like this! Is that consistent behavior?"

"But it was an accident!" I protested.

"Who can say? And where will we get the money to compensate the owner?"

"Maybe from his salary?" I suggested hesitantly.

"Would that be enough?"

"No, it wouldn't," I admitted sadly. "At first, the owner was worried the crocodile might burst, but as soon as he realized it was fine, he became delighted at the idea of charging more for entry."

"Not just double, but maybe triple or quadruple!" Timofey Semyonitch chuckled. "The public will rush to see it now, and crocodile owners are clever businessmen. Besides, it's not Lent yet, so people are looking for entertainment. That's why I say Ivan Matveitch should keep a low profile. Everyone might hear he's inside the crocodile, but it doesn't need to be officially confirmed. For now, people think he's abroad. If rumors start, we'll deny them. The important thing is patience—why rush?"

"But what if something happens to him?"

"Don't worry; he's healthy."

"And afterward, when he's waited?"

"Well," Timofey Semyonitch admitted, "this is an unprecedented situation. There's no guide for handling something like this. It will take time."

A sudden idea struck me. "Couldn't he petition to remain officially employed while inside the crocodile? He could be considered on special assignment."

"Without pay, perhaps."

"But why not with pay?" I argued.

"On what grounds?"

"As part of a special commission—to study the crocodile from the inside. It could be a scientific exploration. Observing digestion or habits—gathering data on the spot."

Timofey Semyonitch thought about it. "Sending someone inside a crocodile for research? It's absurd and not in the regulations. And what exactly would he report?"

"He could study nature—like digestion or behavior. It would advance knowledge."

"But would lying inside a crocodile allow someone to do their duties properly? That would be a novelty and a risky one. Again, there's no precedent."

"Well," I said, "no one's ever brought a live crocodile here before."

"Hmm… yes," he said, thinking again. "Your point is valid, and it might justify taking further action. But consider this: if living crocodiles become commonplace and government clerks start disappearing into them, claiming they're comfortable there, and then expect official approval for staying inside, it would set a bad example. Everyone would want to follow suit and get paid for doing nothing."

"Please, do what you can for him, Timofey Semyonitch. By the way, Ivan Matveitch asked me to give you seven roubles he lost to you at cards."

"Ah, yes, he lost that the other day at Nikifor Nikiforitch's. I remember. He was so cheerful and full of life then—and now!" The old man's voice softened with genuine emotion.

"Help him, Timofey Semyonitch!"

"I'll do my best. I'll inquire informally, as though I'm just gathering information. In the meantime, why don't you find out discreetly how much the owner might accept to part with his crocodile?"

Timofey Semyonitch's tone became noticeably warmer.

"Certainly," I replied. "I'll let you know as soon as I find out."

"And his wife… is she managing? Is she very upset?"

"You should visit her, Timofey Semyonitch."

"I've been thinking of it; this would be a good opportunity. But what on earth made him want to see that crocodile? Though, to be honest, I'd like to see it myself."

"You should visit the poor man, Timofey Semyonitch."

"I will, though I don't want to give him false hope. I'll go as a private individual… Well, good-bye. I'm off to Nikifor Nikiforitch's again. Will you be there?"

"No, I'm going to check on the poor prisoner."

"Yes, now he's truly a prisoner! Ah, this is what comes of being careless."

I said goodbye to the old man. My thoughts wandered as I left. Timofey Semyonitch was a kind and honorable man, yet as I walked away, I found myself reflecting on how rare people like him had become, especially after fifty years of service.

Without delay, I headed to the Arcade to share the news with poor Ivan Matveitch. I was also driven by curiosity to see how he was managing inside the crocodile. Could someone really live inside a crocodile? Was it even possible? At times, the whole situation seemed so bizarre and unreal, like a surreal nightmare—especially since the central figure in it all was such an absurd and monstrous creature.

Chapter 3

And yet, this wasn't a dream but an undeniable reality. Would I be telling this story if it weren't true? Let me continue.

It was late, around nine in the evening, when I reached the Arcade. I had to enter the crocodile room through the back door because the German owner had closed the shop earlier than usual. In the privacy of his home, he was wandering around in an old, greasy frock-coat, looking three times happier than he had that morning. Clearly, he wasn't worried anymore, as more people had been visiting the exhibit. A little later, his wife, the Mutter, came out, likely to keep an eye on me. The German and the Mutter whispered to each other often. Even though the shop was closed, he still charged me a quarter-rouble. Such unnecessary precision!

"You will pay every time. The public pays one rouble, but you only pay a quarter because you are a good friend of your good friend. And I respect friends," he explained.

"Are you alive? Are you alive, my cultured friend?" I called out as I approached the crocodile, hoping my voice would flatter Ivan Matveitch.

"Alive and well," he replied, sounding distant, as though speaking from under a bed, even though I was right next to him. "Alive and well. But we'll discuss that later. How are things going?"

Ignoring his question, I quickly began asking how he was, what it was like inside the crocodile, and what he could see. Both friendship and basic courtesy demanded it. But, as usual, he cut me off with an impatient tone.

"How are things going?" he snapped, his voice high-pitched and, at that moment, particularly grating.

I reluctantly described my entire conversation with Timofey Semyonitch in great detail, making sure my irritation was clear in my tone.

"The old man is right," Ivan Matveitch declared abruptly, as he often did. "I respect practical people and can't stand sentimental fools. That said, your idea about a special commission isn't entirely stupid. I do have a lot to report—both scientifically and ethically. But now, everything has changed unexpectedly, and worrying about a salary seems trivial. Listen carefully. Are you sitting down?"

"No, I'm standing," I replied.

"Sit on the floor if you have to, but listen closely," he ordered.

Annoyed, I grabbed a chair and slammed it down onto the floor before sitting.

"Listen," he began in his usual authoritative tone. "The public came in droves today. By evening, there was no space left, and the police had to come to maintain order. At eight, the owner decided to close early to count the day's earnings and prepare for tomorrow. I already know tomorrow will be like a carnival. All the most cultured people of the capital, ladies of high society, foreign ambassadors, leading lawyers, and others will come. People from the farthest corners of our vast empire will flock here. The bottom line is, I am now the center of attention. Though out of sight, I am at the forefront. I'll teach the idle masses and serve as an example of dignity and acceptance. I will become a kind of teacher for humanity. Even the biological observations I can provide from inside this creature are invaluable. So, rather than despairing, I am confidently looking forward to a brilliant career."

"You won't find it dull?" I asked sarcastically.

Here's the revised text:

What annoyed me most was the overblown way he spoke. Still, it left me unsettled. "What could this shallow fool possibly be so full of himself about?" I muttered. "He should be crying, not acting all high and mighty."

"No!" he shot back sharply. "I'm full of great ideas. Only now can I finally reflect on how to improve humanity's condition. Truth and enlightenment will emerge from this crocodile. I'll develop a brand-new economic theory and take pride in it—something I couldn't do before because of my job and other petty distractions. I'll refute everything and become a new Fourier. By the way, did you give Timofey Semyonitch the seven roubles?"

"Yes, out of my own pocket," I replied, trying to emphasize that fact.

"We'll settle that," he said arrogantly. "I'm sure my salary will be raised. Who deserves it more than me? I'm more valuable than ever now. But let's move on. My wife?"

"You mean Elena Ivanovna?" I asked cautiously.

"My wife?" he practically screeched.

I had no choice. Grinding my teeth, I told him how I had left Elena Ivanovna. He didn't even let me finish.

184

"I have special plans for her," he began impatiently. "If I'm going to be famous here, I want her to be celebrated out there. Scholars, poets, philosophers, foreign scientists, and politicians will talk with me in the morning, then visit her salon in the evening. Starting next week, she must host an 'At Home' gathering every night. With my doubled salary, we can afford to entertain. Just tea and a few hired servants—simple. People will talk about both of us. I've wanted fame for so long but couldn't achieve it because of my modest position. Now, one gulp from a crocodile has changed everything. Every word I say will be noted, repeated, and published. I'll show them what they've been missing! 'This man could have been a foreign minister or ruled a nation,' they'll say. And some will argue, 'Yet he didn't rule a nation.' How am I less deserving than those other leaders? My wife will match my greatness—brains on my part, beauty on hers. Some will say, 'She's beautiful because she's his wife,' while others will argue, 'She's his wife because she's beautiful.' To prepare, Elena Ivanovna should buy Kraevsky's Encyclopaedia tomorrow so she can discuss any topic. She must also read the political editorials in the Petersburg News and compare them daily with the Voice. I imagine the crocodile's owner might even agree to let me attend her salon inside a tank. I'll dazzle the guests with witty remarks prepared in advance. I'll share plans with the politicians, speak poetry to the poets, and charm the ladies without making their husbands jealous—after all, I'm no threat. I'll also serve as a symbol of dignity and acceptance. Elena Ivanovna will become a celebrated literary figure. She'll embody the finest virtues, and if they call Andrey Alexandrovitch the Russian Alfred de Musset, they'll call her the Russian Yevgenia Tour."

I couldn't help but wonder if he was feverish or delirious. It was the same Ivan Matveitch, but now exaggerated beyond belief.

"My friend," I asked, "are you planning to live long in there? Tell me honestly, how do you eat, sleep, or breathe? I'm asking as a friend, and you must admit this situation is unnatural. My curiosity is only natural."

"Idle curiosity, nothing more," he declared pompously. "But I'll humor you. You want to know how I manage inside this monster? First, to my amusement, I've discovered the crocodile is completely empty inside. It's like a huge, hollow sack made of gutta-percha, similar to those stretchy goods sold in Gorokhovaya Street or Morskaya. Otherwise, how could there possibly be room for me?"

"Is it really possible?" I exclaimed, completely astonished. "Can the crocodile truly be hollow inside?"

"Absolutely," Ivan Matveitch insisted with a stern and authoritative tone. "And most likely, this is exactly how nature intended it. A crocodile has nothing but jaws filled with sharp teeth and a long tail— those are its defining features. The middle part, between its jaws and tail, is simply an empty space surrounded by something like gutta-percha. It's probably made from gutta-percha itself."

"But what about the ribs, the stomach, the intestines, the liver, the heart?" I interrupted angrily.

"There's none of that—absolutely nothing. And I doubt there ever was. Those are just fanciful tales from unreliable travelers. Right now, I'm essentially inflating the crocodile from the inside with my body, much like how one fills an air cushion. The creature is surprisingly elastic. In fact, as a close family friend, you could even join me inside if you had the courage and generosity—and there would still be space left over. I'm even considering inviting Elena Ivanovna to join me in the future. But this hollow, empty structure of the crocodile aligns perfectly with the principles of natural science.

Think about it: if someone were to design a crocodile from scratch, they would first need to identify its primary function. The obvious answer is to swallow people. And how can one ensure that the crocodile can swallow humans? The answer is clear—it must be hollow inside. Physics tells us that nature abhors a vacuum. So, the crocodile must have an empty interior, driving it to fill that space with whatever it encounters. This explains why crocodiles swallow humans.

Of course, the same logic doesn't apply to humans. For example, the emptier a person's head is, the less they seem to feel the need to fill it—one notable exception to the general rule. All of this has become perfectly clear to me now. Being inside this creature, I feel as though I'm in the very heart of nature itself, studying its secrets firsthand. Even the word 'crocodile' supports my theory. It originates from 'crocodillo,' an Italian term that likely dates back to the era of the Egyptian pharaohs. The root of the word is connected to the French verb 'croquer,' which means to eat, devour, or absorb. This will form the basis of my first lecture in Elena Ivanovna's salon when I make my appearance in a tank."

"My friend, shouldn't you consider taking some kind of purgative?" I blurted out, unable to hold back my concern.

"Fever—he's feverish," I muttered to myself anxiously.

"Don't be ridiculous," he replied, full of contempt. "Besides, taking medicine would be terribly inconvenient in my current situation. I knew you'd suggest something like that."

"But how are you managing to eat?" I asked. "Have you had anything to eat today?"

"No, but I'm not hungry. In fact, I suspect I may never need to eat again. It's entirely logical. By occupying the crocodile's interior, I'm making it feel perpetually full. Now it won't need feeding for years. At the same time, as I nourish the crocodile, it nourishes me by sharing its vital juices. It's similar to how some coquettes preserve their beauty by sleeping wrapped in raw steak. After a morning bath, they emerge looking fresh and radiant. This mutual nourishment benefits both of us.

Of course, digestion won't be easy for the crocodile—it isn't built to process someone like me. That's why I try not to move too much, even though I could. I don't want to cause unnecessary discomfort to the poor creature. This is one small drawback of my situation. Timofey Semyonitch was right in a way when he said I was lying there like a log. But I'll prove that even lying like a log can inspire revolutionary ideas for humanity. In fact, most of the groundbreaking ideas and movements we see in newspapers and magazines come from people who are, metaphorically speaking, lying like logs. Critics may call them disconnected from reality, but what does that matter?

Right now, I'm developing my own complete system. You wouldn't believe how easy it is! Just retreat into a quiet corner—or in my case, a crocodile—close your eyes, and you can dream up a perfect future for humanity. Since you left this afternoon, I've already devised three different systems, and I'm working on a fourth. True, you have to first dismantle everything that came before, but that's much easier to do from within the crocodile.

There are only minor inconveniences in my position. It's slightly damp, there's a slimy coating, and it smells faintly of rubber—like my old galoshes. But beyond that, there's nothing to complain about."

"Ivan Matveitch," I interrupted, "this all sounds unbelievable! And are you seriously planning never to eat again?"

"Why are you so focused on trivial nonsense, you shallow creature?" he snapped. "Here I am, discussing grand ideas, and you're worried about dining! Understand this—I am sustained by the great ideas illuminating the darkness surrounding me. That said, the kind-hearted proprietor, after consulting with his thoughtful Mutter, has decided to insert a bent metal tube, like a whistle, into the crocodile's jaws each morning. Through it, I can sip coffee or broth with soaked bread. The tube is already being crafted nearby. But honestly, this seems like an unnecessary luxury to me.

I expect to live for at least a thousand years if crocodiles really do live that long. By the way, you should verify this in a natural history book tomorrow and let me know—I might be confusing them with some prehistoric creature. One concern troubles me, though: since I'm wearing clothes and boots, the crocodile obviously cannot digest me. Moreover, I'm alive, so my willpower actively resists digestion. You can understand why I'd rather not become what all food eventually turns into—it would be far too degrading.

However, I do fear that over a thousand years, my clothing, unfortunately made of Russian fabric, might disintegrate. Without it, I could risk digestion against my will, perhaps while I sleep, when one has no control. The idea of such humiliation enrages me! This alone supports revising tariffs and encouraging the import of stronger English fabrics, which could withstand nature longer when one is swallowed by a crocodile. I will share this thought with a statesman or a political writer in Petersburg's newspapers. They should spread the idea widely. This won't be the only concept they'll take from me. I predict that every morning, reporters armed with quarter-roubles from their editors will flock here to gather my thoughts on the latest telegrams. The future, my friend, looks exceptionally bright!"

"Fever—he's delirious," I muttered under my breath.

"My friend, what about freedom?" I asked, trying to understand his views. "You're essentially in prison, and isn't freedom a basic right?"

"You're a fool," he replied. "Savages crave independence; wise men value order. And if there's no order—"

"Ivan Matveitch, I beg you, stop!" I pleaded.

"Silence and listen!" he barked, irritated by my interruption. "My spirit has never soared higher than it does now. In my small refuge, my only concern is the critique I might face from literary magazines or the satire in our newspapers. I dread that ignorant visitors, jealous people, or nihilists might ridicule me. But I'm taking precautions. I eagerly await the public's reaction tomorrow, particularly from the newspapers. You must bring me updates from them."

"All right. I'll bring a stack of papers tomorrow," I promised.

"Tomorrow's too early for the articles; it'll take four days for the news to spread. But starting today, visit me each evening through the back way. I'll need you as my secretary. You'll read newspapers and magazines aloud while I dictate my ideas and assign tasks. Don't forget the foreign telegrams—make sure I get all the European updates daily. But enough of this; you're probably tired. Go home, and don't dwell on my earlier worries about criticism. I'm not truly afraid of it. Critics are in a precarious position themselves. One must simply be wise and virtuous to rise above. Whether as Socrates, Diogenes, or perhaps both combined—that's my destined role for humanity."

Ivan Matveitch spoke with such arrogance and feverish excitement, like someone too restless to keep a secret. Everything he claimed about the crocodile struck me as dubious. Could it truly be hollow inside? I suspected he was boasting out of vanity or to demean me. True, he was unwell, and allowances had to be made, but I must confess I had never been fond of Ivan Matveitch. For years, I had tried to escape his influence, but I always found myself drawn back, as though hoping to prove something or to take revenge. Friendship can be such a peculiar thing! Honestly, nine-tenths of my connection to him stemmed from malice. Still, on this occasion, we parted with a genuine sense of camaraderie.

"Your friend is a very clever man," the German muttered as he escorted me out. He had been listening closely to our conversation.

"By the way," I said, seizing the opportunity, "how much would you sell your crocodile for, in case someone wanted to buy it?"

Ivan Matveitch, who overheard the question, waited eagerly for the response. It was clear he didn't want the German to undervalue the creature; he even cleared his throat in a peculiar way.

At first, the German reacted with outrage. "No one will dare to buy my crocodile!" he shouted, turning as red as a boiled lobster. "I won't sell him! Not for a million thalers! Today, I made one hundred and thirty thalers, and tomorrow I'll make ten thousand, then a hundred thousand every day! I will not sell him!"

Ivan Matveitch chuckled with satisfaction. Struggling to remain calm—for I felt it was my duty as his friend—I calmly pointed out to the delusional German that his calculations might be flawed. If he truly made one hundred thousand roubles a day, then in just four days, all of Petersburg would have visited, leaving no one else to bring him money. I added that life and death are in God's hands, the crocodile might burst, or Ivan Matveitch could fall ill and die.

The German looked thoughtful.

"I will get him drops from the chemist to make sure your friend does not die," he said after some consideration.

"Drops might help," I replied, "but consider that this could become a legal matter. Ivan Matveitch's wife may demand her husband's release. You're hoping to get rich from this, but do you plan to provide Elena Ivanovna with a pension?"

"No, I do not intend to," the German said firmly.

"No, we do not intend to," the Mutter echoed, her tone even harsher.

"Then wouldn't it be better to accept a guaranteed sum now? Something moderate but secure, rather than leaving it all to chance? Of course, I'm only asking out of curiosity."

The German pulled the Mutter aside, and they whispered together in a corner near a case holding the largest and ugliest monkey in their collection.

"You'll see," Ivan Matveitch said confidently.

At that moment, I was overwhelmed by the desire to give the German a beating, then to give the Mutter an even worse one, and finally to deliver the hardest thrashing of all to Ivan Matveitch for his absurd vanity. But all of that paled in comparison to the ridiculous demand the greedy German made after consulting the Mutter.

He asked for fifty thousand roubles in government bonds with lottery vouchers, a brick house on Gorohovy Street with a chemist's shop attached, and, as if that weren't absurd enough, the rank of a Russian colonel.

"You see!" Ivan Matveitch exclaimed triumphantly. "I told you so! Apart from his silly desire to be made a colonel, he fully understands the economic value of this situation. The economic principle comes first!"

"Are you serious?" I shouted at the German, furious. "Why should you be made a colonel? What heroic deed have you performed? What service have you rendered? You're insane!"

"Insane?" the German shouted back, offended. "No, I am very sensible, but you are very stupid! I deserve to be a colonel because I show a crocodile with a live hofrath inside! A Russian cannot show a crocodile with a live hofrath inside! I am extremely clever and deserve to be a colonel!"

"Goodbye, Ivan Matveitch!" I yelled, trembling with anger, and stormed out of the crocodile room.

I could feel myself losing control and knew I couldn't take another minute of their absurdity. The cold night air cooled my temper slightly. After spitting on the ground several times in frustration, I hailed a cab and went home. Once there, I undressed, threw myself into bed, and fumed.

What angered me the most was that I had somehow ended up as his secretary. Now I would be stuck there every evening, bored out of my mind, all in the name of friendship. I wanted to kick myself for agreeing to it, and I did—after blowing out the candle and pulling the blankets over my head, I punched myself several times out of frustration. It helped a little, and eventually, I fell into a deep sleep, exhausted.

All night, I dreamed of nothing but monkeys. By morning, though, my dreams shifted to Elena Ivanovna.

Chapter 4

The monkeys appeared in my dreams, no doubt because they were locked up in the German's display case. But dreaming of Elena Ivanovna was an entirely different matter.

I should admit right away that I loved her, but I must clarify this immediately: I loved her like a father loves a child, nothing more. I know this because I often felt an irresistible urge to kiss her little head or her rosy cheek. Though I never acted on these feelings, I wouldn't have objected to kissing her lips either—or even her teeth, which gleamed so beautifully like rows of tiny pearls whenever she laughed. And she laughed a lot. Ivan Matveitch, during his more affectionate moments, used to call her his "darling absurdity," which was a perfectly fitting name. She was a delightful little creature, like a sweet confection—simple as that. That's why I've never understood how Ivan Matveitch could have imagined his wife as some kind of Russian intellectual heroine.

Anyway, aside from the monkeys, my dream left me with a pleasant feeling. While sipping my morning tea and reflecting on everything that had happened the day before, I decided to visit Elena Ivanovna before heading to the office. As their family friend, it was the natural thing to do.

In a small room adjacent to the bedroom, which they grandly called the "little drawing room" (though their larger drawing room wasn't much bigger), Elena Ivanovna sat in a light, sheer morning robe. She was lounging on a dainty little sofa in front of a small tea table, sipping coffee from a tiny cup and dipping a delicate biscuit into it. She looked stunningly beautiful but also seemed a bit preoccupied.

"Ah, it's you, you naughty man!" she greeted me with a distracted smile. "Sit down, you featherbrain. Have some coffee. What were you up to yesterday? Were you at the masquerade?"

"Me? No, I don't go to those things," I replied. "Besides, I spent yesterday visiting our captive..." I sighed and adopted a solemn expression as I took a sip of coffee.

"Who?... What captive?... Oh, yes! Poor thing! How is he? Is he bored? You know..." She paused briefly, as if considering her words. "I wanted to ask you something... Do you think I can get a divorce now?"

"A divorce?" I exclaimed, nearly spilling my coffee in shock. My thoughts immediately turned bitterly to the swarthy fellow—a certain dark-skinned man with a small mustache who often visited them and had a knack for amusing Elena Ivanovna. I must confess, I despised him. There was no doubt in my mind that he had seen Elena Ivanovna the day before, either at the masquerade or perhaps even here, and had filled her head with nonsense.

"Well," she rattled off quickly, as though reciting a rehearsed speech, "if he's planning to stay inside that crocodile, maybe forever, while I sit here waiting for him! A husband is supposed to live at home, not inside a crocodile…"

"But this was an unforeseen accident," I began, clearly agitated.

"Oh, don't start," she interrupted, suddenly sounding annoyed. "You're always against me, you villain! I can never get any advice from you! Other people tell me I can get a divorce because Ivan Matveitch won't be getting his salary anymore."

"Elena Ivanovna! Is this really you speaking?" I exclaimed, full of righteous indignation. "Who could have planted such a wicked idea in your mind? Divorce, over something as trivial as a salary, is simply unthinkable. And poor Ivan Matveitch is burning with love for you, even from inside the belly of the beast. Why, he's melting with love—like a lump of sugar. Just yesterday, while you were off enjoying the masquerade, he said that as a last resort, he might send for you, his lawful wife, to join him in the crocodile. Apparently, it's spacious enough inside to fit two—maybe even three—people."

I proceeded to relay the most interesting parts of my conversation with Ivan Matveitch from the night before.

"What, what!" she exclaimed, visibly surprised. "You expect me to crawl inside the crocodile too? With Ivan Matveitch? What a ridiculous idea! How on earth would I even get in there—in my hat and crinoline? Good heavens, how absurd! And what would I look like climbing into it? What if someone saw me? It's ridiculous! And what would I eat in there? And… and… what would I even do there? Oh, this is so absurd! And what if there's a smell of gutta-percha? What if Ivan Matveitch and I had a fight—would we still have to sit there together? Ugh, how awful!"

"I agree, I absolutely agree with all of your points, dear Elena Ivanovna," I interrupted, trying to speak with the natural enthusiasm that comes when you know the truth is on your side. "But there's one thing you've overlooked: he cannot live without you. By inviting you to join him, he's proving his love—passionate, faithful, and devoted love. You've underestimated his feelings for you, my dear Elena Ivanovna!"

"I won't listen! I won't, I won't!" she cried, waving me off with her delicate hand, her freshly washed and polished pink nails catching the light. "You horrid man! You'll make me cry! If you like the idea so much, go get in there yourself. You're his friend, aren't you? Join him, and you can spend the rest of your lives discussing some boring science together."

"You shouldn't mock this suggestion," I said with dignity, trying to rein in her frivolous attitude. "Ivan Matveitch has already invited me. You, of course, are called by duty as his wife. For me, it would be an act of generosity. But last night, when Ivan Matveitch described the elasticity of the crocodile, he hinted that there would be room for not just you two, but even for me as the family friend, should I choose to join."

"What? All three of us?" she exclaimed in astonishment, looking at me. "How could we all possibly fit in there together? Ha-ha-ha! You two are ridiculous! Ha-ha-ha! I'll be pinching you both the whole time, you wretch! Ha-ha-ha! Ha-ha-ha!"

She collapsed onto the sofa, laughing so hard that tears filled her eyes. Her laughter and tears were so enchanting that I couldn't resist rushing to kiss her hand. She didn't pull it away, though she did pinch my ear lightly in playful reconciliation.

We soon grew cheerful, and I explained Ivan Matveitch's plans in detail. The thought of her evening gatherings and her salon seemed to delight her.

"But I'd need so many new dresses," she said thoughtfully. "Ivan Matveitch will have to send me as much of his salary as he can, as soon as he can. Only... only I'm not sure about one thing," she added, pausing. "How will he be brought here in the tank? That's just absurd. I don't want my husband paraded around in a tank. It would be so embarrassing for my guests to see that... I simply can't allow it."

"By the way," she asked suddenly, "was Timofey Semyonitch here yesterday?"

"Oh yes, he was," she replied. "He came to comfort me, and do you know, we played cards the entire time. He played for sweets, and if I lost, he insisted on kissing my hands. What a scoundrel! Can you believe he almost went to the masquerade with me?"

"He was overcome by your charm!" I remarked. "And who wouldn't be, you enchantress?"

"Oh, stop with your flattery! Here, let me give you a pinch as a parting gift. I've gotten quite good at pinching lately. What do you think of that? By the way, did Ivan Matveitch talk about me much yesterday?"

"Well... not exactly," I admitted hesitantly. "He's more focused on the fate of humanity now. He wants—"

"Oh, stop right there!" she interrupted. "I don't want to hear it. It sounds terribly boring. I'll go visit him someday—tomorrow, perhaps. But not today; I have a headache, and besides, there'll be so many people there. They'll point at me and say, 'That's his wife,' and I'll feel so embarrassed. Goodbye. You'll be there this evening, won't you?"

"Yes, to see him. He asked me to bring him the papers."

"That's perfect. Go read to him. But don't come see me today. I'm not feeling well, and I might go visit someone. Goodbye, you naughty man."

"It's that swarthy fellow visiting her tonight," I thought bitterly.

At work, I made sure to show no signs of the worries and troubles weighing on me. However, I soon noticed that some of the most progressive newspapers were being passed around the office unusually quickly, and my colleagues were reading them with unusually serious expressions. The first one that made its way to me was the News-sheet, a paper with no strong political leanings but a general humanitarian focus, which meant it was often looked down on by my colleagues, though they still read it. To my surprise, I found the following paragraph:

"Yesterday, peculiar rumors spread through the broad streets and grand buildings of our vast city. A certain well-known gentleman of high society, perhaps tired of the food at Borel's and the X. Club, visited the Arcade, where a massive crocodile recently brought to the city is being exhibited. The man reportedly arranged with the owner to prepare the crocodile for his dinner. After striking a deal, he began carving pieces off the living creature with a penknife and eating them at an extraordinary speed. Bit by bit, the entire crocodile disappeared into the depths of his stomach. He was even said to have been eyeing an ichneumon, a small animal often kept with crocodiles, perhaps thinking it would taste just as good.

"We have no objection to this new culinary trend, which has long been popular among foreign food enthusiasts. In fact, we predicted its arrival. English lords and adventurers in Egypt organize trips to catch crocodiles and enjoy their meat, cooked like steak with mustard, onions, and potatoes. The French, who followed Lesseps, prefer baking the crocodile's paws in hot ashes—a practice mocked by the English. Both methods would likely gain fans here. We welcome this new industry, which our diverse and resource-rich country desperately needs. Within a year, hundreds of crocodiles could be brought here to replace this one, now lost in the belly of a Petersburg gourmet.

"Why not breed crocodiles in Russia? If the Neva River is too cold for these fascinating creatures, there are ponds in the city and rivers and lakes outside it. Why not raise crocodiles at Pargolovo, Pavlovsk, the Presnensky Ponds, or Samoteka in Moscow? They could provide a unique and nutritious option for refined diners, entertain ladies strolling by the water, and teach children about natural history. Crocodile skin could be used for making jewelry boxes, wallets, cigar cases, and other items. It could even hold the bundles of greasy banknotes that merchants seem to favor. We plan to revisit this exciting topic in future issues."

Although I had somewhat expected this kind of sensationalism, the wild inaccuracies of the article left me stunned. Unable to share my frustration with anyone, I glanced across the desk at Prohor Savvitch, who had been watching me quietly. He held a copy of the Voice in his hand, apparently ready to pass it to me. Without a word, he took the News-sheet from me and handed over the Voice. He drew his nail along the margin of an article, marking the section he wanted me to read.

Prohor Savvitch was a peculiar man. A quiet bachelor, he rarely spoke to anyone in the office and wasn't close to any of us. He always had his own opinions but disliked sharing them. He lived alone, and almost none of us had ever visited his home.

This is what I read in the Voice.

Everyone knows that we pride ourselves on being progressive and humanitarian, striving to keep up with Europe. But despite all our efforts and the work of our newspaper, we are still far from achieving true maturity. This was made clear by the shocking incident that took place yesterday in the Arcade—something we had long predicted.

A foreigner arrived in the capital with a crocodile, which he began exhibiting in the Arcade. We immediately welcomed this as a new and useful business for our great and varied country. But yesterday at four o'clock in the afternoon, an unusually stout man, apparently intoxicated, entered the shop, paid the admission fee, and, without any warning, jumped straight into the crocodile's jaws. Naturally, the crocodile was forced to swallow him, likely out of self-preservation, to avoid being crushed. Once inside the crocodile, the man reportedly fell asleep. Neither the shouts of the foreign proprietor, the terrified cries of his family, nor even threats to call the police had any effect. From inside the crocodile came only laughter and a promise to "flay him," though the poor creature, struggling to digest such a massive meal, shed tears in vain.

As the saying goes, "An uninvited guest is worse than a Tartar." But this unwanted visitor refused to leave. How can we explain such barbaric behavior? It only proves our lack of culture and brings shame upon us in the eyes of foreigners. This reckless display of Russian temperament has found yet another bizarre outlet.

What could the man's motive have been? Was he seeking a warm and cozy home? There are plenty of good, affordable lodgings in the city, many equipped with gas-lit staircases, running water, and hall-porters. Why choose a crocodile?

We also want to draw attention to the cruel treatment of animals. It must be extremely difficult for the crocodile to digest such a large meal all at once. Now the poor creature lies swollen to the size of a mountain, suffering unbearable agony and awaiting death. In Europe, laws have long been in place to punish inhumane treatment of animals.

Despite our European-style pavements and architecture, we are still far from shedding our outdated habits.

As the saying goes, "Though the houses are new, the traditions are old." And the houses aren't always new—at least not their staircases. We've often reported in our paper about the decayed wooden staircase in the home of the merchant Lukyanov in the Petersburg Side. This staircase has long posed a danger to Afimya Skapidarov, a soldier's wife who works there and frequently carries water or firewood up the steps. Finally, as we predicted, the inevitable happened: yesterday evening, she fell while carrying a basin of soup, breaking her leg. Whether Lukyanov will now repair the staircase is uncertain; Russians often act only after disaster strikes. In the meantime, Afimya has been taken to the hospital.

Similarly, we've argued that porters in the Viborgsky Side, who clear mud from the wooden streets, should pile it neatly rather than splashing it onto pedestrians' legs. That's how it's done in Europe. And so on, and so on.

"What is this?" I asked in confusion, looking at Prohor Savvitch. "What does it all mean?"

"What do you mean?" he replied.

"Why, they pity the crocodile instead of Ivan Matveitch!"

"So what? Even an animal deserves pity—a mammal, after all. We have to keep up with Europe, don't we? They care deeply about crocodiles over there, too. He-he-he!"

With that, the peculiar old Prohor Savvitch buried himself in his papers and refused to say another word. I stuffed the Voice and the News-sheet into my pocket, along with as many old newspapers as I could find, intending to bring them to Ivan Matveitch for his evening entertainment. Though it was still hours until evening, I left work early and headed to the Arcade to observe from a distance and listen to people's opinions. I expected a large crowd and turned up the collar of my coat to brace for it. Feeling slightly self-conscious—publicity is unfamiliar to us—I resolved to put aside my personal discomfort in light of the extraordinary nature of this incident.

Bobok

From Somebody's Diary

Semyon Ardalyonovitch said to me out of the blue two days ago, "Ivan Ivanovitch, will you ever stop drinking? Tell me, honestly."

What a strange question. I didn't take offense—I'm a timid man—but now they're saying I'm mad. An artist once painted my portrait, saying, "After all, you're a literary man." I didn't protest; I let him do it. He displayed the painting, and I later read a review: "Go see this morbid face, clearly hinting at insanity."

Maybe it's true, but why say it so bluntly in print? There should be some decorum in writing—some ideals—but instead, they've printed this. Couldn't they have at least hinted at it subtly? Isn't that what style is for? But no, no one bothers with subtlety anymore. Humor and refinement have vanished, and insults are mistaken for wit. I don't take it personally, but God knows I haven't done enough in literature to lose my mind over it. I wrote a novel—it wasn't published. I've written articles, all of which were rejected. I took those articles from one editor to another, but everywhere they told me, "Your work lacks salt."

"Salt? What kind of salt do you mean?" I asked, mocking them. "Attic salt?"

They didn't even understand the reference. Mostly, I translate French books for publishers. I also write advertisements for shopkeepers, like "An Unmissable Opportunity! Finest Tea from Our Own Plantations." I even made some decent money writing a tribute for the late Pyotr Matveyitch. I've compiled works like The Art of Pleasing the Ladies on commission. Over my life, I've produced six or so similar pieces. I'm even considering publishing a collection of

Voltaire's witticisms, but I'm afraid people here might find it dull. Voltaire doesn't resonate anymore—these days, people prefer a blunt cudgel. Everyone's knocking out each other's last teeth.

So, that's the extent of my literary career. Though I do write letters to editors for free, fully signed. In them, I give advice, share criticisms, and suggest improvements. Last week, I sent my fortieth letter in two years. I've spent four roubles on postage for them. I can't help myself—it's my temper.

I suspect that the artist who painted me wasn't interested in my writing at all but was fascinated by the two symmetrical warts on my forehead. He probably thought of them as a natural phenomenon. "They have no ideas," he would say, "so now they're hunting for oddities." And didn't he capture those warts perfectly in his portrait? That's what they call realism.

And as for madness, many people were labeled insane last year— and the way they phrased it! "With such original talent... and yet, as it turns out..." or, "However, we should have seen this coming." It's skillfully done, in a way—artistically clever. Yet, those so-called madmen often prove themselves more brilliant than ever. Critics can call them mad, but they can't produce anyone better.

In my opinion, the wisest person is the one who can, at least once a month, admit they've been a fool—an ability you rarely see nowadays. In the past, people might acknowledge their foolishness once a year, but now? Not at all. Everything's so confused that you can't tell the fools from the wise men anymore. They've done that on purpose.

I recall a witty Spaniard once said, 250 years ago when the French built their first asylums: "They've locked up all their fools to make sure everyone else can pretend they're wise." Exactly. Locking someone else in a madhouse doesn't prove your own wisdom. Just because "K. has gone mad" doesn't mean you're sane.

But why am I rambling? I grumble too much, even my maid is sick of me. Yesterday, a friend stopped by and told me, "Your writing style has changed. It's all choppy—sentence after sentence, then a parenthesis, then a parenthesis within that one, and then more chopping."

He's right. Something is changing in me. My character is different, my head aches, and I've started seeing and hearing strange things. Not actual voices, but it's as if someone's muttering nearby: "Bobok, bobok, bobok."

What could that mean? I need a distraction.

I decided to find one and ended up at a funeral. It was for a distant relative, a collegiate counselor. He left behind a widow and five daughters, all of marriageable age. How will they even afford slippers now? Their father managed it somehow, but with only a small pension left, they'll have to make do. They've always treated me coldly, and honestly, I wouldn't have gone to the funeral if not for a peculiar circumstance.

I joined the procession to the cemetery, but they kept their distance from me—probably because of my shabby uniform. It must've been 25 years since I last visited a cemetery, and it's such a dreadful place!

First, the smell. There were 15 hearses, each with palls of varying quality. Two catafalques stood out—one for a general and the other for a lady. There were plenty of mourners, with a mix of false grief and blatant cheerfulness. The clergy must make a good living from it, though I wouldn't want their job—the smell alone is enough to deter anyone.

I couldn't help but glance at the faces of the deceased. Some had peaceful expressions, while others looked unpleasant. Most of the smiles were unnerving, almost haunting. I don't like them—they linger in your dreams.

During the service, I stepped outside for some air. It was a gray day, dry but cold—typical for October. I wandered among the graves, noticing the different tiers. The third tier costs thirty roubles—not too expensive and still decent. The first two tiers, with tombs inside the church or under its porch, cost significantly more. On this occasion, six people were being buried in third-tier graves, including the general and the lady.

I looked into the graves, and it was horrifying—there was water, and not just any water. It was completely green. But why even talk about it? The gravedigger kept scooping it out constantly. While the service continued, I wandered outside the cemetery gates. Nearby, there was an almshouse and, a little farther away, a restaurant. It wasn't a bad little place—they served lunch and everything. A lot of mourners had gathered there, and I noticed a surprising amount of cheerfulness and even genuine friendliness. I ate and drank a little.

Later, I helped carry the coffin from the church to the grave. Why are coffins so heavy? People say it's because the body no longer moves itself—it's all about some kind of inertia. But honestly, that explanation seems nonsensical to me, defying both mechanics and common sense. I really dislike hearing people with only a general education spout theories about things that require specialized knowledge. And yet, it happens all the time. Civilians feel free to talk about military strategy as if they were field marshals, and engineers prefer to debate philosophy and economics.

I didn't stay for the memorial meal. I have some pride, and if I'm only barely welcome, why force myself into their gatherings, even for a funeral dinner? I'm not sure why I remained at the cemetery afterward. I found myself sitting on a tombstone, lost in thought.

At first, I reflected on the Moscow exhibition, but my thoughts soon shifted to the concept of astonishment itself. Here's what I concluded:

"To be amazed by everything is, of course, foolish. But to be amazed by nothing is even worse and, for some reason, considered fashionable. Yet, I think it's much more stupid to never be amazed. In fact, to never be amazed is almost the same as having no respect for anything. And a truly foolish person is incapable of feeling respect."

What I crave most of all is respect. "I long to feel respect," a friend told me recently. Imagine saying something like that publicly in today's world! What kind of reaction would it get?

At that moment, I drifted into a sort of daze. I don't like reading the epitaphs on tombstones—they're always the same. There was even a half-eaten sandwich lying on the one next to me. It seemed so stupid and out of place. I tossed it onto the ground. After all, it wasn't bread, just a sandwich. Although, now that I think about it, I should check Suvorin's calendar to see if it's a sin to throw food on the ground.

I must have been sitting there for a long time—too long, in fact. At some point, I lay back on a long, coffin-shaped marble slab. Somehow, I began hearing voices. At first, I ignored them, thinking it was my imagination. But the conversation continued. The voices were muffled, as though coming through a pillow, yet they were oddly distinct and close. I snapped out of my daze, sat up, and started listening carefully.

"Your Excellency, this is outrageous! You lead hearts, and I follow with diamonds, but then you play the seven of diamonds? You should've signaled about the diamonds!"

"What's the point of sticking to strict rules? That takes all the fun out of it."

"But you must follow the rules, Your Excellency. Otherwise, there's no way to play. We should use a dummy hand—one that isn't revealed."

"Good luck finding a dummy here."

What absurd words! The voices were strange and unexpected. One was deep and commanding, while the other was smooth and refined. I wouldn't have believed it if I hadn't heard it myself. But how could they be playing cards here, in a cemetery? And who was this general?

There was no doubt the voices were coming from beneath the tombstones. I leaned forward and read the inscription on one grave: "Here lies Major-General Pervoyedov, decorated with numerous honors. Passed away in August of this year at the age of fifty-seven. Rest, beloved ashes, until the joyful dawn."

A general, indeed! The second voice seemed to be coming from a nearby grave, one without a monument—just a simple tombstone. Judging by the tone, it belonged to a lower-ranking official, likely a court councilor.

Then I heard a new voice from about a dozen yards away, coming from a freshly dug grave. It was rough and plebeian, dripping with exaggerated piety. "Oh-ho-ho-ho!" it sighed.

"Oh, not again!" snapped a haughty, irritated voice, clearly belonging to a woman of high society. "Why must I be stuck next to this shopkeeper?"

"I wasn't hiccuping! I haven't eaten a thing," the plebeian voice protested. "It's just the way I am. Really, madam, must you hold onto your caprices, even here?"

"Then why did you choose to lie down here?" she retorted.

"They put me here—my wife and children did. I didn't choose this spot myself. The mystery of death! And trust me, I wouldn't have chosen to lie here beside you for any amount of money. But I was placed here based on what we could afford. We could only pay for a third-grade tomb, and that's what we got."

"Ah, so you made your money by cheating people, didn't you?" the woman snapped.

"Cheating? Hardly! In fact, I haven't seen your money since January. You still owe my shop a small bill."

"That's ridiculous! Trying to collect debts down here? It's the height of stupidity. Why don't you take it up with someone on the surface? Ask my niece—she's my heiress."

"There's no asking anyone now, and no going anywhere," he retorted. "We've both reached our limits, and before God's judgment, we're equal in our sins."

"In our sins?" the woman sneered mockingly. "Don't you dare compare your sins to mine!"

"Oh-ho-ho-ho!" sighed the shopkeeper.

"See that?" she said, addressing someone else. "The shopkeeper obeys the lady, Your Excellency."

"Why shouldn't he?" came the reply.

"Because, Your Excellency, things are different here," the shopkeeper explained.

"Different? How so?"

"Well, we're dead, so to speak, Your Excellency."

"Ah, yes. But still...."

What a bizarre spectacle this was! If this is how things are down here, what hope is there for the living? I continued to listen, my irritation growing by the minute.

"I'd like to feel alive again!" a new voice suddenly declared from somewhere between the general and the irritable woman.

"Do you hear that, Your Excellency? Our friend is at it again," someone remarked, amused. "He says nothing for days, then suddenly bursts out with, 'I'd like to feel alive again!' And he says it with such eagerness! He-he!"

"And such thoughtlessness," another voice chimed in.

"It really gets to him, Your Excellency," the amused voice continued. "You know, he's been here since April. He gets sleepy and quiet for days, and then suddenly he's all, 'I'd like to feel alive again!'"

"It does get dull," the general admitted.

"Indeed, Your Excellency. Shall we tease Avdotya Ignatyevna again? He-he!"

"No, spare me," the general replied. "I can't stand that quarrelsome woman."

"And I can't stand either of you," Avdotya Ignatyevna shot back with disdain. "You're both insufferable and can't tell me anything worthwhile. I even know a little story about you, Your Excellency. Don't look so smug! Remember how a servant swept you out from under a married couple's bed one morning?"

"What a nasty woman," the general muttered under his breath.

"Avdotya Ignatyevna, ma'am," the shopkeeper piped up suddenly, "please don't be angry, but tell me, am I going through some sort of trial by torment, or is this something else entirely?"

"Ah, there he goes again," Avdotya Ignatyevna replied, exasperated. "I was expecting it! And there's that smell—he must be turning over!"

"I'm not turning over, ma'am," the shopkeeper protested indignantly. "And there's no smell from me! My body has remained intact, as it should. You, however, are the one who reeks. Even for a place like this, the smell is terrible. I only refrain from commenting out of politeness."

"You disgusting little man! How dare you!" she shrieked. "You stink, and yet you accuse me!"

"Oh-ho-ho-ho! If only my requiem would come quickly," the shopkeeper sighed dramatically. "I'd hear their tearful voices above me—my wife's laments, my children's soft weeping...."

"What nonsense!" Avdotya Ignatyevna interrupted. "They'll cry for a bit, then stuff themselves with funeral rice and go home. Ugh! I wish someone interesting would wake up!"

"Patience, Avdotya Ignatyevna," came the smooth voice of the government clerk. "The new arrivals will speak soon enough."

"Are there any young people among them?" she asked, her tone brightening slightly.

"Yes, there are some young ones, Avdotya Ignatyevna. Some are barely more than boys."

"Oh, how wonderful that would be!"

"Have they started speaking yet?" asked the general.

"Not yet, Your Excellency. Even those who arrived the day before yesterday haven't woken up yet. As you know, some take a week or more to begin. Luckily, they've been bringing in many recently—just today and yesterday, in fact. Otherwise, most of those around us are from last year."

"Yes, this will be interesting."

"Indeed, Your Excellency. Today they buried Privy Councillor Tarasevitch. I recognized it from the voices. I also know his nephew— he helped lower the coffin just now."

"Hmm, where is he buried?"

"Just five steps to your left, Your Excellency—almost at your feet. You should meet him."

"Hmm, no, it wouldn't be appropriate for me to make the first move."

"Oh, he'll come to you on his own, Your Excellency. He would be honored. Leave it to me, and I'll—"

"Oh, oh! What's happening to me?" croaked a frightened new voice.

"A new arrival, Your Excellency, thank goodness! And how quick he is—some don't speak for days."

"Oh, I think it's a young man!" Avdotya Ignatyevna exclaimed excitedly.

"I... I... it was so sudden—a complication!" the young man stammered. "Only last evening, Dr. Schultz said there was a complication, and then suddenly, by morning, I was... gone. Oh! Oh!"

"Well, there's no helping it now, young man," the general said graciously, clearly pleased by the arrival. "You're welcome to our little community here in the Vale of Jehoshaphat, if we may call it that. We're good people—you'll get to know and appreciate us. Major General Vassili Vassilitch Pervoyedov, at your service."

"No, no! Certainly not! I was with Schultz, and he said it was a complication. First, it was my chest, then a cough, then a cold. My lungs... influenza... and then suddenly, without warning—it was over. The worst part was how unexpected it all was!"

"You say it started with your chest?" the government clerk asked smoothly, as if to comfort the new arrival.

"Yes, my chest, then catarrh. Then the catarrh was gone, but the chest trouble remained. I couldn't breathe... and then suddenly... you know...."

"I know, I know. But if it was your chest, you should have gone to Dr. Ecke instead of Schultz."

"I kept meaning to see Dr. Botkin, but then, all at once...."

"Botkin is very expensive," the general interjected.

"Oh, no, not at all! I've heard he's very attentive and can predict everything in advance."

"His Excellency meant his fees," the government clerk clarified.

"Oh, but he only charges three roubles. He gives a thorough examination and writes a detailed prescription. I was eager to see him because I'd been told... well, gentlemen, should I have gone to Ecke or Botkin?"

"What? Gone to whom?" The general's laughter, hearty and resonant, filled the space, echoed by the clerk's falsetto chuckle.

"Dear boy, delightful boy, how I adore you!" Avdotya Ignatyevna squealed with delight. "I wish they'd buried someone like you next to me."

This was too much! These were the dead of our time? Still, I thought it best to listen further before forming any conclusions. The young man, with his sniveling voice and the expression of a frightened chicken, had been insufferable in life, and now in death, he seemed no better. But the scene was chaotic.

Soon, more began waking up. An official—a civil councillor—stirred and immediately launched into a detailed discussion about the creation of a new government sub-committee and the potential reshuffling of various functionaries. The general found this particularly

213

fascinating, and I admit I learned a surprising amount about government affairs. Meanwhile, an engineer began muttering incoherently, so the others left him to lie in peace until he was more coherent.

Finally, the distinguished lady buried that morning under the catafalque began to show signs of waking. Lebeziatnikov, the obsequious clerk beside General Pervoyedov, grew visibly excited, marveling at how quickly everyone was waking this time. I, too, was surprised—some of the awakened had been buried only three days ago, including a giggling girl of sixteen whose laughter had an unsettling, predatory tone.

"Your Excellency, Privy Councillor Tarasevitch is waking!" Lebeziatnikov announced with exaggerated fuss.

"Eh? What?" Tarasevitch mumbled irritably as he woke. His lisp carried a note of haughty displeasure.

I listened intently, intrigued. Rumors about Tarasevitch had been swirling recently, and they were shocking, to say the least.

"It's I, Your Excellency," Lebeziatnikov said obsequiously. "Only I, so far."

"What do you want? What's your petition?"

"I merely came to inquire after your Excellency's health. These surroundings can be oppressive at first. General Pervoyedov wishes to make your acquaintance and hopes—"

"I've never heard of him."

"Surely, Your Excellency! General Pervoyedov, Vassili Vassilitch—"

"Are you General Pervoyedov?"

"No, Your Excellency, I am not General Pervoyedov. I am Semyon Yevseitch Lebeziatnikov, lower court councillor, at your service. But General Pervoyedov—"

"Enough nonsense! Leave me alone!"

"Let him be," General Pervoyedov said at last, cutting off his sycophantic companion in the grave with a dignified tone.

"He's just not fully awake yet, Your Excellency. The novelty of all this has overwhelmed him. When he adjusts, he'll behave differently."

"Let him be," the general repeated.

"Vassili Vassilitch! Hey, Your Excellency!" came a new voice, loud and brash, from near Avdotya Ignatyevna. The tone was full of arrogance and carried the languid drawl that had become fashionable among certain circles. "I've been watching you all for the last two hours. Do you remember me, Vassili Vassilitch? I'm Klinevitch. We met at the Volokonskys'—where you, for some reason, were a guest as well. I can't imagine why."

"What? Count Pyotr Petrovitch? Is that really you? And at such a young age! How sad to hear of it."

"Oh, I'm sorry myself, but I don't mind too much. I intend to make the best of things here as well. By the way, I'm not a count, just a baron. A rather disgraceful baron, too, one of those who rose from being mere lackeys. I don't know why, and I don't care. I'm just a scoundrel from the pseudo-aristocratic society. They call me 'a charming rogue.' My father is a pitiful little general, and my mother once managed to gain favor in high places. With the help of a Jew named Zifel, I forged fifty-thousand-rouble notes last year and then turned him in. Meanwhile, Julie Charpentier de Lusignan took the money to Bordeaux. Imagine this—I was even engaged to a schoolgirl, just three months shy of her sixteenth birthday, with a dowry of ninety thousand roubles. Avdotya

Ignatyevna, do you remember how you seduced me fifteen years ago when I was just a boy in the Corps des Pages?"

"Ah, it's you, you scoundrel! Well, you're a welcome sight in this dull place."

"You were wrong to suspect your neighbor, the businessman, of being the source of the unpleasant smell. I stayed silent, but I laughed. The stench came from me—they had to bury me in a sealed coffin."

"Ugh, you vile creature! Still, I'm glad you're here. You wouldn't believe how lifeless it's been."

"Exactly, and I intend to bring some excitement. Your Excellency—not you, Pervoyedov, but Tarasevitch, the privy councillor! Answer me! I'm Klinevitch. Remember how I took you to Mademoiselle Furie during Lent?"

"I remember, Klinevitch, and I am delighted to see you."

"I wouldn't trust you with a single kopeck, but I want to kiss you, dear old man—fortunately, I can't. Do you know, gentlemen, what our dear grandpa's little secret was? He died just three or four days ago, leaving a deficit of four hundred thousand roubles in government funds meant for widows and orphans. Somehow, he had sole control of these funds, and his accounts hadn't been checked in eight years. Imagine the faces of those left to clean up his mess! What a delightful thought! I've been wondering how a decrepit old man of seventy could manage the energy for his indulgences—and now we know! Those widows and orphans must have been his inspiration."

"I ... I have long dreamed of ... of just such a setting," the general stammered, his voice trembling with eagerness.

"Monster!" cried Avdotya Ignatyevna.

"Enough!" Klinevitch declared. "I see there's plenty of potential here. We'll soon liven things up. But first—hey, you, government clerk, Lebeziatnikov, is that your name?"

"Yes, Semyon Yevseitch Lebeziatnikov, lower court councillor, at your service. I'm very, very delighted to meet you."

"I don't care whether you're delighted or not. You seem to know everything around here. Tell me, how is it we can talk? Ever since yesterday, I've been wondering about it. We're dead, yet we're talking and even seem to be moving. What kind of trick is this?"

"If you want an explanation, Baron, Platon Nikolaevitch could provide one far better than I."

"Who's Platon Nikolaevitch? Be clear and stop beating around the bush."

"Platon Nikolaevitch is our local philosopher, scientist, and Master of Arts. He has written several philosophical works, but for the last three months, he's been quite drowsy, and there's no waking him up now. Once a week, he mutters something completely unrelated."

"Get to the point!"

"He explains all of this with a simple idea: when we were alive on the surface, we mistakenly thought death was the end. Instead, the body sort of revives here, and what's left of life is concentrated in consciousness. Life continues, in a way, by inertia. He believes everything condenses in the mind and goes on for two or three months—sometimes even half a year. For example, there's someone here who's almost completely decayed but still manages to mutter a single, meaningless word, 'bobok,' every six weeks. That tiny spark of life still lingers."

"That's ridiculous. And why don't I have a sense of smell, yet I feel like there's a stench?"

"Ah, well, he-he. On that point, our philosopher is a little unclear. He claims the stench is, so to speak, moral. He says it's the stench of the soul trying to recover itself during these two or three months. He even calls it a kind of mercy. But honestly, Baron, I think these are just mystic ramblings, excusable given the circumstances."

"Enough. The rest is nonsense. The main thing is we have two or three months of this strange existence left before—bobok. I suggest we make these months as enjoyable as possible and set up something new. Gentlemen! Let's cast aside all shame!"

"Yes, let's cast aside all shame!" many voices echoed, and new ones joined in—likely from others just waking up. The engineer, now fully awake, enthusiastically agreed, and the girl Katiche let out a gleeful giggle.

"Oh, how I'd love to cast off all shame!" exclaimed Avdotya Ignatyevna with excitement.

"If Avdotya Ignatyevna wants to cast off shame—" began Klinevitch.

"No, no, Klinevitch, I was still ashamed up there. But here? Here, I'd love to let go of it. I'd love it so much!"

"I see what you mean, Klinevitch," the engineer boomed. "You want to reorganize life here on rational principles."

"Oh, I couldn't care less about that! For that, we'll wait for Kudeyarov, who was brought here yesterday. When he wakes, he'll explain everything. He's such a figure, a real titan! And in a few days, they'll bring in a natural scientist, an officer, and later a journalist— probably with his editor. But to hell with all of them. We've got a group forming already, and things will work themselves out. For now, let's just stop lying. That's all I care about. Lying was necessary on the surface; life and lies were inseparable there. But here, we can amuse ourselves with the truth. The grave has its advantages! Let's tell our stories out loud, with no shame at all. I'll go first—I'm one of the predatory types, you know. Up there, rotten social rules held me back. But here? Away with the rules! Let's spend these months in fearless honesty. Let's strip ourselves bare!"

"Let's strip! Let's strip!" cried the voices in unison.

"I can't wait to strip!" Avdotya Ignatyevna shrilled.

"Ah, I see we're going to have some real fun here. I don't need Ecke after all."

"No, I just want a taste of life!"

"He-he-he!" giggled Katiche.

"The best part," said Klinevitch, "is that no one can stop us. Even if Pervoyedov is in a bad mood, he can't reach me from where he is. What do you say, grand-père?"

"I fully agree, absolutely, and with great satisfaction, but only if Katiche is the first to tell her story," Klinevitch declared.

"I protest! I protest with all my heart!" General Pervoyedov said firmly.

"Your Excellency," Lebeziatnikov murmured, fussing excitedly, "I really think it's to our advantage to agree. After all, it involves the girl ... and all their little affairs."

"There is the girl, yes, but..."

"It's beneficial for us, your Excellency, I promise you! Let's at least try it as an experiment."

"Even in the grave, they won't let us rest in peace," the general grumbled.

"In the first place, General, you were playing preference in the grave. And secondly, we don't care about you," Klinevitch said with a lazy drawl.

"Sir, I must ask you to mind your manners," the general retorted.

"What? You can't reach me, and I can mock you as easily as teasing a lapdog. And another thing, gentlemen—why is he still a general here? He was a general up there, but here, he's just … debris."

"No, not debris … even here…"

"Here you'll rot like the rest of us, and all that will remain are your six brass buttons."

"Bravo, Klinevitch, ha-ha-ha!" roared several voices.

"I served my sovereign … I had my sword…"

"Your sword? Only good for skewering mice, and you never even used it for that."

"That doesn't matter; I was part of the whole."

"There are many kinds of parts in a whole."

"Bravo, Klinevitch, bravo!" more voices chimed in.

"I don't see what use a sword is now," the engineer grumbled.

"We'll run from the Prussians like frightened mice! They'll crush us to dust!" came a distant voice, sputtering with glee.

"A sword, sir, is an honor," the general insisted, though only I seemed to hear him. Chaos erupted—a roar of laughter, arguing, and general uproar. Over it all, Avdotya Ignatyevna's shrill voice rose impatiently.

"Let's get on with it already! When will we finally cast off all shame?"

"Oh-ho-ho! The soul truly goes through torments," sighed the plebeian voice.

At that moment, I sneezed. It happened suddenly and involuntarily, but the effect was astonishing. Everything stopped. Silence fell over the cemetery—a true, heavy silence, like one would expect in such a place. It was as if everything vanished, like a dream dissolving. Not a single voice spoke. Not a sound was heard.

I waited for five minutes—nothing. They weren't ashamed because I was there; they had already resolved to cast off all shame. I couldn't believe they feared I might inform the authorities—what could the police do to them? No, it must be some secret they hold, one the living cannot know.

"Well, my friends," I thought, "I'll come back to visit you again." And with that, I left the cemetery.

No, I cannot accept this. No, I really can't! It's not the "bobok" case that troubles me—so that's what "bobok" meant! No, it's the depravity. Such depravity in a place like that—corruption even in their final moments of consciousness. These last moments were granted to them, a mercy even … and yet, such behavior! No, I can't accept it.

I'll visit other graves. I'll listen elsewhere. Surely, I'll find something better, something to ease my mind. But I will return to them, too. They promised stories, biographies, and who knows what else. Tfoo! But I will go back—it's a matter of conscience!

Perhaps I'll even take this to the Citizen. The editor there has had his portrait displayed, too. Maybe he'll print it.

The Dream of a Ridiculous Man

Chapter 1

I am a ridiculous person. People call me a madman now. That might sound like an improvement, but they still see me as ridiculous. I don't mind anymore, though. In fact, I feel a kind of affection for them, even when they laugh at me. Strangely, I find them even more endearing when they do. Sometimes I feel like joining in their laughter—not at myself, but out of affection for them—if only it didn't make me so sad. I feel this sadness because they don't know the truth, but I do. Oh, how hard it is to be the only one who knows the truth! But they will never understand that. No, they won't.

In the past, I was miserable because I wasn't just seen as ridiculous—I truly was. I have always been ridiculous, and I've known it for as long as I can remember, maybe even since I was seven years old. Later, I went to school and eventually university, and the more I learned, the more I realized how ridiculous I was. It seemed like every subject I studied only reinforced how absurd I truly was. The same thing happened in life. With each passing year, I became more aware of how ridiculous I looked in every situation. Everyone laughed at me, but none of them realized that no one understood my absurdity better than I did. What frustrated me most was that they didn't know that I knew. But it was my own pride that stopped me from ever admitting it to anyone.

As I grew older, that pride only grew stronger. If I had ever confessed my ridiculousness to someone, I think I would have ended my life that same evening. In my younger years, I constantly feared that I might let it slip to my classmates. But as I grew into adulthood, I

222

became strangely calmer, even as I became more certain of my absurdity. I don't know why. Perhaps it was because of a deep, growing despair in my soul, a despair tied to something even bigger: the belief that nothing in the world truly mattered. I had sensed this for a long time, but last year it hit me fully and suddenly. I realized that it made no difference whether the world existed or not. I felt with every part of me that nothing really existed. At first, I thought that maybe things had existed in the past, but then I realized they hadn't. It had only seemed that way. Over time, I guessed that nothing would exist in the future either.

With this realization, I stopped being angry at people. I barely noticed them anymore. This even showed in the smallest things. For example, I often bumped into people on the street—not because I was lost in thought (I had nothing to think about), but because nothing mattered to me anymore. I had stopped caring about everything. And as I stopped caring, all my problems seemed to disappear.

It was after this that I discovered the truth. I learned it last November—on the third, to be exact—and I can recall every moment since. It was one of the gloomiest evenings imaginable. Around eleven o'clock, I was walking home, thinking about how dismal everything felt, both outside and within me. It had rained all day, cold and harsh, as if the rain itself hated humanity. The rain stopped between ten and eleven, but the dampness that followed was even worse. A thick, cold mist seemed to rise from the ground, from every stone and every alley. I remember thinking that if all the street lamps were turned off, it would feel less dreary. The gaslight only made it worse by revealing everything.

I hadn't eaten much that day, and I had spent the evening with an engineer and two other friends. They talked animatedly about something, pretending to be deeply interested, but I could tell they didn't really care. I sat silently, probably boring them. Then, out of nowhere, I said, "You don't actually care about any of this." They weren't offended; instead, they laughed. They knew I wasn't criticizing them—I just didn't care either. My indifference amused them.

As I stared at the street's gas lamps, my eyes wandered upward to the sky. The darkness was overwhelming, but I could make out torn clouds drifting across patches of infinite blackness. Suddenly, I saw a star shining in one of those patches, and for some reason, it captivated me. That star gave me an idea: I decided to end my life that night.

I had made up my mind two months earlier. Despite being poor, I bought a fine revolver on the very day I decided, loaded it, and kept it in my drawer. But for two months, it had stayed there untouched. My indifference held me back. I waited, hoping for a moment when I might feel something—anything—to spur me into action. And now, as I looked at that star, I felt certain that tonight would be the night. Why the star triggered this decision, I couldn't say.

Just as I stared at the sky, lost in thought, a little girl grabbed my elbow. The street was nearly empty, with only a cabman dozing far in the distance. She was around eight years old, her head wrapped in a kerchief. She wore a thin, shabby dress soaked from the rain, but what stood out most to me were her drenched, broken shoes. They were so worn that they etched themselves into my memory.

She clutched my elbow and tugged at me, calling out in a shaky, desperate voice. She wasn't crying exactly, but she was gasping for air, struggling to speak. Her whole body shook with fear as she stammered, "Mammy, mammy!" I stopped and turned to face her but said nothing. Then I walked on. She ran beside me, still pulling at my arm, her cries filled with the kind of despair only a terrified child can have. Though her words were jumbled, I understood: her mother was dying or in some terrible crisis, and she was running through the streets to find help.

I didn't follow her. Instead, I told her to find a policeman. But she wouldn't leave me. She clasped her hands, sobbing, running alongside me. Frustrated, I stamped my foot and shouted at her. She cried, "Sir! Sir!…" before suddenly abandoning me and rushing toward another passerby further down the street. She fled from me to him as though he might help.

I climbed the stairs to my fifth-floor room. I rented a small space in a shared flat with several other lodgers. My room was plain—a semicircular garret window, a worn sofa covered in fake leather, a table stacked with books, two chairs, and an armchair so old it might as well have been ancient. Yet it was still comfortable, made in a sturdy, old-fashioned style.

I lit a candle and sat down to think. Next door, separated from me by only a thin partition wall, chaos reigned. It had been going on for three days straight. A retired captain lived there with a rowdy group of questionable friends. They drank vodka, gambled with old playing cards, and often ended up fighting. The night before, two of them had dragged each other around by the hair. The landlady wanted to complain but was too terrified of the captain to say anything.

There was also another lodger—a frail, nervous woman visiting from the countryside with her three young children. Since moving into the flat, the children had fallen ill, and the entire family was petrified of the captain. They spent their nights trembling in fear, crossing themselves, while the youngest child even had a fit from the stress.

The captain, I knew, sometimes begged for money on the Nevsky Prospect. He'd been refused reentry into military service, but oddly enough, none of this bothered me. Ever since he moved in, I had managed to block out the noise and disturbances from the other side of the wall. Even their shouting and late-night gatherings failed to annoy me. I had become indifferent to everything.

For the past year, I'd been staying awake all night, sitting in my armchair at the table, doing absolutely nothing. By day, I read. At night, I simply sat there, letting scattered thoughts drift through my mind. I let them come and go as they pleased. A whole candle burned down every night, but it made no difference to me.

That night, I calmly placed the revolver on the table in front of me. I stared at it and thought, "Is this it?" And then I answered myself, "Yes, it is." I knew, with absolute certainty, that I would end my life that night. Yet I didn't know how much longer I would sit there before doing it.

And I believe I would have done it—if not for that little girl.

Chapter 2

Though nothing seemed to matter to me, I was still capable of feeling pain. If someone had hit me, it would hurt, and it was the same emotionally. If something tragic happened, I would feel pity, just like I used to when life still held meaning for me. I had felt pity earlier that evening. I would have helped the little girl if not for a sudden thought that stopped me.

When she grabbed my arm and begged for help, a strange question popped into my mind, and I couldn't shake it. The question was pointless, but it frustrated me. I thought, "If I plan to end my life tonight, then nothing should matter anymore." So why, I wondered, did I feel pity for the girl? Why did I care? I remember feeling so sorry for her, a deep pang of compassion, but it didn't fit with how I believed I should feel. The sensation lingered when I got home and sat at my table. It irritated me, more than anything had in a long time.

One thought led to another, and I realized that as long as I was alive—still a person and not nothingness—I could still feel things like pain, anger, and shame over my actions. But if I was about to die, what did the girl or my shame matter? Soon, I would turn into nothing, and everything else would vanish too. Could it be true that knowing I would soon stop existing didn't erase my pity for the child or the shame I felt for how I had acted? It was as though my actions still had weight, even if they shouldn't.

When I yelled at the girl, it felt like I was shouting, "I don't care! I don't even need to act human anymore because, in a few hours, nothing will exist!" Looking back now, I believe that was why I shouted. I had this strange sense that everything in life—the whole world— depended on me at that moment. If I died, the world would end, at least for me. And maybe, I thought, it would end entirely. After all, if my consciousness disappeared, the world might vanish too, since it only existed as part of me. For a moment, I believed all people and things might only be projections of myself.

As I sat there, questions flooded my mind. One thought led to another, and then I imagined something new. What if I had lived on the moon or Mars and committed a terrible act there, something so shameful it haunted me? If I came to Earth afterward and remembered that act, but also knew I could never return to the moon, would I still feel shame when looking up at it from Earth?

These thoughts were pointless—after all, the revolver was right there, and I knew what I was going to do. Still, they consumed me, filling me with frustration. I couldn't bring myself to die without answering some of these questions first.

Meanwhile, the noise in the captain's room next door began to quiet down. They had finished their card game and were settling in for the night, still muttering and arguing lazily. And then, unexpectedly, I fell asleep in my chair—a thing that had never happened to me before.

Dreams are strange, as everyone knows. Some parts are so vivid, with every detail as sharp as a finely cut gem, while other parts blur, rushing past in a haze. Dreams seem to follow the heart's desires rather than reason, and yet, sometimes, they can be incredibly logical in ways that don't make sense in waking life. For example, my brother died five years ago, but in my dreams, he sometimes appears alive, participating in my life. Even in the dream, I know he is dead, but somehow, it feels normal that he is there. My mind accepts it without question.

And now, let me tell you about my dream that night. It happened on the third of November. People tease me now, saying it was just a dream. But does it really matter whether it was a dream or reality? If the dream revealed the truth to me, then what difference does it make? Truth is truth, whether you find it while awake or asleep. That night, my dream showed me something extraordinary—a life I had never imagined, renewed and filled with meaning and strength.

Listen closely.

Chapter 3

While I was drifting into sleep, I dreamed that I picked up the revolver and pointed it at my chest—though I had planned to aim at my head, specifically my right temple. I hesitated for a moment after aiming, and then, all of a sudden, everything around me—the candle, the table, and the wall—seemed to shift and tremble. Quickly, I pulled the trigger.

In dreams, when you fall, get stabbed, or are hurt, you don't feel pain—unless you actually hit something in real life, like a bedpost, and then you wake up. In my dream, I didn't feel pain, but it was as though everything inside me had been violently shaken. Darkness swallowed me, so thick it seemed to blind me. I found myself lying flat on my back on something hard. I couldn't move or see anything. I could hear voices, though—people shouting and walking around. I recognized the captain yelling and the landlady screaming. Then, everything shifted again, and I realized I was being carried in a closed coffin. I felt the coffin sway as it was moved, and I began to reflect on it. For the first time, the thought struck me: I was dead. Utterly dead. I had no doubt of it. I couldn't move or see, but I could think and feel. Surprisingly, I accepted this without protest, as one often does in dreams.

They buried me in the earth and left. I was alone, completely alone. I didn't move. Whenever I had imagined being buried before, I thought it would feel cold and damp. Now, in the grave, I did feel cold, especially at the tips of my toes, but I felt nothing else. I lay there, waiting for nothing, fully accepting that there was nothing for a dead man to expect.

Time passed—or perhaps it didn't. I couldn't tell if it was an hour, days, or even longer. Then, all at once, a drop of water fell onto my closed left eye, seeping through the coffin lid. Another drop followed a minute later, then another. The rhythm was exact, each drop falling like clockwork. A surge of indignation filled me, along with a sharp pang of pain in my chest. "That must be the wound," I thought. "Where the bullet hit." The drops continued to fall, one after another, relentlessly.

Suddenly, with all of my being—not with words, but with everything that made me—I cried out to whatever force was behind this nightmare. "Whoever you are, if you exist, and if there's anything more reasonable than this horror, make it happen now. But if this is your way of punishing me for my foolish suicide by making my afterlife absurd and grotesque, then know this: no torture could match the scorn I will feel for you, even if my suffering lasts a million years!"

I waited. Silence followed, deep and unbroken. Then, another drop fell. But in that silence, I knew, with unshakable certainty, that everything was about to change. Suddenly, my grave burst open— though I don't know if it was dug up or shattered—and I was lifted out by some dark, unknown force. Together, we ascended into space.

My sight returned. It was night—darker than anything I had ever known. We flew far away from Earth, moving through the void. I didn't question the being carrying me. I felt proud, refusing to show fear, and even thrilled that I wasn't afraid. I had no sense of time; we moved as though dreams erase the rules of time and space. Only moments that matter seem to stand still. Suddenly, in the vast darkness, I saw a single star. Impulsively, I asked, "Is that Sirius?" though I hadn't meant to speak.

"No," the being answered. "That is the star you saw between the clouds when you were walking home."

I realized that the being accompanying me had something like a human face. Strangely, I felt an intense dislike for it. I had expected complete nothingness after death—that's why I had shot myself. But now, here I was, in the presence of a creature that wasn't human yet clearly alive. "So there is life after death," I thought with a peculiar detachment, the kind one feels in dreams. Deep down, though, my heart resisted. "If I have to exist again," I thought, "and live under the control of some unrelenting power, I will not allow myself to be defeated or humiliated."

"You know I'm afraid of you, and you despise me for it," I suddenly said to my companion. The words slipped out, admitting my humiliation. It hurt, like a sharp sting, to confess such weakness. My companion gave no answer. Instead, I felt something chilling: not only did he not despise me, but he was laughing at me. There was no pity in him. It became clear that our journey had some mysterious purpose that concerned only me. Fear began to creep into my heart. Though my companion remained silent, I felt a painful, unspoken message flowing from him and spreading through me.

We continued flying through a dark and unknown expanse. The constellations I once knew had disappeared from view. I remembered how there are stars so distant that their light takes millions of years to reach Earth. Perhaps we were now traveling through those far-off spaces. A growing sense of anguish weighed on me, an unbearable ache in my heart as I awaited something unknown. Suddenly, I felt an unmistakable sensation—it was familiar, stirring me deeply. I saw a sun.

I knew it couldn't be the sun that gives life to Earth, as we were infinitely far from it. Yet somehow, I understood with absolute certainty that it was exactly like our sun—a duplicate. A wave of joy surged through me as the familiar light awakened something inside me. For the first time since my death, I felt a spark of life, a memory of the life I had left behind.

"But if that's a sun," I cried, "where is the Earth?" My companion pointed toward a distant, twinkling star with a faint green glow. We were flying straight toward it.

"Could such repetitions exist in the universe?" I wondered aloud. "Could this be some law of nature? And if that is another Earth, could it be the same as ours? Could it be as poor, as flawed, yet as beloved and precious as the one I left? Could it inspire the same deep love, even in the hearts of its most ungrateful children?" Overwhelmed, I was seized by a powerful, aching love for my Earth, the one I had left behind. The image of the little girl I had pushed away flashed through my mind.

"You shall see," my companion said, his voice tinged with sorrow.

As we flew closer, the planet grew larger before my eyes. I began to make out the oceans and the shape of Europe. Suddenly, a sacred, burning jealousy ignited in me.

"How could this be?" I thought. "How could it all be repeated, and why? I can only love the Earth I left behind—the one stained with my blood, where, in my ingratitude, I ended my life with a bullet. Yet, even as I parted from it, I loved it more than ever. Does this new Earth know suffering? On our Earth, we only know how to love through suffering. We cannot love in any other way. Love and suffering are inseparable for us. I want that suffering, because only through it can I truly love. Right now, I ache to kiss, with tears, the Earth I left behind. I want no other life, and I refuse to accept any other Earth!"

Without realizing how it happened, I suddenly found myself standing on this new Earth. The day was bright, the sun shining down on a paradise-like land. I think I was on one of the islands in the Greek archipelago or on the mainland facing those islands. Everything looked just like it does on our own Earth, but it seemed to glow with a special light, as though the entire world was celebrating something holy and triumphant.

The sea was a vibrant green, soft and gentle, washing against the shore as if it were showing love. Tall, beautiful trees stood around me, their blossoms in full bloom. Their countless leaves rustled softly, almost as if they were whispering words of love. The grass was dotted with bright, fragrant flowers, and the air felt alive with their scent. Birds flew in flocks through the sky, landing on my arms and shoulders without fear. They gently brushed against me with their wings, filling me with joy.

Then I saw the people who lived in this wonderful place. They came to me on their own, surrounding me with kindness and kissing me in welcome. They were like children of the sun, glowing with its warmth and light. I had never seen people so beautiful before. Perhaps the closest thing to their beauty might be found in the pure innocence of young children on our own Earth, but even that comparison feels too faint.

Their eyes were clear and bright, and their faces glowed with wisdom and understanding. Yet, there was no arrogance—only a serene happiness. They spoke with voices full of joy, and their words carried a childlike warmth and sincerity. From the very first moment I saw them, I understood everything about this place. This was an Earth untouched by sin, unspoiled by the Fall. It was a paradise like the one in humanity's ancient legends, where the first people lived before they sinned. Here, though, the entire Earth was paradise.

These joyful people gathered around me, laughing and showing me affection. They brought me to their homes and did everything they could to comfort me. They didn't ask any questions, but it felt like they already knew everything about me without needing to ask. It seemed like they were in a hurry to erase all traces of pain and sorrow from my face, as if they couldn't bear to see me suffer.

Chapter 4

Even if it was just a dream, the feeling of love from those pure and beautiful people has stayed with me forever. I still feel as though their love reaches out to me from that distant place. I saw them, I knew them, and I believed in them. I loved them, and later, I suffered because of them. From the start, I understood that there were many things about them I couldn't grasp. As a modern, skeptical Russian from Petersburg, I found it puzzling that, despite knowing so much, they didn't have science like ours. But soon I realized that their knowledge came from a completely different source—something we on Earth couldn't comprehend. They didn't strive for knowledge the way we do because their lives were already full. Their understanding was higher and deeper than ours. While our science tries to explain life and teach us how to live, they simply knew how to live, without needing to explain it.

They showed me their trees, and I couldn't understand the deep love they had for them. It was as though the trees were living beings, their equals, and I'm certain they communicated with them. They treated all of nature this way. The animals lived peacefully with them, never attacking but instead loving them, drawn by the people's love. They pointed to the stars and spoke of them in ways I couldn't comprehend, but I felt they had a real, living connection to them, not just through thought but in a tangible way.

These people didn't insist on making me understand them; they loved me as I was. Yet, I knew they would never fully understand me either. I rarely spoke to them about our Earth, but in their presence, I would kiss the ground they walked on and silently worship them. They saw this and accepted my reverence without embarrassment, for their own love was so great. Sometimes, I was overwhelmed and kissed their feet with tears in my eyes. They responded to my love with joy, and their love, in turn, filled me with happiness.

I often wondered how they never offended me or made me feel envy or jealousy. Even though I was boastful and dishonest, I never felt the urge to show off what I knew—things they couldn't possibly have known. I didn't even try to impress or teach them, which amazed me.

They were as carefree and playful as children. They wandered through their beautiful forests, sang sweet songs, and lived on simple food—fruits from the trees, honey from the woods, and milk from the animals that loved them. Their work was light and not burdensome. They loved, had children, and welcomed them not with selfishness but with joy, seeing them as new beings to share their happiness. There was no jealousy or quarreling among them—they didn't even know what those words meant. Their children belonged to everyone, as they all lived like one big family.

There was little illness among them, though death did exist. But even death was peaceful, like gently falling asleep. The elderly passed away with blessings and smiles, surrounded by loved ones who bid them farewell with bright, loving smiles. There was no grief, only love that seemed to transcend death. It felt as though their connection with the departed continued, unbroken by the end of life.

When I asked them about immortality, they barely understood my question. It was so obvious to them that life continued after death that they didn't see it as something to question. They didn't have temples, yet they lived with a constant awareness of their unity with the universe. They had no formal religion, but they believed that once their earthly joy reached its natural limits, they would move on to an even greater connection with the universe. They looked forward to this with quiet joy, not impatience, as if they already carried a sense of it in their hearts and shared that feeling with one another.

In the evenings, before going to sleep, they loved to sing together in beautiful, harmonious choruses. Through their songs, they expressed all the emotions and joys that the day had brought them. They celebrated the wonders of nature, the sea, and the forests. They even made songs about each other, praising one another like innocent children. Their songs were simple but deeply heartfelt, touching the hearts of everyone who heard them. It wasn't just in their music; their entire lives seemed filled with admiration for each other, as if they were all in love—but not in a selfish way. It was a universal, all-encompassing love.

Some of their songs were so deep and joyful that I could barely understand them. Even when I understood the words, the meaning seemed to reach beyond my grasp. Yet, my heart felt and absorbed their essence, even if my mind could not. I often told them that I had sensed something like this before, a faint glimpse of their joy and beauty on our Earth. It had come to me as a bittersweet longing, a sadness so intense that it was almost unbearable. I told them that, even in my hatred for humanity, there had always been an aching love hidden beneath it. I hated people, yet I couldn't stop loving them. I forgave them even when I didn't want to. And in my love, there was always pain—why couldn't I love them without hating them too?

They listened to me, but I could tell they didn't fully understand. Still, I didn't regret speaking to them about it. I knew they felt the depth of my sorrow for those I had left behind. But when they looked at me with their kind, loving eyes, I felt my heart transform, becoming pure and just like theirs. In their presence, I experienced a fullness of life so overwhelming that it left me breathless. I could only worship them silently.

Now, everyone laughs at me. They say it's impossible to dream of such vivid details as I'm describing. They insist that I only experienced a single strong feeling during my dream and made up the rest when I woke up. When I admit that might be true, they laugh even harder. They find it hilarious. Yes, perhaps my dream was just a powerful sensation, something my wounded heart clung to. But the images and moments I experienced during the dream were so harmonious, so beautiful, so real, that I couldn't fully express them when I woke up. Our human language felt too limited, and my memories began to fade. Maybe I did fill in some gaps afterward, distorting the dream in my desperate attempt to share even a piece of its beauty.

Still, how can I not believe it was real? Maybe it was even a thousand times more wonderful than I can describe. Even if it was a dream, it must have been rooted in some truth. And here's a secret: maybe it wasn't a dream at all. Something happened afterward— something so terrible, so painfully real, that it couldn't have come from a mere dream. How could my small, flawed heart and weak, restless mind have created such a revelation on their own? Judge for yourselves, but I'll confess the truth now. I've kept it hidden until this moment.

The truth is, I ruined them all.

Chapter 5

Yes, yes, it ended with me corrupting them all! How it happened, I cannot fully explain, but I remember it clearly. The dream spanned thousands of years, leaving me with only a sense of the whole picture. I know only that I was the cause of their sin and fall. Like a terrible disease, like a germ of the plague infecting entire nations, I brought corruption to that once happy and innocent world. They learned to lie and began to love it, discovering the thrill of deception. Perhaps at first, it started harmlessly, as a joke, a bit of flirtation, or playful mischief. But the seed of falsehood took root in their hearts and grew.

Soon sensuality arose, and from it came jealousy. Jealousy led to cruelty. I don't remember all the details, but very quickly, the first blood was spilled. They were shocked and horrified, but divisions began to form. They split into groups, but not to unite—rather, to oppose each other. Blame and accusations followed. They discovered shame, and shame gave rise to what they called virtue. The idea of honor emerged, and each group began to wave its own flags. They started torturing animals, and the animals fled to the forests, becoming hostile toward them. They fought for separation, for individuality, for "mine" and "yours." They started speaking different languages.

They came to know sorrow and grew to love it. They craved suffering, declaring that truth could only be found through pain. Science was born. As they became more wicked, they talked about brotherhood and humanity, claiming to understand these ideas. But as they committed more crimes, they invented justice, writing elaborate laws to uphold it. They built guillotines to enforce those laws. They forgot what they had lost and even refused to believe they were ever happy or innocent. They laughed at the idea of their past happiness, calling it a dream. They could no longer even imagine it clearly. Yet, strangely, they longed for that lost innocence so deeply that they worshipped the idea of it. They built temples to their yearning, bowing before it with tears, even while believing it was impossible to regain.

But if they had been offered the chance to return to that innocent and happy state, they would have refused. They told me, "We may be deceitful, wicked, and unjust. We know it, and we grieve for it. We punish ourselves more harshly than any merciful Judge might. But we have science, and through it, we will find the truth. We will reach it with understanding. Knowledge is greater than feeling; the awareness of life is more important than life itself. Science will give us wisdom, and wisdom will reveal the laws. And knowing the laws of happiness is better than happiness itself."

That's what they said. After such declarations, everyone began to love themselves more than anyone else. They couldn't help it. Each person became so obsessed with protecting their own individuality that they destroyed it in others. Slavery followed—even voluntary slavery. The weak willingly submitted to the strong, as long as the strong helped them dominate the weaker still. Saints appeared among them, weeping and speaking about pride, the loss of harmony, and the loss of shame. The people mocked them or threw stones at them. Holy blood was shed on the steps of their temples.

Then came others who dreamed of uniting humanity so that everyone, while still loving themselves the most, could avoid harming others. They fought wars over this idea. All sides believed that science, wisdom, and the instinct for self-preservation would eventually force people to unite in harmony. To speed things up, the "wise" tried to eliminate those who were "not wise" so they wouldn't hinder progress. But the instinct for self-preservation weakened. Men grew proud and selfish, demanding everything—or nothing. To achieve their desires, they turned to crime, and when that failed, to suicide. Religions emerged that worshipped non-existence and preached self-destruction in the name of eternal peace.

Eventually, the people became exhausted by their meaningless efforts. Their faces showed signs of suffering, and they declared suffering to be beautiful. They sang songs glorifying pain, claiming it gave life meaning. I wandered among them, wringing my hands, weeping for them. Yet, despite everything, I loved them more than I had before, when they were innocent and beautiful. I even loved the earth they had ruined, perhaps because it had suffered. I had always loved sorrow and suffering—but only for myself. Now, I wept for them, reaching out to them in despair, blaming myself, cursing myself. I told them it was my fault—that I had brought them corruption and falsehood. I begged them to crucify me, even teaching them how to build a cross. I couldn't bring myself to end my own life, but I longed to suffer at their hands. I wanted them to drain every drop of my blood in agony.

But they only laughed at me. In the end, they dismissed me as insane. They told me they had simply followed their own desires and that things couldn't have turned out any other way. Finally, they said I was becoming a danger and threatened to lock me in an asylum if I didn't stop speaking. Such despair took hold of me that my heart felt as though it were breaking. And then... I woke up.

It was morning, though the sun had not yet risen. It was about six o'clock when I woke up in the armchair. My candle had burned out, and there was silence all around—rare in our flat. The captain and his guests were asleep. I jumped up in amazement. Nothing like this had ever happened to me before. Even the smallest detail felt unfamiliar; for instance, I had never fallen asleep like that in my chair. While I stood there trying to collect myself, my eyes fell on the loaded revolver lying on the table, ready. I immediately pushed it away.

Life! Life! I raised my hands and silently called out to eternal truth—not with words, but with tears. An overwhelming joy flooded my soul. Yes, life and sharing the truth! In that moment, I made a decision to spread the truth for the rest of my life. I would tell everyone. What truth? The truth I had seen with my own eyes. The truth in all its glory.

Since that moment, I have been preaching. And strangely, I love those who laugh at me even more than anyone else. I don't know why, but that's how it is. They say I'm unclear and confused, and they're probably right. If I'm unclear now, how much worse will I be later? I know I'll make mistakes as I figure out how to preach, how to find the right words and actions. It's a difficult task, and I understand that clearly. But who doesn't make mistakes? Everyone, from the wisest philosopher to the most petty thief, is striving toward the same goal, though they take different paths. That's an old truth. But here's what's new: I can't go too far wrong because I've seen the truth. I've seen it, and I know people can live beautiful, happy lives without losing their place on this earth.

I refuse to believe that evil is humanity's natural state. People laugh at me for thinking this, but how could I not believe it? I've seen the truth. It's not something I invented in my mind. I've seen it, and the vision of it has filled my soul forever. I saw it so clearly, so completely, that I can't believe it's impossible for people to achieve. How can I go astray when the memory of what I saw will always guide me? Yes, I may make mistakes and use borrowed words at first, but the truth will always correct me.

I am full of hope and determination. I will keep going, even if it takes a thousand years. At first, I thought I should hide the fact that I had caused harm, but that was my first mistake. Truth whispered to me that I was lying, and it corrected me. I don't know how to create paradise. I don't have the words. After my dream, I lost the ability to express myself fully. But that doesn't matter. I'll keep speaking and trying, even if I can't describe exactly what I saw. The skeptics don't understand that. They call it a dream, a hallucination. But what does that matter? Isn't life itself like a dream?

Even if the paradise I saw never becomes real, I'll keep preaching about it. It's so simple: love others as much as you love yourself. That's all there is to it. Nothing more is needed. Everything else will fall into place. This truth has been told countless times, yet it's never truly been lived. People say that understanding life is more important than living it, that knowing how to be happy is better than happiness itself. That's the real obstacle, and I will fight against it. If everyone wanted to, the world could change in an instant.

And I found that little girl. I will keep going, no matter what!

THE END

Thank You for Reading

Dear Reader,

We hope this timeless classic has sparked your imagination and enriched your literary journey. Now that you've turned the final page, we want to share a vision for the future of reading—one where every classic you've ever wanted to explore is at your fingertips, in a format that best suits your life.

We'd like to invite you to gain immediate, unlimited digital & audiobook access to hundreds of the most treasured literary classics ever written—along with the option to secure deluxe paperback, hardcover & box set editions at printing cost. Together, we can spark a new global literary renaissance alongside our small, independent publishing house called "The Library of Alexandria."

Thousands of years ago, the Library of Alexandria stood as a beacon of knowledge—until it was lost to history. We aim to reignite that spirit of preservation and discovery right now, in the modern age—only this time, it's accessible to all, in every language and every format.

Picture a world where every timeless classic, novel, poem, or philosophical treatise is not only available to read but also updated for today's readers—modernized, translated into any language or dialect, and ready to enjoy in any format you choose, whether that is in an eBook, audiobook, paperback, or deluxe hardcover & box set version a printing cost.

By joining our movement to rebuild the modern Library of Alexandria, you become part of an unprecedented mission to offer:

Unlimited Audiobook & eBook Access to the Greatest Classics of All Time

Instantly explore thousands of legendary works, from Plato and Shakespeare to Jane Austen and Leo Tolstoy. All are instantly ready to read or listen to, giving you a complete literary universe at your fingertips.

Paperback & Deluxe Editions at Printing Costs:

Purchase any title in a paperback, deluxe hardbound, or deluxe boxset edition at printing costs, shipped right to your doorstep. Curate your personal library of Alexandria with editions worthy of display—crafted to last, designed to captivate, and delivered straight to your door.

Modern translations for Contemporary Readers in all languages and dialects

Discover a vast selection of classics reimagined in clear, current language—no more struggling with outdated phrases or obscure references. Next to the original versions, we aim to offer translations in as many languages and dialects as possible.

As we continue our translation efforts and add new languages, readers everywhere can connect with these works as if they were written today. By bridging linguistic divides, you're contributing to ensuring that these timeless stories become more meaningful, accessible, and inspiring for people across the globe.

Your Personal Library of Alexandria:

Over the months and years, you'll curate a unique physical archive of classics—each volume a testament to your taste, curiosity, and love of knowledge. It's not just about owning books—it's about curating a cultural legacy you'll cherish and pass down for generations to come.

Join a Global Literary Renaissance:

Your support fuels an ongoing mission: allowing us to reinvest in offering deluxe print editions (including special boxsets) at their true cost, broaden the range of available formats and translations, and extend the reach of these works to new audiences worldwide. By joining today, you're not just preserving a legacy of masterpieces; you set in motion a powerful wave of literary accessibility.

We are more than a publisher—we're a movement, and we can't do it alone. Your support lets us scale our mission, preserving and reimagining history's greatest works for tomorrow's readers.

Become a Torchbearer of knowledge.

Thank you for picking up this book and allowing us into your literary journey. As you turn the pages, know that you're part of something larger: a global effort to keep these stories alive, share their wisdom across borders and generations, and spark a true cultural revival for the modern era.

If this resonates with you—please consider taking the next step by visiting:

www.libraryofalexandria.com

With gratitude and a shared love of knowledge,

The Modern Library of Alexandria Team

Visit:

www.libraryofalexandria.com

Or scan the code below: